Deadly Secret

by

Joy Brighton

Deadly Secret

Cover Art by *Debbie Taylor*

The Wild Rose Press, Inc.
PO Box 708
Adams Basin, NY 14410-0708
Visit us at www.thewildrosepress.com

Publishing History
First Crimson Rose Edition, 2014
Print ISBN 978-1-62830-599-9
Digital ISBN 978-1-62830-600-2

Published in the United States of America

"I had to talk to you right away.
You have to understand the consequences of not making things right."

Jana dodged around the woman, set her bag on the landing, and planted her hands on her hips. "You should be in bed."

"I can't rest. Not until you change the past."

Jana's skin crawled. Her belly curdled, and she recoiled, slowly shaking her head.

"You must prevent more tragedy. How can I make you believe me?" the woman asked, edging between Jana and the front door.

Despite the tightness in her chest, Jana forced in a deep breath. The poor woman was confused, but hardly dangerous. "Go home. Please, Ms. Redfox. Your meds have clouded your thinking. Mike's dead. No one and nothing can change the past."

"You can. And you must. Until you do, you're in deadly peril. The blight will spread, and many more will die."

"I've heard enough of your scare tactics. You need to leave."

The woman stared, holding her palms out flat. Pain shimmered in her dark eyes and creased her forehead. "But I can help you. I've helped others change history."

Jana clenched her hands and caught hold of the panic inching through her. "I'll call the police unless you go. Come here again and I'll get a restraining order. Is that clear?"

"Yes." The woman shuffled past her and down the first step. Then she turned. "If you refuse me now, within the week you'll come to me, overwhelmed by your grief."

Award Winning Author
Joy Brighton

1st place 2010 Heart of the Rockies contest.
(The Molly)

~*~

1st place 2011 Heart of Denver Romance Writers—
Romantic Suspense

~*~

1st place 2008 Duel of the Delta

~*~

Honorable Mention 2008 Daphne Du Maurier—
Unpublished

~*~

2010 Winner of the Linda Howard

~*~

2010 Winner of the Gotcha! Contest

Dedication

To my husband and family,
who always believed in me.
Thanks.

Chapter One

Sereno, California

January 1, present day, 10:00 a.m.

"Party animals, maniacs, and crazies." Dr. Jana Sutherland shoved her stethoscope into her pocket and headed for the locker room. Her first New Year's Eve in the Sereno General ER had been a double shift straight from hell. Her shoulders ached, and her feet weighed a metric ton each, but she was finally free. Free to sleep a few days straight. Free to clear the stink of unwashed humanity, vomit, and death from her sinuses.

A well-dressed young woman with dark hair swept into a twist waited by the elevator. She carried an enormous vase of flowers with both hands. The pungent scent of 'Stargazer' lilies wafted from the bouquet, fighting the ever-present sting of pine disinfectant.

As Jana approached, the woman turned her head. Above her broad cheekbones, the woman's wide, deep brown eyes shimmered with anxiety, but her lips curved up at the corners.

"Are you headed to surgery?" the woman called.

"No, I'm finally going home. Time for a long soak in a hot tub with the latest thriller."

"You earned it, Dr. Sutherland. You were my

aunt's surgeon. Shirley Redfox."

"Ah, the dissecting aneurysm. She's one lucky lady."

"Thank you for all you did." The woman cradled the vase against her chest with one arm and held out her free hand. "I'm Norah Redfox."

Their fingers touched, and violent energy surged through Jana like a hit from the defib paddles.

Norah's eyes opened wide, and the vase she was holding crashed to the floor in an explosion of ceramic shards, water, and pink blooms.

Jana tried to jump out of the way, but the other woman's clammy hand clenched her wrist.

"Hey! Let go!" She snatched back her hand and shot a frantic glance around the nearly deserted lobby. Her pulse pounded against her temples, and her throat tightened. She searched the hall for the security guard, but he wasn't at his station.

"Why can't I focus?" Norah Redfox shuddered and swiped her palms over her eyes. She let loose a low, eerie groan. "You're more distorted than the others. You really must have screwed up the timeline."

"What?" Jana gaped, rubbing at the goose bumps crawling on her arms.

The P. A. system crackled to life. "Code blue. Rapid response team to the ER."

Norah blinked rapidly, as if returning to her senses. "What did you do to warp time so much?"

Jana staggered back a step. "What are you talking about?"

"I'm talking about a redo. I'll send you back in time to change whatever you did wrong."

"A redo? That's absurd." A ghostly chill traced her

vertebrae one at a time. Jana cleared her throat, fumbling for something professional to say. "Look, y-you must be upset about your aunt..."

The woman's face had gone ashen, and her eyelids drooped, but she stared straight at Jana.

"Are you okay?"

"So many others were killed because your lover died."

The hollow tone of Norah's voice sent another wave of shivers over Jana's skin. Shaking her head, she held up her palms. "I'm sorry, I've got to get back to the ER."

"Ten years ago, he was murdered."

A cold weight formed in the pit of her stomach, and she struggled to draw a breath. Mike's death had been her fault, but how had this creepy woman known?

The elevator bonged, and Jana pivoted toward the sound.

The doors slid open, and a skinny, glassy-eyed punk with long, greasy hair stepped out. He glanced at her nametag. "Doctor Sutherland. I have something for you."

The skin between her shoulder blades prickled. "Do I know you?"

Smirking, he reached under his leather jacket and raised a gun.

Jana froze, lightheaded. How had he gotten a weapon through the metal detectors? Her knees threatened to buckle as her perspective narrowed to the huge chrome pistol pointed at her heart.

The gunman's fingers tightened.

She dived for the floor and hit the linoleum hard. Fire creased her scalp, but she instinctively curled her fingers around the alarm button on her lapel and squeezed.

Blue lights flashed from the walls and sirens wailed.

The punk's head whipped around, and a second shot exploded. Beside her, Norah Redfox screamed.

Jana rolled to her side and searched for the gunman.

His expression rigid, he took a step toward her and braced for another shot.

She gasped.

Footsteps echoed from behind her. "Stop! Drop your weapon!" a male voice ordered.

The punk's face contorted with fury. He gave an incoherent shout of rage, turned, and pounded toward the main hospital entrance.

The security guard raced past with his weapon drawn, but the orderly trailing him stopped and reached out a beefy hand. "Dr. Sutherland? You're bleeding."

When she swiped her forehead, her hand came away sticky. "I...I'm okay." The weak, shaky stammer in her voice made her wince. "I'm okay," she repeated. Every muscle shaking, she glanced around the hall before allowing the orderly to help her to her feet. Behind her, she heard a choking sob.

Norah Redfox had collapsed, grabbing her chest and fighting for air. A red patch blossomed through the right side of her blouse. Her respiration was soggy, almost strangled.

Kneeling, Jana pried the woman's hands off her ribs and ripped the blouse aside. Bubbles gurgled from the exit wound, through exposed flesh. A metallic taste rose in her throat, and she swallowed hard. Shoving both trembling palms flat, she sealed the wound and glanced up at the orderly. "Her right lung's compromised. Pulse is irregular. We need to get her to surgery. Stat."

****

January 3, 4:00 a.m.

"No!" Jana bolted upright and peered at the clock beside her bed. With a groan, she scrunched her eyes shut and burrowed under the comforter, trying to banish the nightmare.

Ever since the shooting and her surreal conversation with Norah Redfox, Mike's funeral had taken over her dreams. Her mind kept replaying the insistent wail of bagpipes, the choke in his dad's voice, and the spatter of dirt on the coffin.

After an hour spent staring at the inside of her eyelids, she grabbed her robe from the bedpost and shrugged it on. So much for catching up on her sleep.

Disgusted, she opened the window shade and gazed out. A thin crescent moon lit the night, but mist had seeped in from the Pacific, blanketing the Santa Cruz Mountains. Shivering, she belted her robe tight around her waist.

Norah Redfox's bizarre statements churned in her mind. How had the woman known? When Jana leaned her head against the cool glass, her breath fogged the window. She closed her eyes and tried to picture Mike, but couldn't. She could almost smell his musky aftershave, almost hear his sexy chuckle. But his face? A blur. She swallowed hard.

Almost ten years later, why did it matter anyway? When had she become a sentimental idiot? She blew a wet raspberry, marched into the hall, and flicked on the lights. Pulling down the heavy folding stairs to her attic, she put a foot on the first step. The hinges squeaked in protest as she climbed.

She knelt before an antique steamer trunk and unhooked the clasps. A whiff of Granny's home tickled her nose and drew a weak smile from the vacant space in her heart. Jana sniffed again. Sandalwood, lavender, and mildew.

Under layers of patchwork quilts, she found Mike's photo next to a clunky old cell phone wrapped in a knitted scarf from her college days.

She returned to her bedroom with the picture and switched on the lamp. She studied his handsome face, wry smile, and curly hair she'd loved to comb her fingers through.

A bulb popped. A frigid ache ballooned deep in her chest and blocked her throat. In the brilliant white flash, she saw snatches of a vision. Her house transformed. Rich color replaced icy white, and a big dog sprawled in front of the fireplace. On her lap, a warm, sleepy toddler sang, "Swing low, sweet chari-o-t. Coming forth to carry me…" A strong hand rested on her shoulder, and a deep voice repeated the words. Stroking the child's dark hair, she inhaled his sweet, just-bathed toddler scent. Tenderness stabbed her.

She shut her eyes and collapsed onto her bed. Clutching Mike's photo in her numb fingers, she waited for sunrise.

Her fiancé was dead. That future was lost forever.

****

January 4, 5:59 p.m.

Sergeant Nate Kapulani rubbed his aching head. "Six o'clock and darker than a sewer rat's gullet."

The evening was clear with only a slice of moon, but half the streetlights on this block were smashed. The one he'd parked his unmarked sedan under had bare wires sparking through jagged glass.

Nate shoved open the door, gritting his teeth against the metallic screech. When he slammed the door behind him, the sedan rocked from the force.

"Piece of garbage," he huffed, and his breath formed clouds. With a shiver, he zipped his jacket and turned up the collar.

Another day.

Another crime scene.

Another corpse.

The coroner's van straddled the broken sidewalk ahead, which was shiny from the earlier drizzle. Three squad cars flashed blue lights, filling the narrow alley beyond with surreal light. Even before he stepped onto the weed-infested gravel, his eyes watered. Like a mouth full of rotten teeth, the passage emitted an unmistakable sickly-sweet reek.

No question some creep had died. Nate drew air through his mouth and waited for his sense of smell to go numb from the overload. Just inside the crime scene tape, two homeless characters slouched beside a shopping cart full of rags. Why hadn't the first officer on the scene secured the perimeter?

Nate slammed his fist against his palm and veered toward them. The short one tucked a bottle beneath his coat and elbowed his buddy. With slumped shoulders, they retreated behind the yellow crime scene tape.

Nate let them go and ducked under the tape. Dodging piles of soggy garbage, he approached the coroner. "What do you have this time?"

Bart Nichols glanced over his shoulder and flashed Nate a grim reaper smile. "A stinker."

"No kidding. How long?"

"Three, four days." The coroner stepped back, running a hand through his frizzy gray hair. Work lights cast eerie shadows on his face. "Left him for you, Kapulani. Knew you wouldn't want to miss the sweet perfume."

The verbal elbow in his ribs made Nate chuckle. He risked a breath through his nose. The vile stench hit the back of his palate, and he couldn't restrain a choking cough. "Yep. Kind of ripe."

Nichols sniggered.

"The photographer through?"

"Yeah, but Detective MacLean's been sitting on his ass."

Holding his hands behind his back, Nate peered into the overflowing Dumpster. A crumpled body lay face up on rotting, rain-soaked cardboard. One bulging, glazed-over eye stared sightless. The other eye and part of his skull had been blasted away.

A muscle in Nate's right cheek twitched. He squinted. What had moved? When he flicked on a flashlight, his skin crawled. A white ball of maggots writhed where the brain should have been. The corpse's tongue protruded, and his skinny neck was bruised. Somebody had really wanted this guy dead.

Somehow his crooked nose and weak chin looked familiar. Nate craned his neck and leaned closer. His gut did a three-point swan dive. Damn. Douggie Wendell? Wonder who he pissed off?

The coroner's assistants rolled up a stretcher and unzipped the body bag. Nate turned back to Nichols, but kept the ID to himself. "I know the days have been in the seventies, but those maggots look pretty active for a four-day-old corpse."

"Probably already there."

"I'll check the date of the last garbage pick-up." Nate scratched the side of his nose. "What else have you come up with?"

"Male, about thirty. Your detective hasn't searched the scene or collected samples yet."

"I'll get him moving." Nate hustled over to the three uniforms smoking and laughing in a doorway. "Flynn. Goldman. Secure this fucking crime scene now," he ordered.

Heads jerked. Heels ground out cigarettes. Two uniforms jogged away.

But one cop stood smirking at him. When he shifted his feet, his paunch jiggled, and the buttons on his uniform gaped.

Nate stopped nose-to-nose with the asshole. "You first on the scene?"

"Yeah." MacLean nodded, inspecting his fat fingers.

Nate fisted his hands on his duty belt. His elbows jutted out, and he inched his boots further apart.

"Yes, sir, Sergeant."

Better. But the cop's tone had set his teeth on edge like chewing tin foil. "Who found him?"

"Those guys stopped my cruiser." MacLean tipped his head toward the two homeless men, now spread-eagled on the pavement for a pat down. "They don't know nothing. Pretty irate, though. Claim the vic's stinking up their alley."

"Fix that for them, will you? Nichols could use a

hand."

"Yes...sir."

Grimacing, Nate walked away. He'd heard that sarcastic edge before. Damn. Another crooked cop? Too fucking many on the force already.

He leaned against the coroner's van while he waited for the coroner to bag the body. Douglas Wendell. Hadn't thought about that douchebag in years. Nate picked up a rock and tossed it from hand to hand. What seemed like a lifetime ago, Wendell and his buddy, Joe Morgan, had topped a short list of murder suspects on a very important case.

Nate chucked the rock. He could never purge the picture etched in his brain of Mike Gordon's dead body. The brutal, unsolved murder of his partner and best friend still kept him awake at night. Nate spat in the dirt, but the sour taste of bile rose in his throat and coated his tongue. Turning, he let his forehead sag against the cold metal and flexed his fists. Open. Closed. Open. Closed.

Nichols clomped over, adjusted his half glasses, and opened the back door of the van. "I'll have a prelim tomorrow. Pretty sure he wasn't killed here."

"Dumped? No surprise." Nate moved behind the door and muttered under his breath, "I knew him."

The coroner shot him a quick glance.

"Name's Wendell. But keep that to yourself."

"One of yours?"

"Cold case. Hang on to the report, and let me see it first."

"Sure."

Tires crunched on gravel. Officer Alex Frost jumped out of his squad car, adjusting his duty belt as he hustled over.

Nate almost smiled.

Mid-twenties, a family man with a nice wife and kid, Frost was only a year out of the academy. And one of the few cops in Sereno PD Nate could still trust.

Grinning, Alex adjusted his blue cap over a military-style crew cut, and they shook hands. His smile gleamed in the dark like a toothpaste ad. "Glad you're here, Sarge. Got an ID on the vic?" he asked, his voice too upbeat for a cop eyeing a stinking body.

"Not officially."

"Heard over the radio the stiff was a male in his thirties. Any chance he's a slug named Douggie Wendell?"

"Why? You looking for him?"

"Got an APB out. Wendell's a suspect in the hospital shooting on New Year's Day. I caught the case."

"Okay. No fatalities, so I haven't waded into the paperwork yet. Made any progress?"

"We got lucky. He gave a fake ID to admissions, but the cameras caught him. He left a partial print on a gurney in the ER, too. Wendell went gunning for a young doc. Just can't figure out why." Frost strung out his words, rubbing a finger along his Roman nose. "Man, was she pissed. Real firebrand redhead."

Nate's radar pinged. "Redhead?"

"Yeah."

Crossing his arms, Nate shoved on his tough cop face. "And?"

"Tall, nice looking woman. Thin, with big hazel eyes. Freaked out, but tried to hide her shock."

No way. Nate's heart thundered like an artillery

barrage. He stretched the crick in his neck and licked his lips. Had to be thousands of beautiful doctors who happened to have red hair and hazel eyes.

"New in town, poor kid."

Shit. It couldn't be her, but he'd ask anyway. What'd be the harm in asking? Nate cleared his throat and stared at his shined shoes like he didn't give a fuck. "What's her name?"

"Uh, Sutherland."

His pounding heart squeezed down into a lump of dry ice. Jana? Damn. Mike's fiancée. What else would the universe dump on him tonight? With a snort, Nate tugged on his earlobe. Maybe his murdered partner would return from the grave.

"Thought I'd ask my wife to give the doc a call, see if she wanted coffee. Katy could use a friend, since her store went bankrupt. Actually, I'm kinda glad to have her at home after she was robbed again. Sereno's dangerous."

"More like the fourth level of hell. Thirteen homicides on New Year's Eve alone."

"And, at the hospital, a bystander got plugged, and the shooter nicked the doc."

Nate's lungs seized. She'd been hurt? He blew on his hands and shoved them in his pockets, but Frost blathered on.

Jana Sutherland, the sexiest woman he'd ever known. Nate clenched his jaw. Dazzled by his blond, charming partner, the only woman who'd ever gotten her hooks into Nate's heart had treated him like a stuffed teddy bear. She'd never even met his gaze all those years ago, just smiled at his top button and given him sexless, pat-you-on-the-shoulder hugs.

Ancient history, Kapulani. Suck it up. He laid a hand on Frost's shoulder and conjured up a hearty but helpful tone. "Mind if I take over your case?"

"Not at all, Sarge. I've got three others to deal with. I'll send you my report." Frost scratched the side of his neck and shrugged. "Say, you don't suppose the doc had anything to do with Wendell's death?"

"Doubt it," Nate lied.

Chapter Two

January 5, 1:00 p.m.

After her second three-hour surgery of the day, Jana stood in the overcrowded corridor, fingering the rubber tubing of her stethoscope. The elevator bonged, and she tensed, glancing around nervously.

They still hadn't caught that damn shooter, but it had to have been a random attack. She took a deep breath to calm her pulse. The guy had looked strung out, like an addict shopping the ER for oxycodone.

So when would her reactions return to normal?

She peeled an antacid off the roll in her pocket and popped the chalky mint tablet into her mouth. New Year's Day had been more like the trailer for a sci-fi psycho-action thriller than her normal, boring life. Now she had to face her crazy patient again. She'd been exhausted the first time she spoke to Norah Redfox, nothing but a walking bundle of imagination. Maybe she could pretend the whole crazy conversation never happened.

Adjusting her lab coat, she stepped inside her patient's room. A soap opera droned from the ceiling-mounted TV, but the old woman in the first bed snored openmouthed. Jana wrinkled her nose. The wilted chrysanthemums did nothing to disguise the musty smell of stale urine.

She poked her face around the blue curtain and yanked it closed behind her.

Norah Redfox lay propped up in bed, staring vacantly into space and twisting her plastic ID bracelet.

Jana cleared her throat. "How are you feeling today, Ms. Redfox? Were you able to sleep?"

"Some." Norah rolled her eyes in the direction of her snoring roommate.

"I'll see if I can get you moved to a quieter room."

"That'd be great. Thanks."

She reached for Norah's wrist to take her vitals. When they touched, lightning seared her fingers, and her pulse spiked.

Jana recoiled. That eerie sensation she'd felt before hadn't been her imagination. Clutching her hands together to stop them from trembling, she sank onto a bedside chair, her stomach reeling. "What happened just then? Did you do that on purpose?"

"Not exactly, but you must be very sensitive to feel the energy."

"I don't understand."

Norah took a deep breath. "I know I sound crazy, but I can sense your life hasn't gone the way it should have."

Jana fiddled with her stethoscope again. Her pulse pounded at her temples, but she couldn't squelch her morbid curiosity. "How can you tell?"

Norah's brows pulled down in a squint, and her mouth pursed. "When I look at you, you're almost out of focus. How did you cause your fiancé's death?"

"What? I didn't do anything of the kind. That's ridiculous." Jana rose, wrapping her arms tight against her body. "Drug dealers murdered him ten years ago.

No one and nothing can change the past."

"Wrong. With my help, you can rewrite history."

Jana gasped. Chilled to her bone marrow, she backed away from the bed.

"You think I'm delusional. Not surprising." A smile quirked Norah's lips. "I didn't trust my gift myself until my brother drowned. I twisted time, went back, and saved him."

"Impossible."

"Hard to imagine, perhaps, but not impossible." Norah winced and grabbed her ribs. "Your fiancé's murder didn't just affect the two of you. His death distorted everything, like a massive earthquake warps the landscape. But your life doesn't have to stay this way. You can change the past."

Dull-edged pain compressed her heart, but Jana kept her professional façade in place. She'd refer the poor woman to the psych team, ASAP. "Excuse me. I have to finish my rounds," she said and shifted the curtain aside.

"No. You have to save Mike."

Every fine hair on Jana's arms stood vertical. She stomped back to the lunatic. "Mike? How did you know his name?"

Norah stared at her for a minute. "Think it through, then come back, and we'll talk."

****

1:45 p.m.

Jana huddled at a corner table in the nearly empty cafeteria. The clang of pots and cutlery echoed from the kitchen, jangling her already rattled nerves.

She crumbled saltines into her chicken soup and swallowed a spoonful of the warm, savory broth.

Comfort food. But the big, frosted brownie on her tray snared her gaze. Leaning closer, she shut her eyes and inhaled the seductive fragrance. Why not? She took a huge bite. Her eyes closed, and her mouth filled with the heady taste of dark, rich chocolate.

Dr. Griffon Raines stalked up. A slight man, the Chief of Staff stood a few inches short of her five-foot-ten. Today a scowl marred his narrow-faced, blond good looks.

"I had another inquiry from Sereno PD. You are a trouble magnet, Dr. Sutherland," her boss said in a high-pitched nasal tone. His thin upper lip rose in a sneer.

Despite the anger rushing through her veins, she dropped her gaze and swallowed, struggling to clear the chocolate from her teeth before she spoke. "Some idiot sneaked a gun past your security guards and shot me. What part of that was my fault?"

"Whenever trouble happens, you're always there."

"So what are you doing to prevent trouble and protect all of us?"

"We hired a top consultant. He's handled it. New metal detectors, extra guards. The whole works." He used both hands to cinch his yellow power tie tighter. "Now tell me why you missed the Trustees' dinner last week."

"I pulled a double shift again that night because what's-his-name left for the job at Cedars Sinai. Remember? You can't expect me to schmooze after nineteen hours on my feet."

"We all have to make connections to keep this place running. Eighty-three percent of our patients are uninsured. You knew that when I hired you."

Jaw tight, she met his aloof gray eyes. The stuffy, paper-pushing misogynist had tripped over his wingtips to recruit her, but had glossed over a few pertinent details. "You left that out of the sales pitch. When you hired me, all you told me was you'd been searching for a thoracic surgeon for almost a year."

Raines held out his palms. "You know what Sereno's like," he said in a slow, even tone. For once, he sounded almost human. "You know I scrounge and grovel for resources, try to keep all my staff safe so we can do our best for our patients."

"Of course."

"You know the people we serve have nothing and can pay nothing."

"But..."

"Without support from the few wealthy people still left in the Valley, this hospital will close." He leaned over the table. "Your job will disappear."

"I'm just not very..."

"Dr. Sutherland." Red mottled his face as he drew to his full height and glared down his aristocratic nose at her. "You're still on probation. Put in your time at the annual gala next Friday." He turned and marched away.

She took another big bite of brownie. Receptions were pure misery. Dressing up for the lechers to ogle. Smiling at insipid conversation. Stroking super-sized egos. But if that's what it took, she'd had lots of practice growing up.

Calmer, she stirred her soup. She'd taken this job hoping to make a difference. Had naïve optimism bit her in the butt again? Or was her father right? Had she chosen Sereno General as some kind of self-imposed penance for Mike's death?

A shadow loomed over the table. Tensing to rejoin the battle with Raines, she glanced up. Her breath hitched, and a surge of warmth brought a smile to her lips.

Her old friend, Nate Kapulani, set down his tray. "Welcome back." Cupping her chin with his warm, calloused palm, he kissed her cheek.

Her gaze locked with his for an instant. His brown-black eyes had a sinful gleam that stripped her soul bare. Lifting her hand to her cheek, she closed her mouth and stood. "Nate, what...?"

He wrapped his arms around her, lifted her off her feet as if she weighed nothing, and swung her in a huge circle. Heavenly warmth radiated from him.

For a split second, her face nestled against the curve of his neck, and she inhaled a trace of his woodsy aftershave. The rough stubble on his jaw scraped her skin, and her breasts flattened against his wide muscled chest. Heat seared her cheeks.

With a nervous laugh, she rested her hands on his shoulders. "Put me down."

Grinning wickedly, he returned her to her feet, and she pushed away. She'd forgotten how tall he was. How solid. Hugged tight against him, she'd felt vulnerable, but almost too good. How many years had passed since a man had held her in his arms?

Nate brushed his thumb across her forehead. "You could have called. Didn't have to get shot to catch my attention."

"This? Only a scrape." Ignoring the lump in her throat, she stuffed her hands in her pockets and backed away. "Why are you here?"

"Checking up on you. Want to tell me what happened?"

"There's not much to tell. Some hyped-up punk with a gun jumped out of the elevator and fired at me. I don't know why. I don't even know who the creep was. I figured he wanted drugs, and I was in his way."

"Have a seat. I'll fill you in." He grabbed the chair next to hers.

Returning to her place, she dropped her hands to her lap, and stared at the worn beige and black linoleum. She could still feel warmth where his lips had brushed her cheek.

No! Forget it. She'd finally escaped her snap-and-salute father when she moved to Sereno from Arizona. She was through with controlling men forever. Especially cops.

She leaned against her chair and dredged up her iceberg-cool smile. She might not like her reaction to Nate, but there was certainly nothing wrong with the view. He had waves in his dark hair, strong and straight brows cutting across his square face, and too much jaw for handsome. His shoulders were broad enough to heft a ton of granite and never notice.

As if he'd read her mind, his slow grin widened. His gaze met hers and held.

Tingles spread over her body like he'd put his hands on her, not just his luscious espresso-brown gaze. Ruthlessly, she tamped down her reaction and kept her smile steady.

"I've got the shooting investigation now," Nate said.

She tipped her head to one side. "What happened to Officer Frost? He seemed like a nice guy, very patient. I was freaked out, but eventually he got a coherent statement out of me."

"I heard." He smiled at her in silence, but a dozen heartbeats later, his expression sobered. "Something else wrong? Patient in trouble?"

"No. Both morning surgeries went flawlessly." She hesitated, fighting the temptation to share her problem, namely one stark-raving delusional patient. She chewed on her lip. She should keep her mouth shut, but was it all connected somehow? The shooting, Norah's claims, and Nate showing up like a ghost from one of Shakespeare's tragedies.

"But?"

Jana trailed a finger through the silky chocolate frosting. A miniscule part of her wanted to ignore the fact he was an alpha male, slide over next to him, and consign that bizarre woman to the cosmic loony bin. Instead, she licked the frosting off her finger, reached for the brownie, and took another bite.

"What's bugging you, gorgeous?" he asked in a rumbling voice.

Her damn heart tripped, but she snorted. Gorgeous? A skinny, freckled redhead with a mouth too big for her face? Yeah, right. "Do you remember the other woman who was shot?"

With a nod, he propped one elbow on the table and focused on her face.

"I just left her room. She freaked me out, knew things about my life—things she couldn't possibly know."

"Like what?"

Jana shook her head to clear her thoughts. "She knew about Mike's murder, knew we were engaged.

She even knew his name."

"How'd she dig that up?"

Cold despite her scrubs and lab coat, Jana chafed her upper arms. "Who knows? Maybe she's a scam artist. She even claimed she could help me change the past."

****

Nate studied her intense expression. Her big hazel eyes were narrowed. She'd pressed her lips together in a thin line, and hot color edged her high cheekbones. "Weird. No wonder you've got the willies."

"The woman's a nutcase, but you haven't heard the totally crazy part yet. She claims she's brought people back from the dead."

Nate's hackles stirred. "Whoa, Jana. Take a deep breath."

Gulping in a lungful, she rubbed her hands on her long, slim thighs. Then she twined her pale fingers together. Short nails. No polish. No rings. But so damn sexy.

He glanced at her lips again. Naked. No lipstick— just soft, bare skin. Her pink tongue darted out, swiping off a frosting smear. His body tightened and heated until he was painfully hard.

He shifted in his seat and hooked an ankle over his knee to ease the sudden pressure. He wanted her mouth and hands on him so badly he felt lust had run over him like a bulldozer.

He stared down at his lunch, but couldn't eat. Damn. What the hell was going on with him? He could've sworn he was over her, but then he never should have gotten hung up on her in the first place. Shoulda, coulda, woulda. Well, he finally had her attention. What next?

Leaning one elbow on the table, he faced her square on. "Try again, Jana. Exactly what did she say?"

"She blamed me for Mike's death."

"Bullshit," Nate growled.

A flush chased up her neck and cheeks, and her bright, hazel eyes shot sparks. "What does that mean?"

Hell. He'd sounded like a rookie. Damned erection had sucked all the blood out of his brain. He scrubbed his hand across his mouth. "Sorry. Didn't come out the way I meant it. We both know Mike was set up, ambushed. You had nothing to do with his murder. But did you listen long enough for the woman to explain?"

Jana slapped her palms on the table and glared at him. "Explain? You didn't hear her. She talked about the impossible."

He angled his head and captured her hand. Her skin felt as soft and her fingers as strong as they looked. "Hey, I'm not arguing here. But did you ever think maybe it's time you gave yourself a break and got over what happened to Mike? Wouldn't he want you to live your life?"

Rolling her eyes, she leaned back and chewed on the inside of her cheek, but didn't yank her hand free. "Whatever."

Nate forced his gaze away from her mouth and back to her eyes. "After the shooting, Frost ran a sheet on Norah Redfox. Standard procedure. I dug deeper into her background, and she's absolutely clean. She's a lawyer for Child Protective Services."

"A lawyer, not a loony?"

"Yeah. Although I guess they're not mutually exclusive." Chuckling, he brushed the back of her hand with his thumb. A delicate shiver shook her. All he could think about was holding her close and keeping her safe. He cleared his throat. "But that's not why I'm here. We identified the shooter."

"Who is he?"

"*Was* he. Last night, patrol found his body in a Dumpster."

All the color drained from her face except for the golden freckles dusting her nose and cheeks.

Nate tightened his hold on her hand. "A small-time hood and drug pusher named Douggie Wendell. Worked for a jailhouse buddy who owns a garage. I've run across them before. No link to Norah Redfox, but I'm investigating his ties to Mike."

She caught one corner of her lip between her teeth again, her fingers trembling in his. "Mike?"

"I have a hunch Wendell sighted on your nametag for a reason."

"That's ridiculous. I just returned to Sereno. I haven't had time to make enemies."

Chapter Three

January 5, 7:15 p.m.

Jana stared at the sixties style building and finally found the gumption to open her car door. Nate was waiting for her inside the morgue, but the thought of having to identify the man who'd shot at her gave her the creeps. The night chill closed around her, and she shoved her hands deeper into her jacket pockets. Ridiculous. She'd seen hundreds of corpses in her thirty-one years, from her first anatomy class to today in the ER.

She dodged another puddle and marched toward the large, darkened building looming in the distance. A fresh batch of goose bumps tiptoed across her skin. Every shadow in the murky, razor-wire fenced parking lot made her think of the hospital shooter.

A car door slammed, and her pulse bumped up a notch. She glanced over her shoulder, squinting into the gloom, but didn't stop.

Something moved next to the jacked-up truck in the far corner, and ice brushed the back of her neck. Footsteps scraped on the asphalt behind her.

Her heart thundered in her ears, and she broke into a run.

Did he have a gun?

She hunched forward, trying to make herself a

smaller target. With cold, sweaty hands, she snatched her cellphone and pushed call.

"Jana?"

"Nate. Help. I'm out front."

"Be right there."

Through the earpiece, she heard his footfalls echo. She stumbled over a chunk of cracked asphalt and went down on one knee. Pain laced through her, and her pants tore, but she scrambled to her feet.

Through the dirty glass door, Nate motioned and buzzed her in.

Trembling, she hurried inside. "Someone was chasing me."

He drew his weapon and pushed her behind him. "Get down."

Jana crouched behind a pillar. Air shuddered into her lungs. She swallowed hard to control the gasps and breathed slowly and deeply. The floor tiles in the dimly lit lobby were cold, and her bruised palms and scraped knee ached.

"Nothing's out there." He relocked the door and extended a hand to help her up. "Damn it, Jana. It's already dark. If you were scared, why didn't you call? I'd have met you at your car."

"I didn't think..."

"Exactly."

Her heart skipped, but she held back her temper to avoid the argument. "Sorry I'm so late. I had patients in post-op and no backup. I had to wait until they were stable."

"Wendell's not going anywhere." Nate raised an eyebrow and slanted her an assessing glance.

She met his deep brown gaze, and her insides

jumped and twisted. Heat flamed her cheeks.

With the ghost of a grin, he ushered her down a long corridor toward a waiting elevator. "How'd the rest of your shift go?"

"The afternoon was hectic. Gruesome. I patched up two preteen girls who got caught in a drive-by shooting."

"Wearing the wrong color?"

"If only. The mom, who wasn't much older than I am, swore they're too young and innocent to be gangbangers."

Nate opened the elevator and followed her in. "Not likely. Eastside gangs rope them in early."

Brushed steel doors slid shut with a teeth-grinding squeal, caging her close enough beside him to feel his heat. The narrow elevator had been built for a gurney, long but with barely enough room for an EMT to squeeze beside a corpse. Her adrenaline-driven pulse still pounded in her throat. She clamped her teeth together and pressed her fists tight against her thighs.

Nate slapped the hold button, stalling the elevator. He turned, looming over her, his jaw tense, his mouth taut and straight.

Nowhere to go, she glanced up half a foot to meet his gaze and swallowed with difficulty. Why had she ever thought of him as a teddy bear? With those muscles and the fierce, dangerous expression on his face, he seemed more like a grizzly.

Fighting the urge to step back, she straightened her spine and drew a slow breath. "Nate, I..."

"You need to be more careful," he barked in an I'm-in-charge tone.

His attitude scorched her exhausted nerves, and she

raised her chin. She did not need an ass-chewing. "I always am. I know how to take care of myself."

"Not in this town."

"What do you mean?"

Nate pursed his lips. "It's not the Sereno we lived in years ago."

"I work in the ER; I've seen the worst." She touched her fingertips to his sleeve. "Look, it's no big deal. I'm not in any danger."

"That's not what you said a minute ago."

"I can't help it. My perspective's skewed." She shrugged and crossed her arms tightly over her chest. "I'm seeing punks with hand cannons around every corner."

He studied her silently, and one corner of his mouth drew down. "Uh-huh." He ran his fingers through his short black hair and poked the down button with the other hand.

The elevator groaned and jerked toward the basement, throwing her off balance. "I must be tired if I can't keep my feet under me."

He laid a big, warm hand on her waist and steadied her, moving closer. Close enough for her to catch the faint, but compelling male scent along with his aftershave. Something low in her body hummed to life, and her long dormant libido started to defrost.

Back when she was dating Mike, Nate had been a good friend. She'd liked both guys from the start and been attracted to both, but Nate had always seemed too intense and a little scary, without the charm and easy charisma Mike could turn on at will. Plus, Mike had pursued her single-mindedly, even while she worked for him as an intern.

But Mike was gone, and she had the rest of her life to live.

The elevator settled with a clunk. The B above the door lit, and a warning chimed.

He followed her out, but grabbed her arm.

Her skin tingled.

"Hold on a minute. The coroner's straight. Nichols has stayed clean, even in this sewer."

"What does that have to do with...?"

Nate tapped a finger on his lips. "Can't make the same claim for his staff. Nichols said we could use his office to talk if we need to. Keep your questions under wraps until then," he said, dropping his voice to a whisper.

She paused for two heartbeats. "Noted. Let's get this over with."

"Good." Replacing his strong hand on the small of her back, he steered her along the dingy linoleum. He stopped to push a square metal button that jutted out from the wall.

The frosted glass double doors swung open. A formaldehyde blast seared her nostrils, drowning everything except the sickly sweet smell of decay. She blinked to clear her stinging eyes.

Nate dropped his hand and waved her into the chilly room. Ahead, a white-coated woman wearing a heavy rubber apron, goggles, and gloves hosed down a stainless steel autopsy table. With a squeegee, she scraped bits of offal into the drain trays that ran along the sides.

At the other end of the room, a man hoisted a body bag from a metal gurney and dumped it into a refrigerated drawer with a squelch. Faintly queasy, Jana winced and drew a deep breath through her mouth.

Half a dozen gurneys, each bearing a corpse, lined the walls. Light filtered through glass bricks at ground level outside and cast eerie shadows. Blocks of specimens preserved and encased in wax were stacked along the top, waiting to be sliced like blocks of cheddar for microscopic examination.

Dr. Nichols glanced at Nate, set aside the bone saw he'd been cleaning, and removed his safety goggles. His eyebrows arched as he surveyed her wrinkled, stained, and torn scrubs. "Hey, Kapulani. You finally learned how to show a pretty lady a good time?"

"Bart Nichols, meet Jana Sutherland."

She forced a quick smile. "Dr. Nichols. Sorry to come by so late."

"She's here to ID Wendell."

"Ah. One of my favorite tenants. We've cleaned him up a bit since you saw him, Kapulani." The tall, bony coroner stood and rubbed his hands together. His light blue eyes sparkled below thick brows. Wisps of grizzled salt and pepper hair brushed his collar. He cast a fleeting look at his two assistants.

Jana's gaze followed his, and she shivered. The woman had shut off the hose and stood silently. Next to the autopsy table, the male aide guarded a body bag.

"Start on the next one, Laura. I'll be there in a minute." Nichols lifted half-glasses onto his nose and grabbed a clipboard from the ledge. He pointed to the wall of drawers. "Let me pull Wendell out for you."

The shiny metal drawer squeaked open, and Nichols unzipped the body bag.

Jana shuddered at the face distorted by a gunshot through the left eye socket. Most of the skullcap and braincase were missing, but a hank of dark brown hair hung limp over the right cheek.

Nichols handed her a pair of nitrile gloves. "We finished with him around lunchtime. Just waiting for the tox screen to come back."

She snapped on gloves, shifted the clump of hair aside, and checked the ears and neck. "There are ligature marks and bruising on the throat. Was the head wound post-mortem?"

"No. Cause of death." Nichols opened the bag the rest of the way.

"And the other abrasions?"

"Rats. He took a short vacation in a local Dumpster."

A shiver ran through her, and Nate stepped closer. "This your shooter?" he asked gruffly.

In the background, the unmistakable screech of a bone saw ripped through a ribcage. She glanced at Nate. "Yes, I recognize his facial structure and the old break in his nose."

"Can I commandeer your office to take her statement, Nichols? I need the ID on paper before this witness disappears."

****

7:35 p.m.

Nate locked the door behind them and flipped the blinds shut. Jana looked like hell. Her lips had a faint bluish tinge, and her teeth chattered. Her skinned knee showed through the rip in her light cotton scrubs. She'd had a rough week, plus this room was only slightly warmer than the inside of a deep freezer.

He took a manila envelope from his pocket, tossed it on Nichols' cluttered desk, and shucked his sport coat.

"What did you mean, disappear? No punk with a gun can chase me away," she said, her hands clenched.

"That performance was for our audience. Gave me a good reason to drag you in here." He draped the coat over her shoulders.

Hazel eyes huge, she started to remove the coat. "Thank you, but you need this."

He held his hands on her shoulders to stop her. "I'm fine. Your jacket doesn't do much."

"I should have stopped at home for something warmer, but I was running late."

When she snuggled into his coat and wrapped it tight around herself, his heart beat faster, heavier. Her ripe, full lips drew his gaze. He wanted to warm her with his mouth, his body, and replace the fear on her face with pleasure. Instead, he drew his thumb down her soft cheek. "No problem."

He pulled out a chair for her and sat in another close by. "I had a hunch, so I rustled up a couple of mug shots I want you to see." He passed her the first two photos.

With a faint frown, Jana leaned forward and laid them on the desk. She pointed at one. "This is the shooter, but he's younger. When was it taken?"

"Ten years ago."

Her brow furrowed deeper, then her eyes lit. "Was he involved in Mike's murder?"

"Can't prove it, but he did time for drug dealing. The case Mike and I were dogging at the time. Sent this character to prison, too." He tapped the other mug shot. "Joe Morgan. Recognize him?"

She shook her head and folded the lapels of his

coat against her slender neck.

Nate fanned several more pictures in front of her.

"That's me!" Surprise and indignation shaded her voice.

"I have shots of everyone who had any contact with Mike that week."

"I think I know that man, but he wears a Rolex now instead of Bermuda shorts."

"Morrie Tomasini, Mike's former snitch. He passed us information about Morgan and the drug ring."

"He's sure come up in the world. The hospital board just named him a trustee."

"He's sharp. Lucky. Midas had nothing on the guy. Built a convenience store into a real estate empire." Nate cocked an eyebrow and stacked the evidence. "Questioned him a couple years ago on a different case, and the captain slapped me around the block."

Her frown reappeared. "But you were always careful. You never made mistakes."

"I did that time. The guy was clean, or at least, well-insulated." A gut deep burn of anger and frustration sparked back to life, but Nate shrugged. "Doesn't matter anymore. Corruption's everywhere. Honest witnesses are harassed, suspects released, evidence does a disappearing act. One week, a cop's a straight arrow, and the next he has a new ride, a fat bank account and an attitude."

"Why doesn't the chief clean out the ranks?"

"Ask him to show you pictures of his new lodge on Lake Tahoe. I've fought nonstop, but the rot is like kudzu. Chop off one vine and the damn stuff grows a foot in six other directions by morning." He slumped back in his chair, rubbing his forehead.

"Why don't you leave Sereno?" She squeezed his hand with her slim, cold fingers. "Don't you still have connections in Hawaii?"

"Yeah, but first I need to finish…to solve…"

"What?"

"Mike's murder."

"And you lectured me about getting over his death." She poked him in the chest with her middle finger. "Am I right?"

"I don't know." He shrugged. "It's hard to leave all this behind, but the islands sound better every day. What do you think?"

Her eyes lit up, and a smile brightened her face. She let out a long, dramatic sigh. "Tropical sunshine. I can already feel the freckles popping out on my skin."

A bikini. Acres of smooth, bare skin. His body stirred and tightened. "Sure. Every time my Dad gets wind of the murder stats in Sereno, he's on the horn, talking up the department in Hilo."

"Very tempting, but only a fantasy. We both have commitments here."

He grabbed the lapels of his coat and drew her closer, trapping her against his chest. "To hell with commitments."

A flush highlighted her cheekbones. Her lids fluttered closed.

He kissed her once, twice, and his mouth closed over hers, fierce and hungry. His fingers shifted beneath her short, soft hair, supporting her head. He slanted his mouth and teased the seam between her lips with his tongue.

She trembled and opened for him. Her silky tongue brushed against his.

He savored her welcoming mouth, sucking her lower lip between his. When she wound her arms around his waist, her needy sound zapped him like a Taser. He smiled and crushed her to him, and she didn't pull away.

The door handle rattled, and someone banged on the wood.

Not now.

Glassy-eyed, she blinked several times. "Nate?"

Bang-bang-bang. The loose glass shook in its frame.

"Kapulani? Get your ass out here," Bart Nichols shouted.

Swearing under his breath, he released her. "Got to see what's gone down."

"Right."

He tucked the pictures into his inside pocket and shifted his jacket back around her shoulders. "Forget you saw these for now, okay?"

She nodded with understanding, and he opened the office door to chaos. The morgue swarmed with EMTs and cops.

Alex Frost staggered up to him, white-faced and dazed. The young cop looked like a zombie.

Adrenaline pumping into his bloodstream, Nate clapped his friend on the shoulder. "What happened?"

Frost's stricken, red-rimmed eyes met his. "Those creeps made good on their threats. Why didn't I cave, Nate? They killed my wife. Killed our son."

Chapter Four

January 5, 8:15 p.m.

Nate opened his front door, Glock drawn, and his insides tied in knots. The warning alarm beeped its sixty-second countdown, while he double-checked the brightly lit house and jammed the deadbolt home.

No intruders. Not this time.

Letting out a huge sigh, he keyed in his security code and slipped his gun back into the underarm holster.

Bruner barked from the back porch. Nate let the dog in and fed him before taking a minute to switch on some music and grab a beer.

Returning to the living room, he lit the gas fireplace and warmed his hands. When he shucked his jacket, he caught a faint trace of Jana's scent. His groin tightened, and he glanced at his couch.

Man, he ached for that woman. Just thinking about her hands, her mouth, and her tight, gently-curved ass made him crazy.

He wanted her here.

Now.

Bruner nudged against his hand, whining. With a sigh, Nate patted the old boxer's head and dug out a rawhide bone.

While the dog chewed, Nate shifted aside two

books and pressed a hidden latch on his bookcase. The small door of a concealed safe clicked open, and he extracted a battered metal cashbox.

He kicked off his shoes and collapsed on his black leather chair, rifling through the pictures he'd shown Jana. He'd never gotten much satisfaction from locking away Wendell and Morgan. Their high-priced lawyer had wrangled a plea bargain, and within six months, the perps were out on parole.

Propping his feet on the coffee table, he twisted the top off his beer. The cold, bitter brew slid down his throat. He licked his lips and took another swallow.

He stared at the picture of Jana with long hair and an innocent smile. Why shoot at her? And why now? She hadn't been anywhere near Sereno for ten years. Nate rubbed a thumb across his stubble-roughened chin. She'd all but disappeared after Mike died. Had someone else tried to find her, but hadn't known she'd headed for medical school on the East Coast? Maybe given up for years, but then stalked her when she resurfaced?

What did Jana do to make herself a target? Even in Sereno, no one sent hit men after innocents.

His stomach dropped, and a wave of cold swamped him. Alex Frost's grief-stricken face flashed through Nate's mind. If he and Jana hooked up, would she be in more danger? He'd refused their dirty money, just like Alex. *Shit. What a disaster.*

Now that he'd gotten a taste of Jana and felt her flash-bang response to him, he craved her. But he couldn't both pursue her and keep her anonymous. Hell, scratching an itch wasn't worth exposing her to killers.

Nate drained the beer and rested his pounding head

against the heel of his hand. His muscles ached like he'd been in a brawl. At the thought of Jana getting hurt because of him, a weight as big as a rhino sat on his chest.

He straightened and set the empty bottle on the hearth. Who said the killers would ever find out? He could pursue Jana on the sly and still keep her safe. He grinned. For a little while, sneaking around might even add an edge to the fireworks.

But hiding their relationship wouldn't work long-term. He had to escape this battle zone and find someplace he could actually make a life worth living. And he would, the minute he closed Mike's case.

Nate plowed through his cache and flipped open the tattered, black leather notebook he'd never surrendered into evidence. He searched through pages of scribbled notes, hunting for a connection.

Crossed-out leads.

Dead ends.

Nothing popped.

But Wendell's murder opened up new possibilities. As his boss, Morgan was a likely suspect. Nate cracked his knuckles.

Maybe he'd track the money closer this time. After Mike died, he'd figured Morgan's cash came from drug sales. The scenario fit, so he hadn't dug very deep.

Nate stared at the flames flickering behind the glass fire screen. Bruner curled next to him for an ear scratch. "What do you think, buddy? Did I miss something the night Mike died?"

Every moment, every sensation of that night ten years ago was branded into his memory. He could still feel the sweat trickle down his spine. A third quarter moon had lit the night sky. With no breeze, the air stank of sewer lines under repair.

Glock in hand, he crept along the chain link fence bordering the construction site. Where was Mike? Why had he come here tonight? And why the hell didn't he wait for backup?

Two gunshots cracked.

His heart pounded, and his senses heightened. Nate turned and raced down the alley toward the noise.

An engine turned over. A few seconds later, a white pickup with blinding high beams rounded the corner, headed straight at him.

He jumped to the side and hit the pavement hard. Before his head stopped spinning, the truck disappeared.

He crept forward, sweeping the area with his weapon at high ready.

Mike's cruiser.

Hyper alert for any movement, Nate peered in the open window. A coppery smell stung his nose, and a vicious chill gripped his gut.

A small wound leaked blood down his partner's forehead. Nate ripped his radio from his duty belt. "11-99! Officer down!"

A rumble from deep in Bruner's throat brought Nate back to the present. Adrenaline buzzed through his system, and his mind cleared.

The hackles on the dog's neck stood up straight, and he bared his teeth. With a loud growl, Bruner sprang off the couch and scrambled for the front door, barking furiously.

Taking a slow, deep breath, Nate drew his gun and followed. An intruder? He checked the security camera monitor in the hall. The motion sensitive floodlights had snapped on. There. A man bent over the squad car hood.

Nate grabbed the dog's collar, braced in a crouch with his weapon raised, and cracked open the door.

The alarm warning beeped.

"Freeze. Police," he shouted from behind the steel door.

No shots, but footsteps pounded down the block.

"Sit. Stay."

With his ears pinned back, Bruner shivered on his haunches, but obeyed.

The yard blazed with floodlights. Searching as he moved, Nate hedged across the porch and around the corner of the garage. No one.

Now what?

Down the block, an engine cranked. *Damn.*

He lowered his gun and shrugged. Probably just a punk. He let out a disgusted grunt.

Blood? Nate sniffed hard. Why did he smell blood?

Squinting, he stalked across the driveway and kicked a spray paint can out of his path. At the clatter, Bruner howled from the front door, then whined.

Butcher shop garbage dripped down the fender. Mutilated organs and bloody offal littered the cement on one side of the cruiser.

Scrawled across his windshield in red paint were the words, "You're next."

****

January 5, 8:45 p.m.

Jana slammed her car door and glanced around the dark road in front of her house. Gang graffiti tagged the fence across the street, and she'd passed two hookers and a drug deal on the drive home. But no suspicious people loitered in the shadows.

No black pickups.

No drug-crazed punks with guns.

She drew a shivering breath of frigid air and flipped up her sweatshirt hood, but her pulse rate hit triple digits. *Chicken.*

Grabbing her gym bag and purse from the trunk, she hitched them onto a shoulder and slammed the trunk. She'd worked up a satisfying sweat kickboxing, but the biting wind hijacked all the warmth from her blood. After battering the pads at the gym, her legs would be sore tomorrow, but at least she'd cranked down her stress level.

She rubbed the dull ache behind her sternum, unable to banish the victims she'd seen yesterday in the morgue from her thoughts. Katy Frost's only mistake had been to love an honest cop, but it had been a fatal mistake.

Jana bit her lip and marched across the street. Would a connection to Nate put her in more danger? Realistically, he posed a potential double threat—first, whoever killed Katy Frost and her son might be after Nate next, and second, he was a do-it-my-way alpha cop. His hot kisses had shut down her brain.

That wasn't necessarily a bad thing, though. She felt alive and aware of her body again for the first time in years. Dropping her chin, she twirled in a tight little circle. Jana Sutherland, former surgical robot, transformed into a real, warm-blooded woman by six amazing, incendiary kisses.

When she'd gone off to med school after Mike died, she'd been too emotionally battered and busy for romance. But she'd hidden behind those excuses long enough.

She ruffled her damp hair. Did she want to date Nate? Probably not long-term. Her reaction to him was so intense, it scared her. He seemed like the kind of guy who'd demand everything from her.

But he had a point. She'd wallowed for too many years. It was past time to bury her grief for Mike. It was time to go after what she wanted, time to actually live her life again. With one last glance around, she hurried up her front steps.

From a dark corner near her door, the chains on her redwood porch swing creaked. "Dr. Sutherland?"

Jana's heart sprinted. She stumbled backwards, and her keys clattered onto the top cement step. She snatched them up, fisting the sharp-edged metal between her fingers for a weapon.

"Sorry, I didn't mean to startle you. It's cold tonight, so I curled up on your swing out of the wind." Norah Redfox rose slowly, bracing her ribs with both arms. In the bleak light, her face looked gray and haggard.

"Why are you here? I just sent you home from the hospital this morning."

"I had to talk to you right away. You have to understand the consequences of not making things right."

Jana dodged around the woman, set her bag on the landing, and planted her hands on her hips. "You should be in bed."

"I can't rest. Not until you change the past."

Jana's skin crawled. Her belly curdled, and she recoiled, slowly shaking her head.

"You must prevent more tragedy. How can I make you believe me?" the woman asked, edging between Jana and the front door.

Despite the tightness in her chest, Jana forced in a deep breath. The poor woman was confused, but hardly dangerous. "Go home. Please, Ms. Redfox. Your meds have clouded your thinking. Mike's dead. No one and nothing can change the past."

"You can. And you must. Until you do, you're in deadly peril. The blight will spread, and many more will die."

"I've heard enough of your scare tactics. You need to leave."

The woman stared, holding her palms out flat. Pain shimmered in her dark eyes and creased her forehead. "But I can help you. I've helped others change history."

Jana clenched her hands and caught hold of the panic inching through her. "I'll call the police unless you go. Come here again, and I'll get a restraining order. Is that clear?"

"Yes." The woman shuffled past her and down the first step. Then she turned. "If you refuse me now, within the week you'll come to me, overwhelmed by your grief."

Chapter Five

January 6, 3:45 p.m.

The loose ends in the hospital shooting still stood out like the tracks on a junkie's arm. Nate threw Frost's report on his desk and speared his fingers through his hair.

Take two bullets, plus one hyped-up druggie with a gun, and a do-gooder doctor. Stir them together, and what do you get? A corpse in a Dumpster.

But why kill Wendell? To shut him up? Or to enforce a point? Nate's gut itched. The scenario didn't quite fit, and he couldn't get his hands on the rest of Wendell's case file to decipher the riddle.

Nate flipped a yellow pencil back and forth between his fingers. MacLean or Captain Greene must be hiding something, but both denied they had the crime scene reports or the physical evidence. Captain Greene was breathing down his ass for grabbing the case from Frost. Maybe he'd been onto something last night. Maybe some creative financial forensics would expose the rot.

Time to hack into the account records of Mr. Douglas C. Wendell, deceased. With his heart banging against his ribs, Nate peered over the top of his cube and surveyed the bullpen. Empty. And the door to Greene's office was closed.

Nate rubbed his sweaty hands on his thighs and flipped open his laptop. He punched in his access code subroutine and tapped his fingers impatiently while the display cycled. Brushing the line of sweat off his lip, he leaned his mouth into his hand.

A minute later, he smiled at the screen. Douggie had stashed away a sizable nest egg. But how? Not too many legal ways for a part-time grease monkey to pull down that kind of loot. Bank statements detailed puny paychecks from Morgan's Garage and columns of cash deposits, all below the federal reporting limit. Drug money?

Frowning, Nate chewed on his lip and reviewed the numbers. The last entry made his gut lurch. Wendell's account had been drained the day he died, and his seven-figure balance had vanished.

Nate shifted to Joe Morgan's accounts. A series of whopper transactions cleared every month. Money laundering?

He scrolled through years of transactions. His heart pounded like he'd just finished a marathon, and his insides twisted. *Damn.* A six-figure deposit from an offshore account the night Mike Gordon died. Had Mike's murder been a paid hit?

Nate leaned back in his chair and tapped the pencil against his knee. Time to get a warrant. He cricked his neck and stood. Across the bullpen, MacLean slouched in Greene's open doorway.

A cold shiver launched between Nate's shoulders. He wished he could read lips. But he understood body language. MacLean looked nervous. The Captain didn't act too happy either. They turned and glared at him in unison, and his gut did a belly flop.

Nate keyed in his overwrite code and pocketed his flash drive. Hunching over his desk, he closed his laptop.

His desk phone buzzed, and his pulse skipped. When he checked the caller ID, his heart kicked into a gallop. What did Jana want?

Frowning, he scanned the noisy bullpen again. MacLean had moved to within fifteen feet and was leaning on the next dirty gray cubicle divider.

He lifted the receiver. "Kapulani."

"Nate, I want to talk to you."

"Where'd you get this number?"

"Dispatch punched me through."

His stomach twisted around his backbone and sloshed acid into his gut. Closing his eyes, he braced his forehead on his palms and mumbled into the phone, "Tell me you didn't give the operator your name."

"No, I said I was a witness calling to make a statement. Why?"

The tension between his shoulders eased. Thank God. "Never mind. What do you need?"

"I decided you were right. It's time for me to face what happened to Mike. Can you get me access to his case file?"

Nate let out the breath he'd been holding. Good thing he had copies at home. "I'll see what I can do."

"Great. I'll be there after work, around six."

He felt the blood drain from his face. "No. Not here," he barked.

MacLean's head snapped around, and his eyes narrowed. The roar of conversation in the bullpen suddenly died to nothing.

"Thank you for your interest, ma'am." Nate cleared

his throat. "Although we're always grateful for tips from the public, that case is closed."

"But..."

Couldn't that stubborn, independent woman take a freaking hint? He'd told her about the corruption in the department, and she knew about Alex Frost's family being murdered. He cupped his hands around the mouthpiece and hissed, "Absolutely not."

Greene signaled from the doorway, and with a last backward glance, MacLean headed across the bullpen toward dispatch.

"I just want some closure, Nate."

"Wendell got closure. You want to visit Nichols dressed in a body bag?"

She clucked her tongue and let out a little huff. "You're exaggerating."

Might as well explain, he thought. He hugged the phone tighter. "Look, we can't risk anybody connecting us," he growled. "If you show up here, you'll leave me exposed and make yourself a bare-assed, please-come-and-get-me target."

"Nate..."

"No. I'm in charge. Too dangerous."

"We can talk later. I'm being paged." *Click*.

****

5:30 p.m.

Jana hunched in her car outside the Sereno Police Station. The sprawling stucco complex was built atop a rise, but some punks had spray-painted gang slogans on one side. She shook her head in amazement. How had anyone gotten away with tagging a cop shop?

She wrapped her coat closer against the twilight chill and finished the last sip of her latte. Her mind flipped back to Norah Redfox. The freak's crazy claims had put down roots in her brain. Last night, true crime nightmares had invaded every single dream.

Jana picked at the paper sleeve on her cup and peeled off a cardboard strip. When she'd called, Nate had warned her away with dire predictions. But no matter what he said, no matter how angry he sounded, she had to see the files before she could move on. She had to see them today. She'd already wasted enough years grieving.

She stuffed her cup in the holder, locked her car, and cut across the damp lawn toward the building. She'd never really been in love with Mike. Infatuation maybe? Lust, for sure. Now all she felt was grief and the vague sense of guilt Norah Redfox had dredged to the surface. Time to exorcise a ghost.

Two teenage toughs wearing droopy pants and green bandanas swaggered out the station doors toward the parking lot. The taller one flicked his cigarette in her direction and nudged the other, sniggering.

Fear tickled the back of her throat, and she increased her pace and dug in her purse. Her shaky fingers closed on her pepper spray.

The two thugs stopped at the edge of the lot and elbowed each other. The shorter kid slid a hand in his pocket. Metal scraped against metal, and a switchblade glinted.

Her breath caught. Her heart raced. "Stay back!" She glared at him and held the pepper spray in her outstretched arm.

The big kid punched his buddy's shoulder with a terse warning and flashed his middle finger.

She edged past them and scrambled backwards up

the stairs.

"Jana?" a sharp baritone voice called from behind her.

She turned and released a shaky sigh. Nate.

"MacLean, that guy just posted bail. Clear him out," Nate ordered, his stance wide, and hands fisted.

The sandy haired, middle-aged cop with a beer belly straightened, frowning at the thugs. MacLean patted the weapon on his duty belt and sauntered toward them, smirking. "Put some hustle into it, boys. Sergeant wants you off his turf, pronto."

Nate glowered at their backs until the kids turned the corner. Then he glared at her. "What the hell are you doing?"

Ignoring the heart pumping madly inside her rib cage, she pulled a face. "I'm standing in front of the police station."

"I told you not to come."

"I know. But I'm going inside, with or without you."

His teeth grated, and he let loose a low growl. "Fine. Damage is done anyway." He took her arm and hurried her up the last few steps.

His big, warm hand cupped her elbow, spreading tingles of heat. Why was she so sensitive to his touch? She fought the awareness and glanced sideways at his square jaw. Date him? She'd been delusional. Maybe their kiss in the coroner's office had melted her brain, because Nate even out-domineered her father.

He signaled a guard inside to open the glass doors and followed her into the crowded lobby. "Never come here alone again. It's not safe."

Jana shivered. Starbursts framed half a dozen bullet

marks in the door. "When I was an intern, Sereno wasn't this dangerous."

"No." He touched her shoulder, and the warmth fanned out. "Wait a minute. I'll arrange a pass."

She handed him her ID and looked around for a seat. A dozen people crowded benches lining the walls. One frenzied woman with a thin face and deep creases on her forehead had three kids with her. The baby fussed, and the toddler wiped his drippy nose on his sleeve. The other kid coughed and sniffled.

Alone on a bench, a man with lanky gray hair muttered into his beard. When Jana walked past him, the stench of vomit and rancid body odor had her craving a gas mask and a giant bottle of hand sanitizer.

She paused before the display case where a faded, black-framed photo of Mike hung. A cold, flat feeling rose in her chest, and she wrapped her arms around her waist. That night she'd told Mike to leave, told him she never wanted to see him again. When he'd stomped out, he'd been too angry to think clearly. Maybe Mike hadn't been her soul mate, but he hadn't deserved to die.

"Jana?" Nate materialized behind her with a visitor's pass in his hand.

She forced down the lump in her throat and looked into his deep brown eyes. A slight frown still creased his forehead, but for a split second, he seemed more strong and protective than angry.

"You okay?"

Though her heart still pummeled her sternum, she shot him a quick smile. Nate narrowed his gaze and ushered her through security. "The observation area's private." He led her past the interrogation room and opened a door. "What's so freaking important?"

Her cheeks heated, and she shifted sideways. "I told you. I need to know what happened to Mike."

Nate didn't respond immediately. His face seemed carved from stone, with a ridge chiseled between his brows.

She hated to push him, but he didn't understand how Norah's words had haunted her. "Ms. Redfox confronted me at my house last night, spouting more hocus pocus."

"Let me guess. She freaked you out, so now you're determined to see the evidence."

"You don't sound surprised."

He slammed his hand on the table, and she jumped. "Damn it, Jana. Someone's gunning for you. By coming here to see me, you've made yourself more of a target. Are you trying to get killed before I can find out why?"

Her stomach knotted, and her nerves coiled into jangled bundles. "You're overreacting."

"You saw what happened to Katy Frost and the boy," he hissed and stalked out.

****

5:45 p.m.

Nate paused outside the observation room. He'd expected Jana to show up tonight, but figured he'd talk her around, and she'd leave smiling, maybe agree to meet him later, someplace private where he could show her the evidence. Instead, when those punks threatened her, he'd caved and let her inside. *Big tough cop*, he thought, disgusted.

He yanked the door open and banged it shut behind him. Since he couldn't turn her over his knee and spank her, he'd scare her bad enough to keep her safe. Opening the flap, he drew the first picture of Mike from a manila envelope.

Jana murmured her thanks and laid the crime scene photo on the table. "Just a trickle of blood from his temple," she said in her doctor's voice. But her forehead wrinkled, and her face tilted sideways, like she didn't quite understand. "He looks surprised."

Nate chose a second picture showing the gruesome exit wound. He hated that shot. Brought back too many memories. Brought back the sense of paralyzed helplessness. Brought back the metallic reek of blood.

When he passed it to Jana, her face blanched, and she cupped her hand over her mouth.

Maybe this would make the danger real enough to drive her away. He handed her the rest, and she pawed through the pile, her expression shifting from shock to horror. She uncovered shots of Mike on the autopsy table, bit a knuckle, and closed her eyes.

His gut twisted, but he straightened his spine and resisted the urge to comfort her.

Footsteps echoed in the hall, and the door handle behind him rattled. Adrenaline slammed into his blood stream, and his heart pounded with sickening force. He swept the pictures into the trash and booted the can underneath the table.

Captain Greene shouldered into the room and swiped a hand over his bald crown. Raising one eyebrow, he bared bleached teeth. "Got a statement from her yet, Kapulani?"

"Working on it, sir. She claims she never saw Wendell except when he shot at her." *Shit*. He had to protect her, but to do it; he'd have to piss her off. No alternative. She'd understand once he explained. Nate glared at Jana like she was dog shit on the bottom of his shoe.

She recoiled, blinking at him wide-eyed.

She got the message.

"Fine. I'll observe," Greene declared. He dragged a metal folding chair over and sat backwards with his arms crossed over the top. "Let's hear your story, Miss Sutherland."

"It's Dr. Sutherland. And you've lost me. I'm not a suspect," she said in a crisp, don't-mess-with-my-head voice.

Greene's brows lifted, and he drew in a breath through the corner of his mouth. "She's a cool one."

Narrowing his eyes to slits, Nate leaned closer. "Where were you the night Douggie Wendell was murdered?"

She shook her head slowly. "At home in bed."

"Alone?" Greene demanded.

She tipped up her chin and nodded. "Yes, of course."

Greene slapped a test tube on the table. "Then prove you're innocent. Give me a DNA sample."

Chapter Six

January 7, 6:30 a.m.

The sun warmed the secluded tropical beach. Surf pounded in the background, and a soft breeze played over her skin. With her eyes closed, Jana snuggled against his broad chest and listened to the slow, steady beat of his heart.

"I want you." Nate turned and kissed her. His big hands stroked her breasts, and his legs tangled with hers, easing them apart.

Her pulse rioted. Pleasure flamed at his knowing touch. She traced her hands over the hard muscles of his shoulders and down his belly.

He whispered enticing words she couldn't quite understand. But his fingers trailed lower and explored her triangle of curls. With the lightest of touches, he traced her folds and parted them gently.

Her blood tingled with awareness. She gazed into his dark eyes, hungry for all of him.

Jana awakened, pulsing with need. An ache burned low in her body. Huffing, she threw back the covers. "Fat chance. Nate Kapulani will always be a pushy, stubborn, macho cop."

Tossing her nightshirt on the floor, she wrenched open the shower door. "Cold water? No way, he's not worth the misery." She cranked the hot tap, stuck her hand under the jet, and stepped in. Luxuriating under the steamy cascade, she grabbed a loofah and scrubbed.

A hollow throbbed in the pit of her stomach. After last night at the station, she never wanted to see Nate again. The big jerk. She was the one who'd been shot, but he and the Captain had treated her like a crook.

Did Nate actually consider her a suspect in the punk's murder? She worried the inside of her lip. She had a compelling motive and, worse, no alibi. Home alone in bed didn't count for much when a murdered thug was rotting in the morgue.

She scrunched her eyes closed and worked shampoo into her hair. Once Raines heard the story, she'd have to find a new job to pay her med school loans and mortgage. She'd probably been a fool to buy this place.

She stuck her head under the hot spray to rinse, shut off the water, and patted herself dry. She'd scrubbed so hard her skin tingled.

Jana dressed in clean flannel pajama bottoms and a sweatshirt. The aroma of fresh coffee enticed her down the stairs.

Bright morning sunshine poured through the kitchen window. She patted her automatic espresso machine and chose an oversized cup from her collection.

Maybe she could find a ripe grapefruit on the tree. She took a gulp of coffee, slipped on her flip-flops, and headed outside.

Huge, yellow-pink fruit hung on the limbs. She picked one, but a long thorny spike pierced her thumb. She yanked her hand back and set the grapefruit on the garden bench.

Noises from the alley sent her heart pounding, and she hurried toward the steps. Could that pack of feral dogs be back?

Thumps. A muffled curse. Nate vaulted her back fence and dropped onto the grass.

With flushed cheeks and pursed lips, she scrutinized the big, domineering jerk-in-blue and sucked a drop of blood off her thumb. "What are you doing here?"

He loped across the yard and examined her hand. "Wicked thorn."

She extricated her fingers without much subtlety and stepped back. "I asked why you're here. Practicing your high jump?"

"Parked in the alley. Can't let anyone see me here."

Her brows hiked. "What's that supposed to mean?"

"I warned you not to come near the station."

The pulse at her temples throbbed. "Well, excuse me for not saluting at your every command."

"I'm trying to keep you safe. Alive."

"Thanks." Gritting her teeth, she turned on her heel and started toward the door. "You let yourself in. You can let yourself out."

He followed her along the walkway. "I get why you're pissed."

"Really?" She batted her lashes at him and made a little kissy noise. "Oh, you're good. Must be why you're a great big ol' detective?"

"Grilling you was Captain Greene's latest brainstorm. No clue where he got the idea."

"No shit? But you both treated me like a lying heap of trash." Her voice sounded loud and a little shrill, and her hands fisted on her hips. "Like a freaking criminal."

Shaking his head slowly, he thrust his chin forward. "You have absolutely no idea."

"I've never even fired a gun in my life, but today I have to tell my Chief of Staff why I'm the prime suspect in a murder investigation."

"Stop." He grabbed her arm.

"Don't touch me." She ripped loose from his grasp and backed toward the twisted oak.

His eyebrows had scrunched together, and the veins in his neck pulsed. He stalked toward her. "Damn it, Jana. Every contact with me pulls you deeper into this mess. Remember Frost's family?"

Her stomach dropped with an almost audible thud. "Yes. Then why don't you leave?"

"I played along with Greene to protect you."

"Fine. I forgive you. Goodbye."

"I'm a cop. Let me keep you safe."

She studied his face and sighed. "Okay, okay. I get it."

Ruddy color scorched his ears. He tipped her chin up until her eyes met his. "I'm worried about you."

She let her shoulders sag. "Do you really think I'm still in danger?"

"We both are." Nate drew her against him and sandwiched her between his hard body and the tree.

Pressed tight against him, she could feel his heart thudding in his chest. "So what do we do next?"

Holding her gaze with his intense brown eyes, he dipped his head toward her. His warm mouth pressed against hers lightly, and then his tongue teased her lips.

She shuddered and parted her mouth for him.

His tongue slipped inside. A mad flutter surged all the way to her center.

She slid her arms to his shoulders, and his muscles tensed under her fingers. Her heart thundered. Trembling, she softened against him.

He angled his lips and deepened the kiss, holding his hand behind her neck while his tongue penetrated her mouth. She expected another greedy, thrusting kiss, expected hard, demanding hands racing over her body. Instead, he savored her intimately, as though intent on exploring and tasting each surface.

The insistent brush of his lips and tongue became gentle nips. Hot blood pounded in her veins. She made a hungry noise and arched closer.

An endless moment later, he broke the kiss, and she leaned back to look at him.

He smiled, and her breath caught. Scents from the small garden mixed with the tart, pungent grapefruit.

A bright glare dashed across her vision, and she squinted over his shoulder. Prickly sensations rasped her nerves. Something moved on the other side of the fence. There, beside the neighbor's garage.

A man.

Adrenaline surged.

A man with a gun.

She stuck her calf behind Nate's knee and wrenched. The hip toss toppled him to the ground under her.

"Oof," he groaned. "What the hell?"

A muffled pop exploded from the alley. Her planter smashed, showering them with soil and pottery shards. The flock of crows perched on the roof scattered.

A shriek stuck in her throat.

"Shooter!" Nate shoved her behind the oak, and they huddled against the thick trunk.

Another pop and a thud. A bullet burrowed into the dirt next to the tree. Grass sprayed the air, and a scent hit her nostrils.

A few feet away, the grapefruit she'd just picked exploded. The yellow rind burst into tattered fragments, and juice cascaded down the bench.

Drawing his weapon, Nate came up in a crouch and returned fire.

Two shots slammed into the tree.

She clamped her hands over her ears, trying to curl into the smallest ball possible, but every muscle shook.

Nate squeezed off four more rounds. Another bullet hit the trunk, and the branches rattled. He pushed her lower and shoved his phone into her hand. "Call Frost. Speed dial seven."

Her heart raced, fast and erratic, and a knot clogged her throat. With clumsy fingers, she punched the number. When Officer Frost answered, she explained quickly and ended the call.

"Why not 911?" she whispered.

Nate shook his head and curled his free hand around her shoulder. "Can't trust anybody else." He shifted and fired two quick rounds. The second shot pinged off the Dumpster in the alley.

Frozen against the rough bark, she listened for movement.

Silence.

Her hands trembled. "Why shoot at me?"

He didn't look at her, just squeezed her shoulder again. "My guess? You know something."

She went cold inside, and her stomach twisted under her lungs. "But what?"

"Some   information   that   threatens   Mike's murderer."

Inhaling a jagged breath, she pressed her fingers to her temples. *Think*. "It must be a mistake. I was a lowly intern, a paper shuffler, when I worked at Sereno PD."

"Then who'd you piss off at the hospital? Kill any patients lately?"

"People die."

He glanced at her sharply, and her cheeks flamed. "I didn't mean to sound callous."

"Realistic." His gaze returned to the alley. "A nutcase?"

A ghoulish chill traced her vertebrae one by one. "The only crazy I know is Norah Redfox."

Nate grunted.

Minutes passed in silence, and the crows settled back on the power lines, cawing their aggravation. Her heartbeat finally stopped throbbing in her ears. "Is he gone?"

"Too soon to tell." Expression grim, he shrugged and returned to his vigil.

"Kapulani?" A man yelled over the side gate. The hinges creaked, and Alex Frost scrambled through the gap, low to the ground. Although he wore civvies, he still moved like a cop, alert and aware. He had quick eyes, but they were bloodshot, and deep grooves framed his tight mouth.

Jana released a long breath and straightened, but Nate shook his head and extended a hand, blocking her behind the tree.

Alex ducked under pine branches, gun drawn.

"I'm moving her inside." Nate scanned the area. "I need to track this guy, but can't leave her unguarded. Can you stick around and escort her to work?"

"Roger." Alex took a defensive posture near in the alley, using one corner of her freestanding garage as protection.

"Thanks. Owe you one."

Alex's face shuttered, and his bleak smile tugged at her heartstrings. "Sure, but I'm outta here tomorrow after the funeral. Resigned last night," he said without inflection.

"Sorry to hear that."

"Maybe you should get out of this hellhole, too."

"Thought about leaving a million times." Nate's mouth quirked as he grabbed Jana's arm. "Ready?"

At her nod, he positioned his body between her and the fence. "Keep low," he ordered and shadowed her across the lawn.

She hurried over the cool grass toward the house, but hesitated, caught by the ruby glint of the mangled grapefruit. Her stomach dipped, and adrenaline fizzed along her spine. That could have been her head. Or Nate's.

"Move," he barked and urged her up the stairs with a hand on her waist.

Inside the kitchen, Nate released her and slid the deadbolt into place. When he turned back toward her with mayhem in his gaze, her joints dissolved into mush. Dragging in a breath, he said her name. A slow, sexy warning.

Her pulse refused to slow, and a totally different type of tension coiled low in her body. She swallowed against the sudden tightness in her throat.

Nate smiled, and his fingers brushed her cheek. "Classy makeup."

"What?" When she touched her face, her finger

came away smeared with mud. She wrinkled her nose.

"Hold still." He smoothed his thumb across the spot, and warmth surged through her.

Avoiding his intense gaze, she took three steps back and ran a shaky hand through her hair. Her fingers dislodged a blade of grass, and she yanked it out. "I...I have to go to work. But how will I get home if Alex drives me?" she asked, her voice shaky and strangled.

"I'll pick you up tonight at the coffee shop off the lobby. We need to talk." He kissed her forehead. "And don't worry. With the new metal detectors and the security detail, the hospital's the safest place around."

****

12:30 p.m.

Nate flexed his clenched hands. Getting shot at had cranked out buckets of adrenaline. The rush sharpened focus, fine-tuned perceptions, and jump-started reactions, but anger blunted his vital edge.

After he called in his location, he glanced around the alley behind Morgan's garage and settled back to wait. Trash stuck in the cyclone fence, and a healthy crop of weeds broke through the asphalt.

The exterior of the auto-repair shop fit the neighborhood. Battered, rust-stained, and tagged by gangs. Weather-beaten plywood covered a broken window. The M in the neon sign blinked off, then fizzled back to life.

A '56 T-Bird convertible purred by, and he slid lower in the seat of his primer-gray cruiser.

Morgan. With his surfer blond hair and a dark, fake-bake tan glowing in the chilly winter sunshine, the son-of-a-bitch tapped his hand to blaring techno metal while the steel door rolled open. Then he drove the tricked-out, turquoise and white car inside, and the garage cranked shut.

Nate crushed his empty coffee cup and tossed the mangled remains into the back seat. He'd rather crush Morgan's scrawny neck.

No, take it slow. Sucking in stale air, he blew out a controlled hiss and forced his heartbeat down from triple digits. Stay focused. He'd never snag this asshole unless he finessed him just right.

He slammed his car door and scanned the area. No movement. No sound, except the distant roar of the expressway. Stretching his neck, he moved toward the building.

With his hand on his gun, he edged through the unlocked front door and whistled under his breath. Not a grease spot on the floor. Painted walls, intense lighting, every tool precisely placed. Half hidden behind the convertible, a gleaming repair bay held a shiny black truck.

Nate checked the perimeter, and his shoulders relaxed a fraction. Wearing immaculate denim coveralls, Joe squatted by a jacked-up Jeep.

"Police." Nate held up his shield.

Morgan pivoted and rose slowly. He knew the routine and kept his hands in view. But his expression registered shock for a split second before his Texas Hold 'em face slid into place. "I remember you. What do you want? I'm clean."

Yeah, right. Hands fisted, Nate doused his smirk and let his gaze roam the shop. "Got a nice setup here. Want to show me around?"

"Why should I? I'm busy. Need to finish a job." Morgan pointed to the flat tire.

"Just a few questions. Won't take much of your valuable time." He kept his voice conversational and wandered over to inspect the convertible. "Nice. This your T-Bird?"

Frowning, Morgan crossed his arms and didn't reply.

"Do the restoration yourself?"

He got a quick nod out of the guy, but Morgan's gaze bounced around the room, and his Adam's apple bobbed like a yo-yo.

Warmth bloomed in Nate's chest, along with a gut feeling he'd found his quarry. But he couldn't push the creep too hard. He rocked back on his heels and played it friendly. "So, last time I checked the junkyard, a rusted-out T-Bird frame cost a bundle. How much did she set you back?"

Color mottled Morgan's face under the tan. "Why the fuck should I tell you?"

Blood pressure pounded at his temples, but Nate ground his molars and pretended not to hear. He picked up a clean rag and polished a spot off the gleaming chrome. "Man-oh-man. I'm in the wrong business. Couldn't manage this cherry ride on a cop's paycheck."

"What the fuck does that mean?" The words exploded from Morgan's mouth. Then his lips thinned to a tight line.

Nate leaned against the fender and pulled on his earlobe. "Remember your buddy, Wendell?"

Morgan's eyes went flashbulb wide, and his skin turned a putrid green. "Douggie's dead. Murdered. A uniform already took my statement, and I got an air-tight alibi."

"I read the report. Girlfriend swears you were

humping her. But I'm checking the guy's finances. Judge signed the warrant today." Nate edged closer, raising an eyebrow to bolster his lie. "Know anything about Wendell's stash, buddy?"

Morgan backed up a step and shook his head.

There went the perp's Adam's apple again. Nate snickered silently. "Seems kind of strange to find a grease monkey with so much money."

Morgan rubbed the nape of his neck.

The guy should work on his tells. Nate snapped his fingers and pointed. "Hey, I got it. Wendell must have freelanced."

Morgan's face turned bright red. "Listen, cop. Show me your warrant or get the fuck out."

Nate cranked down his temper. "Don't get your balls in a wringer, Joe. Don't need your permission to trace the cash."

"Maybe not, but I'm not helping you."

Shrugging, Nate showed his palms and edged closer to Morgan. Close enough to smell the guy's nervous sweat and something else over the axle grease. He drew in another deep breath through his nose and smiled. Gunpowder. The guy reeked.

Whistling a striptease, Nate drew his weapon and released the safety. "You're coming with me, Morgan."

****

2:05 p.m.

"What's the problem? My nurse said you called." Jaw clenched, Jana faced the Chief of Staff's sneering receptionist.

The pasty-faced matron dipped her nose and glared over her half-glasses. "It took you long enough to get here. Dr. Raines is a busy man. Have a seat, and I'll see when he wants to fit you in."

"I'd rather reschedule."

"Sit. I'll ask Dr. Raines after he finishes this meeting."

"But I need to..." Her stomach growled. She never did get lunch today.

"Your legal difficulties are your first priority," the woman snapped. She pointed at a chair. "Sit."

Restraining the urge to snap back, Jana sank onto the leather seat and flicked a glance at the uniformed cop outside the office door. She'd seen MacLean at Sereno PD the other day. Was he here because of her? Maybe Nate arranged a guard.

She scraped her damp bangs off her forehead and smacked her surgical cap against her thigh. Hell of a day. And now she had to cooperate while the paper pushing Chief of Staff interrogated her. A chill stole her breath. Thank goodness Griffon Raines didn't know about the ambush this morning.

Why had Nate picked her backyard for a place to get shot at? If he had to file paperwork for firing his service weapon, ballistics would invade her home searching for evidence, and Raines would ratchet up the pressure. She grimaced. Someone was after Nate, and she'd been in the way. Just bad luck she'd become collateral damage, but the subtlety was hard to explain to her boss.

The knot in her chest tightened, and she fought rising anxiety. She glanced at the cop again. Shit, why was MacLean here?

Jiggling one foot, she pointedly checked the time while the receptionist avoided her gaze. She could almost see the words "murder suspect" rolling through the woman's mind.

The door to Raines' office opened to rumbling masculine laughter. He emerged, thumping a burly, middle-aged man on the shoulder. The blond Chief of Staff's slight build and preppy appearance contrasted sharply with his visitor's curly, dyed Reagan-brown hair, barrel chest, and coarse features. But both men wore flashy watches and hand-tailored suits.

Jana rose, and the men turned toward her.

"Dr. Sutherland, have you met our newest trustee, Mr. Tomasini?"

"Yes. Last fall at the hospital benefit. Pleasure to see you again."

Morrie Tomasini's sharp brown eyes flared briefly then narrowed. "Dr. Sutherland. You look well." Smiling slowly, he crowded closer.

A blush heated her cheekbones, and she stepped back. Was he hitting on her? The guy gave her the creeps.

Raines waved his hands frantically at her from behind Tomasini's back.

"Uh, thanks again for your generous donation to the hospital foundation, sir. Your money made a huge difference for so many people." She lifted the corners of her mouth in a stiff smile.

His eyes narrowed again, and a dark look oozed across his face. "Just doing my part," he said and turned to Raines. "See you later, Grif." Glancing sharply at her again, he hustled away.

Griffon Raines tapped his foot. "You're hopeless."

"What did you want me to say?"

He joined the admin in a headshake and checked the calendar on his phone. "Glad you finally decided to show."

"We had a busy morning in the ER. Again. Tough to break away when I was up to my elbows patching some guy's aorta with synthetic pipes."

Her boss's face flushed, and his jaw clenched. He gave her a frigid nod. "In my office, now. Explain to me how you became involved in a murder investigation. Captain Greene just called. He says you're the prime suspect."

****

2:15 p.m.

Nate's fist mangled the creep's collar. He tossed Morgan in the interview room.

Straightening his shirt, Morgan sauntered over to the empty bench. He sat and hooked one ankle over his knee, brushing some imaginary lint off his khakis. There were grass stains on the cuffs, and a chunk of gravel embedded in his sole.

Nate turned his back, slammed the steel door, and left the creep to stew. Morgan's smirk twisted his guts. Nate snorted, and the air practically singed his nostrils. He'd need absolute control before he could handle this interview.

He slipped into the observation area to cool down. Grabbing a cup of coffee, he rotated his shoulders and shook the kinks out of his fingers while he kept one eye on the scumbag through the one-way mirror.

Morgan lounged on the bench, his arms spread wide. No nervous twitch, no sweaty armpits on his pale green polo. The creep wasn't worried. Why not? What had changed during the silent ride to the station?

Nate's hands fisted around his mug, and he took a gulp. The guy should've been squirming in his seat.

Probable cause or not, he still had to tease the truth from Morgan to find out who pulled the marionette strings. The money trail he'd followed would never hold up at trial, but gunpowder residue on a convicted felon should buy a few hours of investigation time while Jana was safe at work.

Nate unclenched his jaw. Anger still simmered, but his pulse had slowed.

Morgan tapped his fingers on the metal table. "When do I get my phone call?"

"When I say," Nate growled through the intercom. He walked over to the coffee pot and topped off his cup.

"I got an alibi." Morgan sneered through the one-way mirror.

"What's your whore charging for the alibi? Wonder what she'd say if I slipped her a grand?" There. A twitch. Grinning, Nate shoved back from the microphone.

Morgan ran a hand along the side of his spiked blond hair. "Why you hassling me? I did my time."

Nate paused in the observation room doorway and eyed Morgan again. That tic in his left cheek twitched like crazy, and he swiped his mouth with one hand.

Finally, he'd rattled the creep.

He kicked the door open, strolled over, and leaned across the table, nose-to-nose with Morgan. "Where were you this morning? And where'd you pick up the fucking gun powder?"

Morgan's fingers jerked back over his mouth just as Captain Greene barged through the door. "Kapulani? Morgan lawyered-up."

"When?"

Greene shrugged. "You'll have to wait to question him."

Morgan flashed him a smile.

Chapter Seven

January 7, 6:45 p.m.

"You're obsessing. My house looks exactly the same as this morning." Jana fisted her hands together on her lap. Her jaw was so tight the joints ached.

"Wait here," he ordered, his face grim. He slammed the squad car door and stalked toward her front walk.

Jana stared out the passenger side window and blew a raspberry at his back. The drapes were closed, but she'd left a light on inside, and a faint glow leaked out from the edges. A bare-branched sycamore centered a lawn littered with unraked leaves.

Nate aimed the flashlight up the stairs, illuminating the corners of her porch, and shined the beam around her tiny front yard. He gave her a crisp nod and crooked his finger.

"Yes, sir!" she snapped and unlocked the car door. "This is ridiculous." Her first instincts were right. She should stay away from any man in uniform. The minute you smiled at them, the jerks started giving orders. Kiss one and he'd take over your life. Or he'd die and rip your heart out. She drew a slow breath, but couldn't ease the tight ache in her chest.

"Never again," she muttered and gathered the bag of fragrant takeout cartons.

By the time she mounted the stairs, Nate had the front door open.

Clenching her teeth, she snatched her keys out of his big hand. "Thank you, Detective. I'll take it from here."

"No." He herded her inside and rammed the deadbolt shut behind them.

Her mouth dropped open. All she could do was sputter.

Nate drew his weapon and scanned the space. "Don't move."

"Damn it! Don't make my life into some stupid cop-on-steroids cliché."

He glanced down his nose at her, his mouth twisted in disgust. Turning, he prowled silently from room to room and flicked on every light he passed.

"You're making me more nervous, not less. And my electric bill can't stand the strain," she called to him.

No response.

She thumped her purse and the Chinese food onto the entry table, hung her coat in the hall closet, and waited at the base of the stairs.

Finally, he clomped back down and holstered his gun. "You need to upgrade your locks and alarm system. I'll have my security guy come by."

She pursed her lips. *No, never again*, she reminded herself. But how could she get him out the door without a fight? "Look, Detective…Nate, I appreciate what you're doing, but—"

He took two steps closer and loomed over her. A predatory gleam lit his chocolate eyes.

Her heart began to sprint. She backed away, then

caught herself and stood firm. "I don't think I need that much protection. I refuse to live behind barred windows."

"You'll do what's necessary to stay safe."

"Fine. I appreciated the ride this morning. The sniper terrified me. But why'd you sic creepy Officer MacLean on me?"

His eyes narrowed. "I didn't. When did he show?"

"Mid-afternoon."

"Can't trust him. He's on the take."

She combed her fingers through her hair. "Then why did he shadow me?"

"Shit. Don't know. Probably Greene's orders, and I don't like it much." Frowning, Nate gave her a calculating squint. "But a bodyguard's a damn good idea."

"No! My boss threatened to fire me if I cause any more uproar."

His jaw did that freaking granite thing again. "Someone shot at you. Twice."

"Once." She pointed a finger and poked him in the sternum, hard. "In the hospital, yes. But Wendell is dead. They could have been shooting at you this morning."

"True, but I'm not willing to take that chance." He closed his fingers over hers and took another step forward.

Her back bumped against the wall, and he faced her with his arms braced on either side of her body. Adrenaline rushed through her.

He circled her wrists with his strong fingers.

She tried to swallow, but her throat was dry as sand, and her captive hands balled into fists. "Let me go, Nate."

"Will you listen?"

Barely blinking, she stared at the arrogant, but mesmerizing, cop. "Okay."

He released her, and she rubbed her wrists. "My gut tells me someone's gunning for you. You need to take your safety seriously."

"Fine."

"Will you let my guy upgrade your system?"

"Fine."

"Tomorrow?"

"Yes." She sighed. "Thank you, Nate. I appreciate your help, especially since you know a security expert I can trust."

"Great." The tension around his dark eyes eased. He kissed her forehead and threaded his fingers through hers. "What's on your schedule this week besides work?"

"Nothing." She heaved a harsh breath and frowned. "Hell. I forgot the fundraiser Friday night. Raines insists I go and schmooze."

"Where?" he demanded, his upper body angled toward her.

Her head tilted back, and she met his gaze, but her pulse hammered in her throat. His face was only a couple inches from hers. She gritted her teeth together. Nate was off-limits. She didn't want a pushy, headstrong, and protective cop in her life, but her treacherous body heated in spite of her brain, and she fought the urge to kiss the frown from his mouth.

Damn, she wanted him. "The Mountain Winery, but—"

"Shoot me the details, and I'll send a couple

guards."

"No-freaking-way." She tried for a calm, reasonable tone, hiding her building tension and awareness. "I can't afford to lose my job. Especially if I have to pay for new locks and alarms."

He grunted. "Then, for now, I'll back off on the bodyguard."

"Good."

He pressed against her. Silently, he stared down at her face while his warmth seeped through her.

Hot, electric shivers pulsed over her skin. She licked her lips and squeezed her eyes shut for a minute.

When she opened them again, he gave her a sexy, marauder-holding-a-very-tasty-captive smile that sucked all the air out of her lungs.

He drew his hands down both sides of her body. His thumbs grazed her breasts, and her nipples pebbled into sensitive, achy points.

Her breath came back in jerky gasps. When he shaped the sides of her hips, her hands fluttered against his chest. "Nate..."

Cutting off her protest, his mouth closed over hers.

No! She wouldn't kiss him back.

Wouldn't respond.

Wouldn't surrender.

But his kiss sent exquisite shockwaves through her. She damped down each tantalizing sensation, but her hunger built and spread, mushrooming into a hot, wet throb.

A needy cry tore from her. She curled her hands around his neck, and kissed him back.

He growled deep in his throat, and his mouth demanded more, consuming her response.

Damp heat gathered low in her body. Wildly alive and aware of every touch, every sensation, she strained closer. Her breasts flattened against his firm, muscled chest, aching for his touch. His slick tongue rasping her lips, he coaxed her mouth open and sank inside.

His kiss turned gentler, but still thorough and possessive. His arms loosened, and his fingers spread wide, cupping her bottom. He pulled her to her tiptoes, flush against his very hard body. When his rigid length rubbed against her, a wave of molten pleasure flowed through her.

With a shudder, he released her lips and eased back, letting her slide to her feet. His mouth grazed her jawline and moved lower to nibble at the tight cord on her neck.

Jana let out a shaky moan and tongued the curve of his ear.

He murmured, "You hungry?" His voice was deep and resonant, and his breath warmed her neck.

"Mm."

"Me, too." One hand slipped beneath her sweater and cradled her breast. He gently pinched the nipple into a harder point and kneaded.

Sharp licks of pleasure swirled through her. Gripped by a compelling need, she trembled and leaned toward him.

"I can smell dinner. Let's eat first," he whispered, toying with her breast.

Jana stilled. "First?"

"Before I carry you upstairs and make love to you all night." His pupils were dilated, and his eyes were half-closed, but the grin on his swollen lips held an unmistakable glow of masculine triumph.

The conceited, manipulative bastard. He thought five minutes under his hands could turn her into a simpering playmate?

He'd learn. She adjusted her sweater and slid away from his grasp. "Sure."

The grin on his self-satisfied face widened. "Need to build up our strength."

"Good idea. I left the takeout on the entry table." She turned, but he followed her across the living room, his strong fingers possessively cupping her right ass cheek.

With each step, her sex pulsed. God, she was a freaking puddle of need. She swallowed, trying not to remember how incredible his hard length had felt rubbing against her. *Be strong.*

Stopping near the door, she faced him and grabbed his tie to pull him closer. She swiped her tongue over his lips, giving him a wet, open-mouthed kiss.

He shuddered and reached for her, but she broke the kiss, sidestepped, and turned the deadbolt.

His brow furrowed, and he gave his head a half shake.

Yanking the door open, she shoved him out onto the porch. "Thanks for the ride. I'm eating alone."

She slammed the door and locked the deadbolt. Heaving a sigh, she braced her back against the door and ran her fingers through her hair.

Chapter Eight

January 9, 10:15 p.m.

A husky voiced diva in sequins crooned a classic rock ballad, backed by a twelve-piece band. Tiny white lights twinkled in the ancient oaks rimming the winery courtyard, and a platoon of space heaters blazed into the chilly night.

Clustered palms and potted camellias bordered the dance floor. At the far edge, a sheltered outdoor alcove reeked with cigar smoke from a gaggle of lechers.

Jana took a sip from her glass, and bubbles did a happy jig on her tongue. The champagne was cold, crisp, and delicate. She sniffed and caught the sharpness of citrus and yeast. She popped the last bite of a prawn canapé into her mouth and closed her eyes to savor the rich, spicy sauce.

She smiled and took another drink. Maybe Raines did know how to fundraise. This gala provided the perfect excuse to loosen the most moth-eaten checkbook. Inside, the silent auction tables were crowded with happy, laughing people intent on indulging themselves, while also making a contribution. Raines was right. For an upgrade to the diagnostic imaging center, she could manage the required hour of schmoozing in these killer heels.

A just-barely-legal server, long and lean with

black-lashed blue eyes and a rakish hint of beard stubble, poured another flute for a patron wearing too many diamonds and slinky lavender lace. The woman's hair might be a youthful blonde, but her Botox-and-collagen face only emphasized the papery skin of her cleavage.

The waiter laughed and gave the woman a conspiratorial wink, earning at least hardship pay, if not membership in the Screen Actors' Guild. The woman blushed an unflattering shade of fuchsia.

Across the courtyard, an overweight man with triple jowls caught Jana's eye and toasted her with his glass. The red veins on the guy's nose almost glowed above his entitled leer. Yuck. She did not need her grandmother's tea leaves to predict gout or cirrhosis.

She pretended to wave to a friend, gathered up her long, slim skirt, and merged into the crowd around the caviar table.

"Dr. Sutherland." A powerful hand tapped her bare shoulder.

She flinched, and her heart pounded in an uneven rhythm. Pivoting to face him, she showed some teeth and her dimple. "Mr. Tomasini."

The designer tux fit his barrel chest perfectly, but his flinty brown eyes glittered below a double-wide, furry brow. Wiry black hair poked out of his white cuffs and furred the backs of his hands and fingers. With a smile that didn't reach his eyes, he sidled up one step too close. "Glad to see you tonight."

"Sure." She cleared her throat. Why had this guy decided to hit on her? He gave her the creeps, but there was Raines, waving and grinning from a spot beside the shrimp cocktail table. Watching. Waiting for her to screw up. "Th-thank you for your generous contribution, Mr. Tomasini. We're hoping to upgrade our catheterization lab equipment."

"Admirable. Such true dedication." He captured her hand in an unyielding grip and bent it to his lips. His giant pinkie ring gouged her wrist.

Heat rose on her neck. A crawling sensation started at her nails, climbed up her arm, and shivered down her spine. She let her hand go boneless and slipped free. "How kind of you to say so."

"Grif told me what a wonderful surgeon you are."

"He did?" She glanced over his shoulder, and her stomach plummeted. Her suck-up-to-the-donors boss was making shooing motions toward the dance floor.

"Raved about you. Said he didn't know how he'd run the hospital if you disappeared. Dance with me, Dr. Sutherland."

"Uh..." She stepped back. Would Raines really make good on his threat to fire her? She couldn't take the chance, but Tomasini scared her, and she didn't want him to touch her. She had to finesse him. "Thanks, but I'm not much of a dancer." She sipped her drink, but her hand trembled, and some of the bubbly drink splashed onto her dress.

Tomasini's eyebrows rose, and his grin widened. "With me? Sure you are." He seized her arm and yanked her toward the dance floor.

In her heels, her eyes were level with Tomasini's. He probably outweighed her by a hundred pounds. A swift sidekick to the rear end still might teach the grabby jackass some manners, but Raines would never miss that move, and anyway, her skirt was too tight. She planted her feet and shrugged free. "No, thanks."

"It's a rumba." Tomasini chuckled smugly. "You might never have another chance."

Tossing back the last of the champagne, she set down the glass and nodded at him. "Fine. One dance."

He led her to center floor and took her into his arms. His hands were damp, and his breath smelled like fish and vodka.

Her stomach did a double axel. She snapped her head around and breathed over his shoulder. Raines was still watching from the sidelines. He rocked back and forth in his spit-shined patent leather shoes, grinning like a pimp eyeing his favorite hooker.

Tomasini focused his cold, flat eyes on hers, and then he cinched her close. Against her ear, he whispered, "See, you're doing great."

Her jaw clenched. Enough. No new equipment was worth being mauled. She stomped on the creep's foot with her stiletto, and he let out a squeal.

Thankfully, Raines had his back turned.

"Oh, I'm so sorry, Mr. Tomasini. I got the moves mixed up."

Groaning, he threw her a lethal glare. His black brows met in the center of his forehead. "Watch your step."

"I try, but I warned you I'm not a very good dancer. Sit down, and I'll send you a fresh drink." She hurried through the crowd on shaky legs.

With his back turned toward her, Raines was talking to Captain Greene and gesturing wildly.

She grabbed her black silk duster and a tall, frothy mug of coffee. Aiming for nonchalance, she skirted a knot of overweight, loud-voiced, cigar-puffing robber barons.

Triple Jowls turned toward her and winked. "Ah, our sexy little surgeon." Smoke leaked out his nose and between his teeth.

The pungent reek hit her nostrils. Gagging, she coughed loudly in his face. When his head jerked back, she wiggled her fingers. "Nice to meet you. Excuse me."

Her challenge for the night was to avoid filthy-rich mashers, but she refused to cower in the ladies' room for the next half hour. Not only cliché, but too predictable. The alcove just outside the door made a perfect place for some slimy rattlesnake to linger and strike when she emerged.

On the edge of the courtyard near the mountain overlook, she took up a defensible position and slipped on her coat. The coffee she'd grabbed on the way over should help keep her warm. She'd wait out her time beside this oversized vase of tropical flowers.

She drew in a deep breath of their exotic perfume to chase away the lingering smoke. Better, but that clump of orchids alone would have bought a new heart monitor for the ER.

She rubbed her arm. Unlike that bullying asshole, Tomasini, Nate would never hurt more than her pride. He might act controlling, but even though he'd reduced her to a puddle of swirling lust, he'd left her house when she'd told him no.

A leather sole scraped the cement behind her, and Nate chuckled. "Are you hiding?"

Her pulse skittered again. She jumped and turned, staring straight into a pleated shirt. Her gaze followed the trail of shiny black studs to his face.

She let out a little huff and took a half step back.

Nate in a tux? Unexpected, maybe, but not bad. He filled out the shoulders nicely. His alert-and-poised-for-action stance still telegraphed his badge, but the delivery was smooth and powerful.

His grin propelled her heart rate into a slow, heady climb, but she tipped up her chin. "You surprised me. I'm not hiding. Just admiring the flowers."

He nodded, like he understood she was lying, and stared out at the view.

She followed his gaze. Below their perch, city lights sparkled in the night, but clouds massed around the almost full moon. "I'm not much for the posh crowd either."

"Then why are you here?"

"You're in danger."

"Here? Do you think someone's going to poison my canapés?"

"I'm not taking any chances."

"Look, the only danger I'm in tonight is being mauled by horny billionaires."

Nate chuckled.

She searched his face. His melted-chocolate eyes met hers, and her blood swam. "Anyway, I thought you were sending your minions on bodyguard duty."

"Decided to protect you myself and not risk your job."

Her head spun so quickly, she had an instant of dizziness. "You listened to me?"

He shrugged, but a grin teased his mouth. "Took notes."

Heat swirled low in her body. "An alpha male actually paid attention? Didn't just bark orders?"

"Yep. Hidden talents."

She put the back of her wrist against her forehead and sighed dramatically. "What next? Pink elephants? Dancing crocodiles?"

"Good idea. Let's dance." He took her coffee mug and set it on a nearby table.

Her brow scrunched. She peeked around the shrubbery and didn't see Triple Jowls or Tomasini or Raines, but a cloud of cigar smoke hovered over the crowd between her and the dance floor. "I don't think..."

"Not there. Here." Nate gathered her in his powerful arms and swung her to the beat. "I like this song." His breath whispered against her ear, and warm shivers raced over her skin and threaded through her system.

She glanced up into his smiling eyes. Her three-inch heels helped even their heights, but he still towered over her, surrounded her with his strength. For once she didn't feel like a beanpole. "How's your, uh, tie?"

He chuckled appreciatively and twirled her around twice. "Took a while to recover."

Breathless, she giggled. "But no permanent damage?"

"Wouldn't matter. I was out of line."

She stumbled and missed a step. "You're really not mad?"

"Nope." Humming the melody, he edged her further from the crowd and dipped her over his arm. "Just don't get used to holding the reins."

The glint in his eyes sparked a prickly feeling all the way down to her toes. She pulled her lips into a pout. "You want a doormat?"

"No. Pushing back is kind of sexy, says you respect

yourself."

Closing her eyes, she relaxed into the music. Into him. His muscles shifted and flexed as his warm, strong hand at her waist guided her through the steps. On the dance floor, he made it easy to follow, easy to trust him. But could she trust him enough to let herself be vulnerable?

The song ended too soon. They stood face-to-face, very close together. Her heart beat in a funny syncopated rhythm. She wanted him to kiss her like he had the other night. She angled her face toward him.

He drew his thumb down her warm cheek. "So soft."

More lovely shivers zinged through her and coiled low in her body, melting the frost. She ran her hand over his satin lapels, itching to undress him. "I need to wave at my boss one more time, but I can leave at eleven."

Nate's eyes glimmered in the starlight. "Go do your job. Make Raines happy. I'll keep watch."

"Does Captain Greene know you're here?"

Nate shook his head. "No. He's crooked. I have to play games to keep him off my ass."

His cell phone buzzed. He kissed her lightly on the nose, then glanced at his screen. "The bald-headed devil-in-blue himself. I have to answer the captain's call. Meet you back here in half an hour. I'll walk you to your car and make sure you get home safely."

****

11:10 p.m.

With a clink of crystal, the boy-toy waiter circulated another tray of champagne flutes. Although the caviar bowl had been scraped clean, the crowd still boogied to the band.

Even Dr. Singh was up dancing with her husband. Jana had never seen Parvati in anything but her scrubs, a messy bun, and a harried expression. But tonight she looked beautiful dressed in a bright orange and gold sari with her dark, wavy hair worn loose.

Jana slid off one shoe and wiggled her cramped toes. Her feet hurt, but she'd done her part for the hospital tonight. She grabbed one last chocolate truffle from the dessert table and waved goodbye to Dr. Peterson and his gaggle of pretty nurses.

She chuckled. At six-five, Andy Peterson was a tall, lanky, blue-eyed blond hunk. And from the rumors flowing around Sereno General, more than one nurse had enjoyed his bedside manner.

After parading past Raines one last time, Jana searched through the crowded winery. Nate should be easy to spot, but he'd vanished.

Avoiding the outdoor smoking area where Tomasini was now holding court, she headed across the patio toward the overlook and waited.

Silicon Valley's latest tech-wonder-kid-in-jeans danced by with an ER nurse. He caught Jana's eye and winked. He'd amassed double digit billions before he was thirty and still seemed like a nice guy. But when she'd danced with him, she'd wanted Nate's arms around her instead.

She checked her watch. Eleven fifteen, but still no Nate. Cloudbanks had massed on the Western horizon, partially obscuring the moon. The temperature had dropped into the low thirties. A brisk wind stirred her hair, and she smelled rain.

Dampness from the incoming storm blew through

her light clothing and raised goose bumps. She needed to get off this mountain soon. When slick, the winding road could be treacherous.

Jana worried her lower lip and checked her cell again. Nothing, not even a text. Nate was over fifteen minutes late, and she couldn't wait much longer. He must have been dispatched on an emergency, or maybe he was stuck placating his crooked captain.

She should leave him a cell phone message and talk to him tomorrow, but she really didn't want to hike down the hill alone. By the time she'd gotten off work, changed, and driven all the way out here, she'd had to park in the boonies. No, she was safer here with people around.

"Dr. Sutherland, may I have a word?"

Jana pivoted. Her blood pressure and pulse doubled, and she felt lightheaded.

Norah Redfox stood beside a potted camellia, a slight frown line between her brows. The woman looked elegant and otherworldly in a floor-length black cape with cobalt blue lining. A triangle of her beaded gown showed below the bottom clasp. "I'm sorry to intrude..."

"Then why are you bothering me again?" Jana gave her a frosty stare.

A flush colored Norah's cheeks. Rubbing at her forehead, she glanced down at her shoes. "My spirit guide has been pressuring me. He says the window for change is narrowing fast. The suffering has mushroomed, and you're the only one who can reverse the blight in Sereno. You must undo Mike Gordon's murder."

Frissons of alarm raced through Jana, triggering

jitters in her belly. She pulled herself ramrod straight and narrowed her eyes. "I've already wasted ten years of my life on guilt and grief for Mike."

Norah's head jerked, and her mahogany-colored eyes went wide. With one hand extended toward Jana, the woman stepped closer. "He deserved to live his whole life, not have it cut short."

"Absolutely. Mike was a good cop who died tragically in the line of duty." Jana grimaced and squeezed her eyes shut to fight back the tears. "But he wasn't a superhero. How could one man's death possibly have the huge impact you claim?"

"But it's true."

Jana snorted. "Fine. If you want him alive, go back and save him yourself."

"That's not possible." Norah looked at her with sad, dark eyes. "You're in danger yourself, and if you refuse, people you love will die."

"Whatever. I won't argue with you anymore. Just leave me alone." Pulling her car keys from her evening bag, Jana brushed past the woman and stomped toward the parking lot.

She hurried along the uneven, sloping walkway and around a blind corner. Stilettos and gravel. Not a great combination.

A chill arced between her shoulder blades. Nate had wanted her to wait, but she'd had to get away from that nutcase, and there was no real reason she wouldn't be fine by herself. Jana pulled out her phone and sent him a text while she hurried to her car.

She rounded a curve, and the path widened into rows of parked luxury sedans and SUVs. In the dim light, their colors faded to pale gray, maroon, and black.

Dark clouds raced across the moon and sent eerie shadows sprinting and dancing.

About fifty feet away, she beeped the lock on her ancient hybrid. When the interior lights came on, she exhaled in relief. No one close by. No monster trucks or punks with guns.

She quickened her pace. Norah's dire warnings had frazzled her already frayed nerves. "Coward. Get inside and lock the doors. Once you're on the road, you'll feel safer."

She approached her car, and a cold weight cramped her stomach. Shivers erupted on her nape and along her spine. Her car seemed different. Lower. She inspected the front tire and then the back.

Flat.

All four tires had been vandalized.

Shit. Shit. Shit.

Should she run for it? No, the party was too far away. Whoever did this could catch her long before she could reach any other people. Her best bet was to lock herself in and call Nate again.

While fumbling for the handle, she checked the back seat. No boogeyman. Hiking up her long skirt, she jumped into the driver's seat and locked the doors. Squeezing her eyes shut, she held her cell phone in shaky hands. She was alone and stranded. Did someone want her defenseless? Or dead?

Chapter Nine

January 9, 11:20 p.m.

Only fifteen minutes late and that damned woman had taken off on her own. Tension chewed Nate's insides. Just once, he'd love to grab Jana and shake her. He snorted loudly. Right. Then she'd knock him on his ass.

He jogged around the blind corner and scanned the winery parking lot. Limos clogged every aisle, but where had Jana left her little silver tin can?

Ahead, gravel crunched. His throat knotted, and his heart slammed fitfully against his ribs. Footsteps—stealthy and purposeful. Staying low, he drew his weapon from his shoulder harness and swept the area.

In the far corner, a hunched shadow stalking between cars suddenly froze, then veered away and disappeared up the wooded slope. A chauffeur ducking out for a smoke? Possible, although his gut bellowed a warning. Not far from where the guy had been lurking, he spotted Jana's old hybrid and bumped his pace to a trot.

When he knocked on her window, she jumped in her seat and glared at him. "You scared me half to death. Where were you?" she yelled through the glass.

He held his palms out flat. "Relax. Been looking for you. Why'd you come out here alone?"

Obviously still fuming, she stepped out of her car and slammed the door. "I got tired of waiting. You didn't answer your phone."

"Couldn't, Greene kept blathering on and on."

"I was cold. I wanted to go home." She toed a pebble.

"Why didn't you?"

She huffed at him. One corner of her mouth screwed up crooked. "Because every single one of my damn tires is flat."

Flipping on his small flashlight, Nate examined her left front wheel and grimaced. "They've been slashed."

"Great." She rested her forehead on her palm and shook her head.

Instead of tossing her over his shoulder, he moved between Jana and the wooded slope and gently touched her cheek. She was trembling. In the moonlight, her face looked nearly white, and deep lines framed her mouth. Damn. He'd told her to wait. "I'll take you home and order a tow truck."

She gave him a quick nod and retrieved her bag and keys.

"Come on. I'm parked near the edge there." He swung an arm around her waist.

He'd backed his SUV into the slot for a quick exit. When he opened her door, she hiked up her skirt and climbed in, revealing her long, curvy legs in silky stockings and shiny heels. A glimpse of slim thigh above her pantyhose tops cranked the aching tightness in his groin up a notch.

What would it take to get her to listen to him? For starters, he'd take her to bed and make love to her until she went blind with pleasure.

Her gaze darted around the cab as if she thought the bad guys were hiding in the back seat. When he slid behind the wheel and locked his doors, her shoulders visibly relaxed. She drew in a deep breath, held it, and then flashed him an apologetic smile. "Sorry I yelled. I got scared and kind of freaked out."

He stifled a frustrated growl. A few minutes alone in this parking lot had finally made her recognize the danger better than any warning he'd given her. "About time."

Her lips drooped in a controlled frown. She wove her strong, sexy hands together on her lap and stared at them. "You were right. Apparently someone is after me. What should I do next?"

Trying not to think about what he wanted her to do next with those hands, he hooked a finger under her chin and brought her face around so she'd meet his gaze. Her big, wide, hazel eyes were almost all pupil. Blood surged into his groin, swirled in a hot seething eddy, and urged him to ease her back and plunge into her over and over until he drove out the fear.

But he gave her a quick, hard kiss and released her. Rain spattered on the windshield. "Next, I'll drive you home. Probably safe enough for tonight."

She nodded and dropped her gaze.

"We need to get moving." He started the truck and pulled out. "You might think about leaving town until Wendell's case gets settled."

"But I have to work."

"Won't do your patients much good if you're dead. Take a few days of vacation."

"I only have one, maybe two built up."

"Take them now."

She rubbed her knuckles up and down her thighs. "I hate this. But I'll do it and maybe ask for some leave."

"Good. Tomorrow I'll arrange a safe house." He couldn't take her home with him. He never took women home. It gave them the wrong idea. "You could always stay at my place." Hell. He frowned, surprised at what had come out of his mouth but also shocked at how right the words sounded.

She blinked at him. "We can talk tomorrow." Her gaze darted sideways, but he didn't challenge her, just gave a noncommittal grunt.

The two-lane highway started a gradual descent through the dark oak and redwood forest. No lighting other than the occasional cabin driveway. He hadn't seen another car in over a mile. The rain started to pound down in earnest, so he flicked on his wipers.

Bright headlights flashed in his rearview mirror, and he grimaced. Someone was in a big hurry. He slowed and eased along the gravel shoulder to let them pass. The narrow road ahead had steep spots, and he didn't want some impatient SOB on his tail all the way into town.

The driver behind him closed the distance, but didn't take the invitation to pass.

"Can the brights," Nate grumbled, raising a hand to shield his eyes from the reflection. He squinted. The glare made it tough to focus on the wet, slippery road, but no point in scaring Jana.

Then the macho creep gunned his engine, probably a bored out hemi from the roar, and moved closer, to within a length of the back bumper.

An itch started at his tailbone and slowly crept up

each vertebrate. Not your everyday road hog. The itch tickled the back of his neck, and Nate tightened his hands on the wheel. "Got your seatbelt on?"

"Sure."

He punched the gas and skidded around the next curve. Gravel sprayed into the air. "We've got a pushy asshole on our tail. Can you make out the license plate?"

"No, he's too close. Should I call 911?"

"No point." Bile stung the back of his throat. A mile ahead, a set of switchbacks wound through the narrow canyon. The other driver would be crazy to keep up this pace. Nate let his foot off the gas, but the truck stayed on his tail. "Now can you see his tags?"

Jana turned part way around. "No. There's no front plate. It's a pickup. Dodge Ram, dual cab, I think. Maybe black or blue."

Nate tapped his brakes, and for an instant, the truck backed off.

"The only thing I can see is the chrome silhouette of a naked woman on his bumper." She faced front and tightened her belt.

"Okay. Hang on." Nate set his jaw and swung into the first hairpin. He stomped on the gas.

Tires squealed, and Jana gasped.

Cold sweat trickled down his back. He fought the force of his vehicle and pulled out of the turn. Great. Only six more to go.

The roads were slicker here in the forested canyon. Rain dripped from the branches overhead and splashed across the windshield in fat drops. The second hairpin loomed a hundred yards in front of them. "Got your eyes closed?"

"No. I'd rather know when we go off the edge."

"We won't."

"Okay, you've got a deal."

Was that a chuckle in her tone? Nate wiped his palms on his leg.

The second curve wasn't as steep. They skidded around and onto a short, straight section of road, where the edge fell off steeply and dropped to the creek.

He gunned the engine and glanced back. "Damn. He's not having any trouble keeping up."

The truck rammed into his tailgate. The SUV lurched forward, throwing both of them against the seat.

His pulse roared in his ears, and the veins in his neck throbbed.

"What do we do?"

Breathing harshly, he glanced at her. Her eyes were wide, but her face looked surprisingly calm. "We lose him."

They headed for the next sharp curve that hugged the canyon wall. Sweat dripped down the side of his forehead, but he wasn't letting go to swipe it off. At the apex of the curve, Nate cranked the wheel to his left and stomped the brake. On the slick road, the back tires lost traction and went into a skid. He held on, steered the SUV through the one-eighty, and accelerated uphill.

The black truck barreled past them down the canyon road.

Only a few seconds to hide. Nate flipped off the lights and dodged up a narrow driveway. He slid around a curve, slammed on the brakes, and cut the engine. "Down!" he shouted as he jammed the gearshift into park.

Ducking, he drew his weapon from his underarm

holster and double-checked the load. If the creep found them and wanted a firefight, he'd get one.

When Nate lowered the window, the frigid wind blew raindrops onto his face. Out on the highway, the truck roared past.

A sudden silence blanketed the air, undisturbed except for the rain sheeting down.

Nate concentrated on keeping his breathing even, but his heart hammered against his breastbone. "We have to get out of here before he doubles back."

****

January 10, 12:10 a.m.

"I can come in while you pack a bag." Nate pulled his key from the ignition.

Jana's garage door cranked shut behind the SUV. She studied his intense expression and bit the inside of her cheek while she weighed the danger.

Which was more dangerous? The anonymous bad guy in a pickup? Or the protective alpha cop in a gone-in-thirty-seconds tux? She unbuckled her seat belt with shaky hands. "I'll be fine. You said I'd be safe at home tonight."

"That was before someone almost ran us off the road."

"I'll be fine," she repeated and reached for the door handle. "I'll call you tomorrow morning, and we can work out where I'm going to stay."

Nate took her by the shoulders and turned her toward him, giving her a crooked smile. "Hold on a minute." The white tips of a few teeth showed, and his impossibly dark eyes gleamed, adding a dazzling edge to his lethal grin.

Heat seeped over her cheeks, and her stomach

jittered. But her gaze stayed locked with his while he slid her across the bench seat and gathered her against his side. The pad of his thumb grazed her lips. He bent over her, and his firm lips brushed hers, stealing her breath. He swept gentle kisses over the corners of her mouth, cheeks, and nose.

Her heart leaped at the raw emotion in those brief contacts. Moaning, she closed her eyes and met his lips. Hot sensation muted the lingering shock and fear shot through her limbs like a brushfire.

He nudged her closer with pressure at the back of her neck and head, angling his mouth to cover hers. She shuddered and relaxed against his strong hands.

"Adrenaline," he muttered, nibbling down her throat to her collarbone. The roughness of his cheek on her tender skin and the hunger of his urgent mouth sent shivers through her system.

"Exactly. Adrenaline," she repeated. Sliding her hands over his broad shoulders, she laced them behind his neck and guided his lips back to hers. Her tongue invaded his mouth and stroked, tangled, and danced with his. Pleasure pulsed through her, and she went all soft, trembling.

Nate broke the kiss and tilted the steering wheel out of the way. Grasping her waist, he lifted her sideways onto his lap with her back against the car door. The delicate silk of her narrow skirt bunched above her knees.

Nestling her head against his shoulder, she drew a fingertip along his jawline and traced his ear. When she sucked the lobe into her mouth and nipped, he shuddered.

His fingers roamed her legs, stroking the bare skin

above her thigh-high hose. "Nice," he said in a gravelly voice and shifted her gown higher, exposing more flesh. Tingles shadowed his touch and cascaded over her skin.

He cupped her breasts through the silk, and pleasure spiraled toward her center. With his warm hands, he pressed, pinched, and rolled both peaks.

Her natural moisture dampened the satin of her panties. When she moved, the slick, moist slide teased her already swollen and sensitized sex.

With her mouth open and wet against his neck, she drew in a shaky breath, loving the feel of him holding her, loving his muscled arms and thighs, and loving the tantalizing hardness jutted against her hip.

The ache between her legs blossomed into a yearning hunger. She craved his touch, needed his lips and hands on her body.

He slid his fingers inside her strapless bodice and over her cool, naked skin. "What's under this?" Nate rumbled.

Aching with desire, she grinned at him. "Nothing."

One eyebrow rose, then he squeezed his eyes shut and shook his head. "You're going to kill me."

Laughter bubbled up in her throat. "I know a cure."

He bent his head and kissed her collarbone and the top of each breast, but then he drew back. "Tell me. Tell me what you want."

She touched his face, her fingers playing with the strong lines around his eyes and mouth. "I want you to touch me."

His hand delved lower, splayed over her breast, and caged the nipple between two fingers. He plucked and squeezed until the nipple formed a hard peak, then moved his hand to the other breast. "Do you like my hands on your skin?"

"Yessss."

Reaching between her knees, he drew one finger over the moist silk of her panties and brushed her aching nub with a nail. Fierce sensation traveled through the damp, delicate fabric, and she moaned his name.

His light strokes robbed her of thought. Everything inside trembled with need. She scooted forward, but he didn't increase the pressure.

Instead, he stilled his hand, his expression suddenly serious.

"What?"

"I've been half hard since I saw you in that damn cafeteria, Jana. But I'm too old to steam up a car. I want you naked on a bed so I can see and touch and taste every part of you. But you have to ask."

Shivers rippled uncontrollably along her spine. Her hands fluttered against his chest, and she cleared her throat. "Um..." Blood sang in her veins, and her whole body vibrated with possibilities. The damp, throbbing emptiness deep inside her ached to be filled.

He grinned and took her fingers in his, kissing the sensitive tips, one after another. "This time I don't want to end up bouncing down your steps on my ass."

Her lungs took a vacation, and she braced to keep from falling over. Could she make love with him, but guard her heart? She studied his aching, yearning smile. She could damn well try. With a slow, answering smile, she kissed him lightly and crooked her finger. "Please, Nate, come inside."

"You got it." He smoothed a hand through her hair before gently setting her back onto the car seat. With rapt attention, he watched her gather her coat and purse, not exactly drooling, but definitely zeroed in.

When she was ready, he rounded the car and opened her door. He handed her out and stepped away. Arms at his sides, he stood before her, seeming easy and confident in his very sexy skin.

Tilting her head to the side, she let her gaze roam his body. Long, strong limbs. Massive chest. Powerful shoulders.

Too big. Too powerful. Too dominant.

A ripple of panic tickled her throat, but she swallowed it. Letting him take charge felt wickedly tempting, but also oddly safe. Reaching up, she traced his square jaw, shaded and rough, and took his hand. "Come on. Let me show you my sexy, new alarm."

"With motion detectors?"

"Loads of motion detectors."

Nate laughed and kissed her eyelids. With an arm around her waist, he escorted her through the back gate and up the walk.

She unlocked the deadbolt and turned her key in the knob. "Welcome to my fortress."

After locking up behind them, Nate drew his weapon. "Wait here for a minute while I check the house."

She rolled her eyes and watched him creep through the kitchen.

Opening the utility closet, she beeped in a code to reset the alarm.

"All clear." He moved close behind her and drew a finger down the arc of her spine to her bottom.

Goose bumps danced along her arms. He turned her and kissed her.

Her heart pounded with the thrill. She walked her fingers up his chest and loosened his bow tie.

With his lips a breath from hers, he whispered, "Jana?"

She blinked once. Twice. A final chance to say no? Forget that. She shot him a wicked smile. "I have plans for you." She led him into the living room and up the stairs, flicking on lights as she walked.

Inside her bedroom, she turned to face him, and his eyes glittered.

Dropping his jacket on her bedside chair, he stepped toward her. "Turn around and raise your arms."

"Are you going to frisk me, Sergeant?"

"Thoroughly."

Jana chuckled, but complied. "No handcuffs in my bedroom."

"Maybe not tonight." He drew her zipper down and lifted off her dress, leaving her standing in her black silk panties and thigh-high hose.

The cold air hit her skin, but her face heated.

"Gorgeous." His lips traced her nape and along her shoulder, while his hands curled around her waist and settled on her breasts.

She arched her neck and leaned back against him. Her eyes closed as he kissed and nipped every inch. Delectable please-take-me-now tension swept over her and pooled between her thighs.

He turned her toward him and drew a nipple into his mouth.

A high voltage thrill shot straight to her sex, and she sucked in a breath through her teeth.

His long fingers stretched and toyed with the other nipple, and the sight of his dark head bent to her breast stoked the thrill into a raging fire.

He caressed her until she squirmed. She rubbed against his leg and whimpered frantically, "Touch me, Nate."

His hand snaked under the leg of her panties. Grinning, he slipped the satin to the side and teased her nub. Every time he circled and flicked the sensitive bundle of nerve endings, luscious lightning bolts seared her. She moaned at the exquisite pressure, let her head fall back, and her lids fluttered closed.

He kissed her hard and stepped back to rip off his tie, dropping it on the carpet. His eyes, black with passion, locked with hers.

Taking his hand in hers, she kissed his palm. She nibbled each finger before sucking on the pad of his thumb. She slowly undid his cufflinks and kissed the inside of one wrist. He hissed but didn't touch her.

She fumbled with his shirt studs while he stood impatiently, his hot gaze still focused on hers. Pushing back the starched cotton, she ran both palms over his hard chest, tracing the well-defined muscles. Her lips quirked in a mischievous grin, and she swiped his flat nipple with her tongue.

He hitched in a harsh breath and shucked the shirt. When she reached for his belt, he walked her backwards, and they tumbled onto her bed, side by side. He kissed her and cupped her breasts. Molten streaks seared her blood.

He broke the kiss, and his hand crept lower, trailing across her belly, caressing her waist and the flare of her hips.

"You're so beautiful. I love the light on your skin." He brushed a finger over her nose and cheeks. "Your freckles look like gold dust."

Curling her leg over his, she shifted on top and straddled him, excruciatingly aware of his hardness pressed against the moist, needy part of her. She reached down to measure his rigid length through his trousers.

Oh, God. Her imagination hadn't done him justice.

He let loose a deep groan; his eyes squeezed shut for a second. "Not yet." Taking both her wrists in one of his hands, he rolled her onto her back.

He tugged off her panties and sucked a nipple into his mouth while he gently explored her moist folds. One finger entered her, his thumb pressed against her sensitive nub.

She arched to his touch while his tongue mirrored the movement of his finger inside her. Electricity swirled within her, focused, hot, and slick. She spread her legs wide, and he drove her higher.

"Open your eyes, Jana. Look at me."

She met his fierce, urgent gaze and smiled. "Nate." She couldn't breathe, could barely think.

When he inserted another finger and flicked, she melted into explosive, throbbing warmth. She gasped his name again and clutched at his shoulders.

Smiling, he watched her recover her sanity.

"Damn," she drawled and ran her palms along his strong arms. "Make love to me."

"Gotta get my wallet. I'm healthy, but we need protection."

She dodged his gaze and said, "It's okay. I'm on the pill."

One eyebrow rose.

Heat seared her cheeks. "For medical reasons.

There hasn't been anyone for years," she blurted.

He didn't quite hide his grin as he rose and loosened his trousers.

Jana tucked a pillow under her head and enjoyed watching the play of his muscles while he shed the rest of his clothes. Gorgeous tanned skin covered a taut belly, and his jutting erection lay tight against his abdomen, nearly reaching his navel. She licked her lips, grateful for the cool sheets beneath her.

He joined her on the bed and settled between her thighs, running a palm down her side and under her bottom.

Warmed by his heat, she tunneled her fingers into his hair and raised her knees.

He traced a finger around her moist opening and nudged the broad tip of his erection inside.

The pressure drove her wild. "Now, Nate, now." She wrapped her legs around his waist and levered him closer.

He surged into her, and she cried out, her muscles stretched to the limit.

Taking his weight on one elbow, he brushed her hair out of her eyes. "Okay?"

"Perfect."

He found a slow rhythm, pulling almost apart and then slowly returning.

His cell phone buzzed, and he stilled, gritting his teeth. "Damn."

Sweat beaded on his skin, and she could see the tense cords in his neck—the power he fought to control. She tightened around him. "Don't stop. If it's important, they'll call again."

Nate shuddered and thrust again, his face rigid with

concentration and his muscles bunching.

The thick fullness inside her was exquisite torture. She tipped her hips to drive him deeper. "Harder."

"God, you're tight. Don't want to hurt you."

She raked her nails down his back. "Never. Fuck me, Nate."

His fingers dug into the tender skin of her hips. He moved hard and fast, but lingered deep inside her with each plunge, stoking the fire at her core.

She trembled with the pounding force of his thrusts, reveled in his need for her, in her power.

Brilliant colors burst from behind her eyes, and she cried out.

He thrust once more, threw his head back, and shuddered. Intense pleasure slammed through her.

She smoothed her hands over his shoulders and down his broad back to his firm butt.

His heart pounded. Breath ragged, he rested his forehead against hers. "I wanted to do this right, take it slow. Make it better for you."

Still quivering with aftershocks, she tightened her inner muscles around him, and he squeezed his eyes closed with a groan. "Better?" she purred.

"Oh yeah, so much better. I've never made love skin to skin. Couldn't hold out." He pushed in tighter, rubbing against her.

She gasped. Delicious tension coiled within her again, and she rose to meet the hot, sweet ache.

"I want to taste every inch of you," he rumbled, hardening rapidly.

In the background, her landline rang.

Please, not now.

"I want to drive myself deep inside you." He

twined his fingers through hers and kissed her, with their joined hands framing her face.

"I want to make love to you every single way we can imagine." Nate kissed her languidly, his tongue stroking hers. He moved again.

She moaned at the sheer pleasure, like liquid music.

"All you have to do is enjoy." He thrust powerfully and rocked against her.

Another, stronger climax overtook her, and she screamed.

"That's right. I want to feel you come again and again, until you lose count and only remember my name."

Ecstasy burst through her in long, undulating waves, stole her breath and blacked her vision.

He covered her mouth and pulsed his release inside her.

The answering machine kicked in. "Kapulani? It's important. Meet me at the morgue ASAP."

Chapter Ten

January 10, 1:45 a.m.

Jana sat cross-legged on her bed and sipped peppermint tea. Heat danced across her cheeks. What had she been thinking when she crooked a finger at Nate? A smile teased the corners of her mouth, and she shook her head. Silly question.

She sighed and leaned back against the pillows. Dodging bullets and monster trucks must have weird side effects. No question the adrenaline aftershocks had kick-started her dormant libido, but when Nate touched her, wow! Like sparks to a Roman candle. Instant pyrotechnics.

Not that she'd had much experience, but she'd never guessed her body could respond so fast, so sexy, so shameless.

Who'd ever heard of a three-peat in real life? And that didn't count third base in the car. But he insisted he'd make it better? She folded her hands behind her head and grinned.

Only problem? She craved him again already. Just one scary step away from playing doormat to an alpha cop. Even with brain-numbing, oh-my-God-fantastic sex, she refused to let him control her, and on his own turf, he'd take over. She couldn't risk going home with him, not even for a few days, so she'd called the hotel near the hospital. Her credit card could take the strain.

Across the street, the neighbor's dog barked, and Jana startled. Then she laughed self-consciously. She'd double-checked the windows and triple-checked the locks. The alarm was set.

"I'll be fine. Nate said he'd return as soon as he could." Her grin widened. Just one more night with him wouldn't have her hooked forever. She smoothed a hand over her dark green Katharine Hepburn pajamas, hoping he'd appreciate the retro look. No question he'd appreciate the wispy bra and panties underneath.

Tossing aside a medical journal, she slipped under the covers and opened her latest romance. Until they could restart the fireworks, she needed distraction. Greedy girl. She squirmed, rubbing her thighs together, loving the sound and feel of silk against her skin.

Four scenes later, her paperback thumped to the floor. She yawned and rubbed her gritty eyes. She thought she heard glass break, but it almost seemed like part of a bad dream.

The smell of gasoline jerked her awake. Her nostrils burned and goose bumps crawled up her arms like a platoon of stinging ants.

Almost twelve thirty. Where was Nate?

An explosion shook the house. The windows rattled, and the walls flexed like a 6.8 had hit the San Andreas. She froze, her pulse pounding. A whiff of smoke curled into the room, and the fire alarm screamed.

She pulled on her robe, then covered her ears against the screech while she raced for the door and yanked it open. Thick smoke was filling the downstairs. Strange lights flickered across the living room walls.

She needed her keys from the entry table and the bag she'd packed. Could she reach them and get out? Coughing, she covered her mouth and nose with the edge of her robe and hurried down the six steps to the landing.

Below, the fire crackled and flared like a demon. The flames had spread so fast. With her lungs aching, she ran back up the stairs and slammed her bedroom door.

How could she get out? She searched frantically for an escape route. Her window wasn't too far from the ground. She could climb out onto the porch roof and jump if she had to. She cranked it open, punched out the screen, and drew a deep breath of cold air.

Across the street, a strange, dark colored truck was backed into her neighbor's driveway. The chrome silhouette of a naked woman glinted from the bumper. A man dressed in black stood beside the cab. Was it the same guy who'd followed them?

She squinted, but still couldn't see his face in the shadows. When he shifted, metal flashed from beneath his jacket, and he started toward her house with a drawn gun.

Icy panic jolted her. She was trapped.

The fire roared louder, but didn't drown out the piercing racket. She grabbed her cell phone from the nightstand. Crouching on the floor, she dialed Nate and cupped the phone tight against her head, plugging the other ear. "Please. Please. Please."

He answered, "Kapulani."

She sobbed in a breath. "Fire. Someone's outside with a gun."

"On my way." His line went dead. She tucked the

phone in her pocket and peeked out the window.

Why didn't she hear sirens? By now the alarm signal should have reached the fire department. Shit. Was her system still connected? Her new security service hadn't called to verify the problem. She picked up the landline receiver. Dead.

Black smoke seeped under her door and collected near the ceiling. The cloud grew and thickened.

The bedroom smoke alarm started to shriek. Adrenaline pumped through her veins. She wouldn't be able to breathe much longer. *Get out fast.*

Pushing past her terror, she pressed a hand against the wood. Hot! No chance to reach the stairs in the hall. She crammed a pillow into the gap beneath the door and held her breath while she crawled on all fours to the bathroom. She soaked a towel and wound it over her mouth and nose to filter out the smoke.

Moving into her closet, she barricaded the door shut, climbed on a suitcase, and heaved the attic access open. She grabbed the edges and hoisted herself up and through, sliding the trap door shut behind. Thank heaven she'd done her pull-ups.

Smoke oozed in the front eave openings, but the air up here was still breathable. She scooted across the plywood flooring, groping for the light cord and yanked. Nothing.

But a glimmer flickered through the small window at the side of the house. Could she squeeze out unseen and hide in the trees? Or jump into her neighbor's yard?

She ran to the window and grabbed the crank. It came off in her hand. Screaming in frustration, she pulled the towel off her face, wrapped it around a fist, and smashed the glass.

Behind her, more smoke poured in.

More heat.

No more time.

She gulped in fresh air as she cleared the broken shards. Her heart pounded against her sternum, but she paused and took a few deep breaths while her vision adjusted to the dark.

The neighbor's huge, old Monterey pine grew over her side fence. Could she get out the window and reach a branch?

She tore off her robe and covered the slivers of glass still wedged in the casing. Carefully, she sat with her legs dangling over the sill and peered down at the ground, twenty-five feet below. Her stomach heaved.

Although thin tree branches scraped against her house, the closest limb that might hold her was at least three feet away. She hung on to the window frame with one hand and stretched. Her head spun, and white spots swam before her eyes.

She couldn't reach. Her only chance was to jump into nothingness and pray she'd be able to grab a branch.

Impossible.

With hands clenched on the wood, she listened. No sirens yet. Damn. She didn't see the gunman. And where was Nate?

Her chest constricted around her pounding heart. Behind her, smoke poured into the attic. She coughed again. No going back.

She gritted her teeth and leaped. Her pajamas snagged and ripped, but her hands caught a limb. The branch bowed, and a distinctive crack sounded. She scrambled hand over hand toward the center, but the rough bark tore through her palms and scraped her hands raw.

The branch broke, and she dropped another foot.

Grunting with effort, she braced a foot on a lower limb and flung herself toward the trunk. She hung on, gasping. Cold, smoke-tinged air filled her lungs. Clinging to the pine, she muffled her choking coughs, so the guy with the gun wouldn't find her.

Sirens wailed, distant, but closing fast.

Through pine needle clusters, bright headlights flashed. She grabbed a thick branch and balanced, leaning out for a better view. The pickup truck was speeding away.

Flames roared through the front roof of her home, and thick smoke billowed into the night sky. Pain like a dull-edged scalpel twisted in her stomach. The anguish welled up and choked her. Every muscle in her body quivered with rage, and hot tears streaked her face.

Two fire trucks screeched to a halt at the curb. The loud beeping of the rigs and the firefighters' voices shouted in the night.

An odd numbness swept her. She huddled against the tree trunk and closed her eyes for a moment, hoping her pulse would settle. After a moment, the fresh scent of pine filtered through the acrid smoke and filled her with hope.

Water blasted her house, and the hiss of steam almost masked Nate's shouts.

"Here," she choked. "Nate, I'm here."

He peered over the side gate. She scooted lower and dangled her bare feet from a limb. "Help me down. I'm in the pine tree."

"Hang on a minute." He unlatched the gate and

shoved through.

She swung down, two hands gripping the branch, but her legs still twisted about six feet off the ground.

He caught her and carried her around the back corner into the shadows. With her heart pounding against his chest, she clung to him, warm and safe and alive.

"Thank God." He wrapped her in his sweatshirt and zipped it closed. "They're soaking your house, but I don't think there's much left to save. You okay?"

Her lip quivered, and she started to shake. "I'm fine. Really," she said, teeth chattering.

With his hands tangled in her hair, he kissed her hard before he broke away and checked for injuries. "Except for scrapes and bruises you're in one beautiful piece."

"I was so scared. You said you'd be here at midnight. Why were you late?" she demanded.

Even in the dark, his eyes glittered angrily. "I got conned."

Chapter Eleven

January 10, 3:05 a.m.

"We'll talk after you shower." From the master bathroom doorway, Nate pointed at the big glass, brick, and slate enclosure.

Hanging on to the basin, Jana gave a series of deep, rasping coughs. She sucked in a breath, frowning at him. "Tell me what you meant by conned."

He handed her a dark gray towel. "Shower first."

Jana had an angry red graze along her jaw and reeked of smoke. She looked like she belonged in some old blackface vaudeville review. He made an effort not to smile, especially with her standing there, her fists bunched on her hips and her eyes blazing.

One pale thigh and the curve of her ass showed through the big triangular rip in her filthy pajama pants. Arousal flared hot, and his pulse thrummed in his groin. His fingers itched to touch her soft skin. He wanted to kiss every bruise and scratch.

He edged away and braced himself against the doorframe. Careful, or she'd catch him drooling.

The darkest, most primitive part of him needed to throw her onto his bed and make love until dawn to prove they were both still alive. Tonight had been rough, and she needed to rest, but he craved her beneath him, screaming her pleasure.

Craved everything she'd surrender.

Craved even more.

Bruner nudged his hand with a cold, wet nose. Nate scratched the dog's head and wrenched his focus back to her question. "Nichols wasn't at the morgue and his assistant swore he left at six."

"Then who called?"

"Couldn't tell."

"You said the message sounded garbled."

"Yeah, sort of like a strangled hiss, but I figured he was freaked out or maybe your machine distorted his voice. Call came from Nichols' desk phone. I spent some time searching for him. No luck. And his phone was off. Must have been a hoax."

"Why? That doesn't make sense." She bent over the sink and splashed water on her face with bruised, scraped hands. "Nothing makes sense. Unless..."

"Unless someone wanted me out of commission tonight while they torched your place with you inside."

Trembling, Jana straightened and tipped her head. "Is that why you checked me into a seedy motel but then brought me here?"

"Yeah. Can't let whoever's after you suspect where you're hiding."

"If they knew I was with you, I'd be in even more danger. Just like Katy Frost. Tomorrow I'll go to a nice, safe hotel."

"Maybe, but the fancy place by the hospital's too obvious. Too dangerous. How about your parents?"

"No, I have to work tomorrow," she said. Her tone bristled.

He shrugged. "Then a safe house would be best. We'll figure out something in the morning."

She searched his expression in silence. When she nodded, the twist in his gut relaxed.

Soot dripped from her face onto his University of Hawaii sweatshirt. She must have followed his gaze, because she looked down. "Sorry."

"It'll come clean. I'll stick everything in the machine while you shower."

She wiggled out of the sweatshirt. The shimmy bared her belly button and hipbones and sent his Adam's apple bobbing. The rest of his blood deserted his brain for his erection. He shifted to ease the pressure. He couldn't take much more.

When she hooked her thumbs under her waistband, he hustled into the bathroom. Bruner followed close behind. "Hop in and throw your stuff to me." He herded her toward the shower and ducked back.

Through the translucent glass bricks, he heard rustles and saw dark silk slip away, revealing pink skin. Jana giggled, and her pajamas came flying. He slam-dunked them straight into the trash.

Another rustle, and a black bra followed. Bruner must have thought he was playing a game. With his tail wagging and claws clattering on the tile, the boxer snatched the bra on the fly.

"No. Drop it." The dog obediently sank on his haunches, and Nate took the scrap of silk and lace. His mouth went dry. Had she worn that for him?

Her tiny black thong sailed over the shower wall next.

He snagged it in midair and examined the delicate lingerie. His cock ached, painfully hard. God, she was naked. His mind hazed. A sudden rush of water covered his low groan.

He took two steps forward, then stopped and cleared his throat. "Uh, my sister, Lani, left some clothes here last summer. I'll dig them out while these wash."

"Thanks." Jana peeked around the glass bricks and caught him readjusting his trousers. Her face and shoulder glistened with drops of water.

She grinned and flashed one small breast and pert nipple.

"Jana."

"I'll be quick, so you can have a turn." She ran her hand over her breast and down her belly with a moan. "The hot water feels incredible."

****

3:30 a.m.

Jana ached for Nate's touch. She tiptoed back into the bathroom. Bruner was in his crate for the night, and Nate had just gotten into the shower. A cold shiver raked her body. Nate had acted noble, but she needed an inferno in her veins to drive out the terror.

Through the glass bricks, she watched him stick his head under the spray and rinse. She stripped off her T-shirt and panties and dropped them on the tile. "Nate? You've been in there a long time. Are you okay?"

"Fine. You have the guest room. Go to bed."

She chuckled softly. The poor guy sounded like he might swallow his tongue any second.

Her heart raced, and a flare of arousal seared her. She stepped in behind him. Slipping her hands around his waist, she pressed against his broad back.

"Jana, what are you doing?"

"I started thinking about you in here all by yourself. Naked."

117

He turned and kissed her quickly. "You're wiped out. You need rest."

"Later. Right now, I need you." She kissed him back and licked his full lower lip. "I want to forget all about the fire. Forget the shootings. Forget the whole ugly mess. I want to feel alive."

"You sure?"

"Hand me the soap, and I'll wash your back."

He gave her the white bar with a grin that took over his face.

"Turn around." After lathering her hands, she passed him back the soap and massaged the tense cords in his neck until he groaned. Her fingers kneaded his slick shoulders and muscled arms. A sweet ache pooled between her thighs.

He held the soap clenched in his fist and stretched sensuously under her roaming hands.

"Put that down so you can relax."

He set the mangled bar on the soap dish and braced his arms against the slate tiles.

She smiled and sluiced hot water over his back. Big, strong, powerful cop, but she could drive him nuts with a flick of her tongue. She trailed open-mouthed kisses along his spine, and her fingers shifted below his waist, flexing as she worked the muscles in his buttocks and upper thighs.

When she nipped the top of one cheek, he rewarded her with a full body shiver.

She reached around him and combed her nails through the hair that arrowed to his groin. Fondling gently, she weighed his sac, and his balls drew up tight against his body.

Her arousal built, hot and urgent and exquisite. She

caught her lower lip between her teeth. "I like that," she said, her voice husky.

"Yeah," he groaned the word and leaned his brow against the shower wall.

She brushed her fingertips over his length before circling the head lightly with her thumb and index finger. She stroked him slowly, savoring the heady freedom he allowed her.

"Jana, if I spread your legs and touched you right now, would I find you hot and slick?"

His words jolted her, and a quick thrill raced from head to toe. Heat spread over her cheeks, and her lids fluttered shut.

"Yes," she hissed. Breasts pressed against his back, she gave a throaty growl and curled her wet fingers tighter, gliding them up and down. "Nate, I've never been like this before with anyone."

He sucked in air through his teeth and thrust against the pressure of her hand. "Want to feel me nudge between your thighs? Shove inside you?"

The gravel in his voice sent a shiver up her spine, even before she processed the words. Her blood thrummed in her veins. He pulsed, weighty and tight in her hands. "More than anything."

He thrust against her fingers again. "Enough." He swiveled and turned her back against the shower spray.

His dark gaze smoking, he soaped his hands and caressed her breasts, leaving trails of lather and fire. He rolled her nipples between his fingers, tugging and tweaking until they jutted toward him through the suds.

Shivering tendrils of heat curled through her, hotter than the water streaming over her. He only had to touch her, and she'd go up in flames.

Squeezing her bottom, he pulled her toward him, and his erection jutted against her belly. One soapy hand explored her rear while he sank to his knees and sucked a peaked nipple into his mouth.

He brought his hand around to tangle in the thatch between her thighs and drew tantalizing circles, spiraling in on exactly the right spot.

A mewling cry escaped her lips. "Yes," she moaned. "Yes. There."

He parted her folds. Easing first one finger inside her and then a second, he stretched and stroked.

Waves of pleasure hit. She cried out, and her knees threatened to give way as her muscles relaxed into a pool of soft butter.

He rose and held her until her shudders subsided. Then he kissed her gently and shut off the water.

Stepping out of the shower, he toweled them both dry and lifted her in his arms.

Nate laid her on his unmade bed and stood over her smiling, but silent.

Her heart pumped madly. She met his gaze, feeling exposed and needy.

Wanton.

She bent her knees and parted her thighs. "Make love to me."

Cradling her chin, he kissed her forehead. Then he stroked her, starting with her neck and shoulders. He drew his hands over her, all the way to her arches and back to her lips. Within her, a spring coiled tighter with every caress.

He lowered his head and planted open-mouthed kisses. Lips. Shoulders. Breasts.

When he tongued her navel, she moaned and

arched her back.

"I love tasting you," he rumbled. "I want your scent and flavor on my tongue."

A surge of pleasure burst through her. She spread her legs wider, giving him what he wanted without hesitation.

He hooked her heels over his shoulders and caressed her thighs. "You're swollen and wet, ready for me."

"I want you inside me, every inch of you."

His eyebrows rose. "Soon." Parting her softness, he covered her with his mouth. Lightning shot through her, and she hissed a long sigh.

But Nate moved away and blew gently on the damp, sensitive flesh. His hands raised her hips and held her tightly as his tongue raked over her.

She dug her nails into his shoulders.

His teeth grazed a tender spot on her inner thigh, and she twisted and whimpered, stabbing her fingers into his hair.

Pulsing waves of heat radiated from her core, spreading like fire to her limbs. If only he'd touch her once, just once where she needed him.

But he held her balanced on the brink.

Then he circled her nub, drew it between his lips and flicked with his tongue. The world shattered in slow motion, and she screamed his name.

Nate covered her body and drove inside.

Sensation blasted through her. She arched beneath him, crying out her pleasure, and convulsed around him.

He took his time, loving her with slow, deep thrusts.

Need built. Her legs wrapped around his waist pulling him deep, meeting every stroke, matching the rhythm he set.

She exploded into a white-hot orgasm that pulled him over the crest.

Chapter Twelve

January 10, 8:45 a.m.

Sated and sore in spots she hadn't noticed for years, Jana sprawled across Nate, still straddling him. His heartbeat bumped against her ear, slower now than a few minutes ago.

Morning light peeked through a crack in his bedroom drapes. The straight lines of his oak bed and highboy had a rich, mellow surface and looked solid against the matte blue walls.

What a night. Cataloguing all the luscious, tender places, she took a deep breath of his warm, masculine scent and smiled at him. "My muscles feel like rubber bands."

Laughter rumbled through him. He drew the rich green comforter over them and kissed her forehead, cradling her. "You don't have to get out of bed. Catch up on your sleep."

"Unfortunately, I need to be at work by noon." She sketched her hand across his chest, and the muscles underneath his tanned skin rippled. "I'm scheduled for the post-op clinic this morning."

"Your safety comes first. Call in sick. Have Andy Peterson take the shift."

"No, there are patients I have to see." Her fingers meandered over his ribs, but his swift hand snapped out and blocked her. She giggled and reached for his taut belly. "You're ticklish?"

"No. Just sensitive." Nate kissed her fingertips, but didn't release her.

"Big, tough guy like you." She turned her head and kissed each flat brown nipple.

He groaned, but flipped her and pinned both her wrists with one powerful hand before she could yelp.

His eyes took on a wicked glint, and she pretended to struggle, laughing while he teased her bare skin with the lightest of touches. He circled her navel. "What happened to your bellybutton ring?"

She grinned. "You remember that?"

"I remember wanting to tongue the sexy silver bar."

"Mm. Sorry, I let the piercing close up after college."

His mouth covered hers, and a sweet, throbbing emptiness rose inside her.

How could she want him again so soon? Where would she find the strength to leave him when his interest cooled?

He nibbled gently on her ear and smoothed a hand over her hip and bottom.

Warm, languid shivers chased over her skin. Maybe she could think more clearly alone. She needed space and perspective. She sighed and tilted back her face to smile at him. "Let me up, Nate. I need to take a shower."

"Sure." He rolled onto his side. "But first we need to talk."

An uneasy pang tightened her chest, but she met his gaze. "About what? We already agreed no strings."

"Of course." He framed her face with his big hands and kissed her. "Walk me through your last night with Mike."

Frowning, she shifted away from him. "That was the last thing I expected you to ask. Why?"

"Can't help thinking you know something."

She sat up and swung her legs off the bed. "I don't have time now."

"Just a few minutes; it's not even nine yet." His chin jutted forward, his jaw joints flexed, and the muscles of his face solidified into granite.

She slipped out of his hands and stood, surveying the room. What could she put on to help her feel less exposed? Less vulnerable? She reached for his uniform shirt draped over the chair and shrugged into it, closing a few buttons. The sleeves hung to her knees, so she rolled them and padded across the wood floors to a wide bedroom window.

"Maybe we can figure a way out of this mess and get our lives back," he coaxed.

Lifting a corner of the heavy drapes, she squinted into the bright sun and swallowed the sudden lump in her throat. Bars on the windows? She dropped the curtain. Sereno was a grimy slum, but did Nate feel threatened, too? She turned toward him. Time to face the danger. "Fine. What do you want to know?"

He sat on top of the sheets with his back against the oversized headboard. Naked. Muscled chest and arms, wide shoulders and long brown legs with big feet. And poking up between them, his tantalizing erection.

Jana swallowed the drool and fought to drag her gaze back to his face.

With a wicked smile, Nate pulled the sheet up and

patted the mattress next to him. When she sat and scooted close, he slung an arm over her shoulders and said, "Mike came over for dinner that night..."

"Okay. Right." She closed her eyes. "He picked me up from my last class. I fixed him enchiladas, the burn-your-taste-buds-off variety, but we got into a fight after dinner. He wanted me to give up med school, or at least postpone it for a few years."

"Slow down, Jana. Try to remember the details."

She pushed out a long breath through her nose.

"What were you doing when Mike called me and cancelled surveillance?"

Blushing, she cleared her throat and stared at her hands. "My roommate, Liv, had left with her date, and Mike, um, wanted..."

"You." Nate tipped her chin and kissed her, slowly and thoroughly.

Her heart raced, and she reached for him, arching her neck and opening her lips. When he broke the kiss, she nestled her head against the hollow of his shoulder.

"You're the sexiest woman I've ever met, and I can't get enough of you. I understand Mike wanted you that night. Can't say I blame him."

"Nate..."

"Happened a long time ago. Doesn't bother me." He drew his thumb down her cheek, but he blinked, and the tiny crease between his brows gave him away.

Jana licked suddenly dry lips. "Good. Because it doesn't matter to me anymore." Stretching one arm around Nate's waist, she met his gaze and felt a magnetic pull. Her will to resist him evaporated. She touched his jaw, his nose, and traced his ear. When she ran her fingers over his moist, swollen mouth, he caught her hand and kissed her palm.

Languid warmth spread through her, and her blood swirled in her veins. The emptiness low in her body throbbed. Why had she ever wanted another man? She must have been delusional.

Sweat popped out on her upper lip, and dew formed between her thighs. She licked the rough edge of his chin and nibbled her way to his ear.

When he groaned and kissed her, she reached under the sheet and curled her hand around his hard penis. Her nipples pebbled against the starched cotton of his shirt, and she stroked the hot, velvet skin stretched tight over steel.

His tongue tangled with hers, and she shuddered.

She wanted nothing more than to straddle him and take him inside her again and make him part of her. She no longer wanted to break free. Instead, she wanted what they had found to last.

Grinning, he dislodged her hand. "Focus, Jana. Did Mike leave anything at your house?" With the lightest touch, he ran his fingers over her hips and cupped her bottom. As if he'd read her mind, he lifted her onto his lap, facing him.

Jana braced her hands on his shoulders. Her legs were spread wide, her knees resting against the pillow behind his back. Her moist, empty sex was exposed and open to the chilly air. Open to his gaze. The sheet covering his erection tented between them, but didn't touch her. Didn't fill her empty ache.

Nate tilted up her chin. "Look at me. Did Mike leave his notes? Contact info? Anything that might still be stashed away in your stuff?" He eased his big warm hands back under her hips, holding her with his strong fingers spread wide. His hands moved, massaged, and caressed.

Hunger radiated through her, fuzzed her brain. She blinked and tried to concentrate. "I...I can't imagine what. I never found anything."

He rubbed the small of her back, drew his fingers around her bottom, followed the cleft, and stroked down the outsides of her thighs. "Did he get any phone calls? Voice messages?"

"You were the only one he talked to."

Nate frowned, but his fingers finally delved into her triangle of curls and brushed her almost too sensitive flesh.

A tiny burst of pleasure rippled from her nub. She hissed and couldn't help spreading her legs wider, pressing closer to him. "I can't think when you do that. I want you inside me too much."

He chuckled and kept his fingers moving gently, sending more blissful twinges. "In a minute. We're almost done talking. Did Mike spend time by himself? Or were you together the whole evening?"

"Yeah. M-mostly. He used the bathroom once, but..."

"Did he take his cell phone?"

"Maybe. He wore it clipped on his belt."

"I know someone else called him." He circled her clit with his thumb.

"I was in the kitchen with the music turned up." She moaned. "Oh my God, Nate..."

"Makes sense you didn't hear anything. Traced the number to a payphone, but never could identify the caller."

The delicious circles spiraled closer. All her nerve

endings tingled and luscious tension built. "W-why?"

"His cell phone was missing. I'd hoped you overheard something. Did he mention any names?"

"No." Jana closed her eyes, trying to ignore the broad finger slipping inside her. She sucked in a ragged breath. "Mike...he said something about getting a break, but he wouldn't...Oh God, that feels good...wouldn't explain."

"A phone call set him up." Nate eased a second finger inside, stretching her while rubbing against just the right spot.

A tidal wave of contractions seized her, and she threw her head back with a tight little scream. Before the pulses died out, she rose on her knees and jerked back the sheet. His erection jutted free.

"No more." She shot him a narrow-eyed look. "I'm done. I'm done talking about Mike. I'm done thinking about Mike."

Nate's eyes, dark as midnight, glittered at her. "Yeah? Then what do you want?"

"This." She guided him into her, rising and sinking as she worked his stiff, thick erection inside, inch by inch.

She dragged his mouth to hers for a hot, deep kiss, and the dark waves of his hair covered her fingers. Tensing her inner muscles, she held still, but the strokes of his tongue set off frissons of energy, and his heartbeat echoed through her sex.

With his hands gripping her thighs, he lifted her and plunged her down again, impaling her. He broke the kiss, but his teeth grazed her lips. Harder, faster, he pumped and lifted. Each stroke was more intense, penetrating deeper.

Their bodies were slick with sweat. She grasped his biceps; her hips grinding against his driving thrusts.

"Jana." He threw his head back and bucked into her.

Electricity spiked, and her world shattered into rapture. Darkness overtook her, and she collapsed against him.

With each aftershock, tears welled in her eyes.

An eternity later, she stirred and drew a halting breath. "Wow."

Smoothing her bangs off her cheek, he kissed her nose lightly. His penis twitched inside her. "Wow is right."

From the bedside table, his cell phone trilled. "I need to check the caller ID." Grinning, he pulled the phone free from its charger. "The coroner's office. I have to answer. Might actually be Nichols this time."

"Sure." She kissed him and rose up on her knees. "I need to take a quick shower and get ready for work."

****

Smiling, Nate watched her jog from the room, her long, slim legs naked below his shirt. The shoulders hung almost to her elbows; the dark blue tails caressed her thighs. What was it about that woman? Felt like he was a teenager again, and sex was an emergency. He'd just come so hard he should be spent for days, but it wouldn't take much to prime him for another round with her. His phone rang again. "Kapulani," he answered.

"Something weird's going on," Bart Nichols stated.

"No kidding. Where the hell were you last night?"

"What do you mean? I worked until six, ordered in pizza, and had a couple beers. Why? Did something happen?"

"Got a call from your office just before midnight. Wasted the next hour chasing you around while I should have been protecting Jana." Nate quickly described the fire. "Someone's after her."

"Looks like it," Nichols said. "When I autopsied Wendell, the only fibers were from the rope burns on his neck. The corpse had been sanitized, nails bleached."

"Happens. Too many lowlifes watch cop shows."

"No kidding. Makes my job tougher." The sound of rustling papers came through the phone. "But this morning I got a forensics report with info on hairs supposedly found on Wendell. Plus blood traces from fingernail scrapings. B negative. DNA analysis is pending."

"Could there be a screw up? CSI put the wrong name on a report?"

"No. All the supporting paperwork magically appeared in my files. Says here my office initiated everything."

"Who's responsible?"

"Signature's mine, but I never saw the report before today. Kapulani, the hairs are red."

A giant vice tightened around Nate's chest. He stood and paced the room. "Shit. Greene had her do a cheek scrape. Thought he was harassing her, but she's being framed."

"That's what I figured. I'll stash the evidence and the report in my bottom drawer until you can get here."

"Thanks."

"If you want to keep her alive, pick up this garbage and get out of Sereno fast."

Ice formed on the back of Nate's neck, and chills spread down his spine.

"Hey, someone's banging on my door. It's my assistant. I gotta go." The connection broke.

Nate tunneled his hands through his hair. The big question was why Jana? Was someone just trying to scare her away? Or worse?

Last night she could have died.

Only one way to find out. He made a quick call to the seedy motel he'd checked Jana into as a decoy. With his every muscle growing tenser by the second, he alternatively flexed and clenched his hands while listening to the desk clerk weasel to avoid giving out any information.

Fighting to keep his breathing even, Nate promised to pay the guy another hundred bucks. The desk clerk caved. Jana's room had been trashed early in the morning, but "nobody knew nothing."

Nate broke the connection and swore. He'd known all along Jana was a target, but whose? No way to tell for sure without a personal visit and a bigger pile of cash. The security cameras at that dumpy motel hadn't worked in years, and the night-shift guy was witless.

The fire and the motel break-in could be Morgan's work. If so, was he acting on his own? Did he give the orders? Doubtful. Someone else was the brain behind the attacks and Morgan the muscle. Dragging him downtown again would ramp the pressure on him, but also might expose her to more risk.

Too many freaking questions. Nate searched through the highboy for clean clothes and pulled on boxers and uniform pants before heading to the back porch.

He held open the door for Bruner. The dog greeted him with a full body wiggle and a cold nose to his palm, then bounded ahead into the bedroom and curled on the bedside rug.

With his gut churning, Nate slumped on the bed and blew out a frustrated breath. Fear sliced through his belly. How could he protect her when he didn't even know why she was in danger?

Jana had become so much more to him than he'd ever expected.

He'd tried to focus on the danger by questioning her, but it hadn't taken much before he'd gone deaf and blind and stupid as a box of boulders, panting to be inside her again. And when she'd blushed and stammered about sex with Mike, all he could think about was claiming her. Nate slammed his fist against the mattress, and Bruner raised his head.

Nate reached down to scratch the dog's ear. "You're fine, buddy. I just have to forget about my damn cock and think."

He rose and grabbed a clean shirt. First, he'd pick up the so-called evidence from Bart Nichols and destroy it. Then he'd convince Jana to hide until this mess blew over. Without the physical evidence, the case against her would vanish.

But short of tying her up and stuffing her in his trunk, how could he get her to leave town? Or even keep her safe at work this morning?

The water shut off, and a moment later, she wandered back in wrapped in a towel. She gave him a wide smile as she crossed the room. "Did you and Dr. Nichols figure out how you missed each other?"

"Not exactly."

She dropped her towel and turned her back to him while she tugged the scrap of black silk between the pale globes of her ass. Bending forward, she wiggled into her tiny bra and hooked it behind her.

A quick pulse of heat curled through his veins.

She stepped into the jeans and zipped them, but they sagged down around her hips, leaving a glimpse of black silk visible above the belt loops until she drew his UC sweatshirt over her head.

Blood surged into his already hard cock. Didn't matter what she wore, she was the sexiest thing he'd ever seen.

Frowning, she studied herself in his mirror. "No curves, no style. Except for my hair, I look like a teenage boy."

"No way." He moved behind her and circled his arms around her waist and under the sweatshirt. He covered her bra with his hands, caressing her breasts until her nipples hardened and she moaned. "What if I tugged these jeans lower, bent you over, and buried myself inside you?"

She gave a delicate shiver, turned, and spiked her fingers into his hair. "Yes, please."

Her husky voice sent electricity all the way to his toes and made his blood pulse. He wrapped her in his arms and devoured her mouth as if they had forever.

When she broke for breath with a sigh, he licked the curve of her cool, wet ear. "Delicious."

"I want your hands and mouth on me again already. I don't understand."

"Me neither." He nuzzled her neck briefly, but pulled back, determined to ignore the urgent siren song calling his penis. "But we can figure it out later. I have to meet Nichols at the morgue ASAP. Something I need to take care of."

"What?"

Fear gnawed at the edge of his guts again. Tugging her onto the mattress, he settled beside her and took her hand. "Stay here today. Spend some time thinking about what Mike might have told you, or left at your place. I hate to leave you alone, but with the alarm on and Bruner guarding, you'll be safe for a few hours."

"Why?" Her gaze locked on his. "You're scaring me."

"Tell you when I get back."

She edged away and that stubborn expression gripped her brow, jaw, and chin again. "No, explain now."

"Fine. Nichols found a forensic report on Wendell with doctored evidence. Bet you have a rare blood type, don't you?"

She nodded slowly, her frown deepening.

He knew the answer, but checked anyway. "B negative?" When she gasped, he added, "Just so the danger's crystal clear, Jana, they're framing you for murder."

"How can they?"

"Remember the DNA swab Greene wanted?"

Her face paled. "Yes."

"Nichols got back the reports. If we're lucky, I can destroy the evidence they've manufactured. But you've got to leave town today."

She angled a quizzical look at him. "You want me to run away? But you know I didn't kill Wendell."

"Of course."

"If I run, everyone will think I'm guilty."

"Sereno isn't safe. I can't protect you here."

"This is crazy. I have a contract, an important job."

"I used to feel the same way, like I had a mission." His heart pounded against his ribs, and a dark scowl gathered on his face.

"But I can't just quit. I have patients..."

"There are other doctors."

She stared up at him with her mouth open, and her big hazel eyes were full of questions and full of trust, but also full of fear.

Silently, he pulled her back into his arms. "Someone else can handle your shift today. It's not worth the risk."

She started to speak, but he held a finger across her lips. "Listen. Call your boss. Demand a leave of absence. Somebody wants you dead."

She stood and shook her head. "Even if I do leave, I can't resign over the phone. I'd never work again."

Frustration churned his guts. He took a deep breath. Jana was no doormat. He liked her strength, her willingness to push back. Maybe too much. It might rip him up inside, but he had to respect her.

Keeping her safe took first priority. Hell, he'd even give up his obsession with closing Mike's case for her. Even if he put Morgan and whoever was paying him behind bars, Mike would still be dead. Let somebody else clean up this cesspool.

He grabbed his baseball cap off the doorknob and placed it on her head. "If you're determined, make the trip in disguise. I'll drop you at the hospital, pick up the file from Nichols, and turn in my own resignation."

"You're serious."

"If you won't go stay with your parents, come with

me. I know a mile of private island beach we can enjoy while we straighten out this disaster."

She considered his suggestion for a long moment and then nodded again. "Okay."

Finding her mouth, he nudged her lips open and sank his tongue inside. He eased his hands under the sweatshirt and popped her nipples out of the half cups, rolling them between his fingers. His balls tightened, and an irresistible craving burned through his cock and overtook his brain. He kneaded her breasts and nipped a line of love bites along her neck.

Her fingers roamed all over him, his face, his chest, his arms. Her nails scraped his shoulders, ramping his painful hunger. But what sweet pain.

He snaked his hands inside her saggy jeans. Pulling her to her toes and tight against him, he pressed against her belly. "One last time?"

Grinning, she ran a short nail up his zipper and popped the snap.

When the pressure eased, he groaned. Slanting her a heated look, he shucked his pants and leaned closer.

She twisted her arms around his neck, and the jeans she wore drooped lower, flashing the triangle of black silk and taut, pale belly.

He gathered her against him, taking her mouth, and reached under the sweatshirt to smooth the curve of her ass.

She just grinned wider, shoved down her jeans and panties, and stepped out of them. "Make love to me again," she murmured against his lips, her tongue stroking his.

"Oh yeah. Once more." He lifted her onto the bed, spread her thighs, and pushed into her damp heat.

Violent pleasure swamped him, and his eyelids drooped from the rush of sensations. He shuddered, and a groan tore from his throat.

"Nate," she purred, drawing out his name.

Fierce need gripped him, and he started to thrust, fast and hard.

Her legs tightened around his waist, locking him in deep. When he drove against her again, her neck arched, but her eyes stayed open, and her gaze fixed on his.

"Before you, I've never made love like this," he whispered against her lips. "No barriers between us, nothing holding me but you."

"I love the feel of you inside me." Her hips made small grinding movements.

Electric current zinged through him, and his control thinned. His body tight and one with hers, he rocked into her.

Jana's nails dug into his shoulders as her breath caught on a silent scream. Her inner muscles pulsed around him like a steely, silken fist.

His mouth closed fast over hers, and he exploded in a mind-bending rush.

Chapter Thirteen

January 10, 12:05 p.m.

Across the street and half a block from the hospital entrance, Jana tucked a stray hair beneath Nate's University of Hawaii baseball cap and checked the rearview mirror. Her cheekbones heated. Nate had marked her. Love bites paraded up her neck, and her lips were so swollen she looked like she'd injected a triple load of collagen.

A little obvious she'd been busy? But thank heaven nobody could see how her tender sex stabbed with almost blissful pain every time she shifted. "Will I pass if I show some attitude?"

"You look fine. Nobody else knows what you have on under that getup." One eyebrow raised, Nate lasered her with his melted chocolate gaze and chuckled. "Can't think about it too hard or I'll hit the door locks and drag you to the nearest motel."

She laid a hand on his chest. "Later. This won't take long. I have my leave of absence letter all ready."

"Sure you can't mail the sucker?"

"Positive. Anyway, I need to clean out my locker. I'll grab my stuff and be waiting by the security station when you get back from talking to Nichols."

"And?"

"Let's see. Skip the post-op clinic. Do not examine

any patients. Do not take any shit from one soon-to-be-former boss." She ticked the list off on her fingers.

Nate scrubbed a hand across his face. "Wish I could ask Nichols to toss the evidence in a bonfire."

"Wouldn't that put him in danger?"

"Realistically? Yeah." Nate let out a sigh. "We should have a couple hours to spare before Greene can cop a warrant. But be careful. My gut's screaming danger."

"Got it." She squeezed his hand and slid across the seat. With a loud, "Dude," and two thumbs up, she jumped out and slammed the door.

Slumping along the sidewalk, she craned her neck forward and let her chin bob with every stride. But her slouch threw off her center of gravity, and she stumbled over a chunk of concrete. She lost one of her flip-flops and had to toe it back on.

Saunter, don't rush. Like she could anyway, the way her knees were shaking. She took in a slow, deep breath. Think like a teenaged punk. Just stroll into the hospital lobby like nothing's going on, and the world's your ashtray.

No manufactured evidence.

No pending murder charges.

No sex-fiend alpha cop trying to run her life.

Nate. Her pulse did a breakdance. Although she summoned a little righteous, I'm-an-independent-woman resentment, she couldn't restrain a grin. She closed her eyes and pictured Nate parading across the bedroom naked, smiling wickedly, his penis huge and hard and glorious, even though they'd spent all night making love.

She gave a little shimmy. They'd had sex every

possible way except hanging upside down and backwards. Well, not hanging upside down, anyway.

The hospital's wide, bulletproof glass doors loomed fifty feet ahead. Her stomach jittered. She slowed her steps and dawdled behind a skeletal potted cypress. How could she get past security without being recognized?

A big, blue-collar family with four rowdy kids marched by. Perfect. Jana trailed the herd through the automatic entrance. When they stopped at the security desk, the guard raised his head and gave her a hard stare. Her heart did a wild hip-hop, but she averted her gaze and shuffled closer, sticking her hands in her pockets while the white-haired, pigeon-breasted matriarch-in-purple asked directions.

At the x-ray scanner, Jana shucked her backpack, belt, and flip-flops and sent them through. Then she tipped her cap down low and waddled into the metal detector with her thumbs through her belt loops to hold up her pants.

No earth-shattering alarms screamed. She didn't even lose her jeans and flash the crowd. Better yet, from here the physicians' locker room was only two short corridors away, and she could get there without passing the nurses' station. Nonchalantly, she swiped at the moisture on her brow, yanked the jeans up, and belted them tight.

She shivered and shuffled past the elevator. Damn that trigger-happy asshole. And double damn the firebug. Her life had gone from struggling-but-under-control to totally buggered in less than two weeks.

Her cell buzzed. A queasy feeling rammed her stomach as she stared at the text message on the screen.

Her hands curled tight, and the nails made half-moon depressions in her palms. Raines was demanding to see her in ten minutes. Fortunate coincidence? Probably not. She shouldered into the locker room.

Andy Peterson glanced at her from a bench with one of his size fifteens in his hand. "Hey, buddy, this is the doctors' lounge. You lost?"

She snatched off her cap with a wide grin and shook her short, feathery hair free. "Nope. How was the ER last night?"

"Jana?" He thumped his shoe onto the bench. "What are you doing in that outfit?"

"It's a long story."

"Be careful. Raines is on a rampage."

"Why? He texted me, but I have another fifteen minutes before my shift." She dialed her combination and opened her locker, grabbing fresh scrubs and a lab coat.

"Dunno, but when he asked me where to find you, he sure was pissed."

"His typical, sour-mouthed, constipated expression?" She clenched her teeth, lifted her nose in the air, and glared.

Andy hooted.

"I guess I should check in with him first." Stripping off her sweatshirt and jeans, she dressed in scrubs and draped a stethoscope around her neck. "Shoot. I forgot about shoes. I can't see Raines in my flip-flops."

"Might not notice if they're under surgical booties."

"It's worth a try." Jana dug around in the bottom of her locker and came up with a used pair of the blue paper slip-ons.

"You seem frazzled today. Everything okay?"

"I'm making progress." She tucked the envelope with her leave of absence request into her lab coat pocket. On impulse, she grabbed the spare cash she kept at the hospital and stuffed the bills and her disguise into her backpack. She slung the pack over her shoulder before slamming her locker.

Andy unfolded to his full height and crossed his massive, tattooed arms over his chest. A slight frown wrinkled his forehead. "That heartbreaker cop got past your defenses last night."

Her head jerked up, and she met his deep blue gaze with a sigh. "How did you know?"

"The underwear." He twisted the ring in his eyebrow. "And I know Nate when he's on the prowl. Good guy, but he earned his rep as a player."

"A wolf alert from Dr. Andrew Peterson, master seducer of nurses?"

He grinned and shrugged. "When everybody knows the rules…"

Although nagging tension tightened her stomach, she matched his grin. "Don't worry. Nate and I want the same thing from this affair."

Andy waggled his eyebrows and gave her a blatant once-over. "Works for me. Let me know if you decide you want some variety."

Heat seared her cheeks, but she chuckled. "Um, no, I don't think so. But seriously, I'm taking a leave of absence. I don't have time to explain, but I might not see you again before I go."

"You're leaving?" At her nod, he heaved a huge sigh. "Man, we'll miss you. Fill me in on the details one of these days? And be careful. There've been some weird characters hanging around the ER today."

"Thanks for the heads up." She stood on tiptoes and gave him a peck on the cheek. "I have to run."

With her white coat flying, she raced for the elevator and squeezed in just as the doors were closing. Smoothing her hand behind her neck, Jana poked the fifth floor button. She flattened into a corner and jiggled one heel up and down.

Nate, a notorious player? That wasn't a huge surprise. She'd known his reputation years ago, but why did his past bother her so much? He was a virile hunk in his thirties. What did she expect? Just because she didn't have much of a sexual résumé, didn't mean he shouldn't. She snorted. If she wanted a physically satisfying, emotion-free affair with a my-way-or-the-handcuffs cop, so what?

Her stomach did a crash landing, and she wrapped her arms around her middle. What an idiot. Emotion-free, my ass. She'd fallen in love with him.

But Nate had dictated the terms of their no-strings affair and taken complete control in bed. Well, mostly. And now he'd commandeered her life. The leave of absence. Hiding from danger, even though she was innocent. Abandoning her responsibilities to run off with him and make freckles in Hawaii.

Shit. She'd not only turned into a lovesick doormat, she had footprints on her back.

The elevator door bonged, and she heaved a gigantic sigh. Okay, first see what Raines wanted. Then she could strategize, maybe get some help to stay safe and regain control of her life. She'd survived the past ten years alone, and she could do it again, but not without her work. Practicing medicine was her life, her calling. She couldn't afford to give up everything and trail him to Hawaii. There had to be alternatives where she could salvage her career.

Even letting her dad order her around might be a better choice. At least the Colonel wanted her long-term happiness. She cracked her knuckles. Maybe she should hop in her car and head south for home.

She straightened her backbone and smiled at her boss's overbearing receptionist. "Dr. Raines wants to see me?"

Smirking, the woman poked the intercom. "Dr. Sutherland finally arrived."

Raines' door burst open. His pale eyes glittered, and a flush mottled his cheeks and neck. "Get in here."

Cold sweat trickled down her spine, but she obeyed.

He slammed a stack of papers on his desk. "Exactly where were you?"

Jana managed not to roll her eyes. "Getting ready for my shift, which starts in exactly two minutes."

"Officer MacLean was waiting for you. He just left for Judge Pascal's chambers."

Goose bumps paraded across her neck and shoulders. Jana stared at her boss. "Why did he want me?"

"Are you an imbecile?" Raines shrieked. "He has to question you for murder and arson."

Her ears buzzed, and her stomach turned to molten metal. Silence stretched for two heartbeats, then a guttural growl burst from her throat. "That is so totally ridiculous, I can't even…"

He raised his nose and gave an aristocratic little

sniff. "You've shown zero discretion and until last night, no cooperative spirit."

Tapping the tip of her finger on her the desk, she let out a snort. "Well, there you go. Murder is pretty damned uncooperative."

"Obviously, you're suspended without pay. Effective immediately."

Her pulse broke the speed record. "Obviously, you bureaucratic chicken shit, I quit." She pivoted on her heel and stalked toward the elevator.

"Stop! Where are you going? Officer MacLean wanted you to wait."

Jana stepped into the elevator, turned, and flashed her former boss both middle fingers.

****

12:55 p.m.

The morgue elevator creaked open, and a snoot full of formaldehyde seared Nate's sinuses. Squeezing his eyes shut, he cleared his throat, but his nose still stung. He hurried down the deserted corridor into ghoul central.

"Nichols?" his voice echoed around the tile room.

No answer.

Nobody around.

Frowning, Nate rubbed his chin. The glistening autopsy tables had been hosed down. Even the corpses were stowed away. He knocked on the office doorframe and waited.

Nothing.

He knocked again.

"Nichols?" Nate tried the knob. Unlocked.

A chill whispered across his neck. He drew his gun, pressed flat against the wall, and kicked open the door. All clear.

When he flicked on the overhead light, his muscles knotted. The office had been tossed. Files emptied. Desk ransacked.

Nate entered, closed, and locked the door. A computer mouse dangled above a pile of papers, but where the fuck was that evidence? Nichols had said something about his desk.

After a quick check of the drawers, Nate blew out a breath. Hopeless, but Nichols was a real tech nerd and kept copies of everything on his computer. Nate searched the room twice. No laptop.

His gut bottomed out as he surveyed the wreckage. He'd never find anything fast in this disaster zone. The evidence against Jana would have to wait. He needed to get out of here and take her someplace safe. But he could leave a message for Nichols.

On the way out the door, Nate punched in the coroner's cell phone number. He turned toward the sound of distant ringing, and his breathing spiked along with his heart rate. The Star Trek theme song? Maybe Nichols was still around. Hiding? Hurt?

His insides knotted. The call went to voicemail. Adrenaline roared through his system. His thoughts calmed. His hands steadied. He pressed redial and followed the sound to drawer number sixty-eight.

He yanked the cold steel handle.

He inhaled through his mouth so he wouldn't gag. Nichols? Nate stared for a long moment, hoping he was wrong. Not much left of his face, but the body still wore the coroner's long white jacket, now doused with fresh blood, and a stupid Starship Enterprise tie. Nate recognized the Stanford med school class ring on his friend's right hand. Nichols had raised a lot of beers with that hand.

Nate smashed his fist into drawer number sixty-seven and turned away. Dry heaves caught him, but after a few moments, he could think again.

Gritting his teeth, he dug for Nichols' cell phone. Why leave evidence of their calls behind? Nate wiped his prints off the drawer handle and cleaned everything he'd touched in the office. No need to invite a murder rap.

He hurried out of the morgue to the elevator, punched, and then swiped the up button. They'd killed Nichols. They were eliminating every obstacle.

A cold weight slammed into his chest. That meant he and Jana were next on the list. He had to warn her. A gunman had gotten loose in the hospital once before. Even with new security in place, a determined shooter could sneak in again. Especially if he had help.

The elevator doors ground open. Nate squeezed through and hoofed it outside, punching in her number on the run. One ring. Pick up, Jana.

What would he do if he lost her? A wrenching pain slashed through his heart, and his blood iced in his veins. He couldn't imagine life without her.

Two rings.

His lungs seized. Itching prickles of agony ran up his spine.

Fuck, he couldn't imagine life without her?

Sure, he enjoyed her company, admired her strength and intelligence, and loved having sex with her. She was gorgeous and fun and hadn't lost her sense of humor, even after she'd been ambushed by disaster after disaster.

He had to face it; he loved her. Had loved her for years.

He didn't know how she'd react, but he wouldn't let her go, ever. First priority? Keep her alive.

Three rings.

"Hello?" Jana answered.

"Get out of there, now!"

Chapter Fourteen

January 10, 1:15 p.m.

Jana's stomach twisted, and her throat clogged. She clutched her cell phone closer. "They murdered Nichols?" she choked.

"Yeah, and you're next," Nate said.

"But who?" Hurrying toward the locker room, she grabbed a patient file from a door holder to shield her face.

"Has to be Morgan. He'll be gunning for you. Don't depend on Sereno PD."

She glanced toward the nurse's station. Gooseflesh crept over her, and her pulse rate doubled. A man wearing a designer leather jacket and pressed-to-a-razor-edge khakis leaned against the counter with his back to her. She sidestepped and checked his profile. Where had she seen him before?

She bent over the water fountain and flipped up the collar of her lab coat to hide her red hair. Her heart pounded so fiercely against her ribs, she couldn't catch her breath much less swallow the icy water. "Didn't you show me Joe Morgan's picture?" she whispered into the phone.

"Mug shot."

"Shit. He's here."

"Did he see you?"

"I don't think so, but I can't get to the locker room without going past him."

"You still in disguise?"

"No."

Nate gave a growly rumble. "Get moving. Dr. Jana Sutherland has to vanish."

She wanted to run, but hitched her backpack higher and strolled away as casually as she could by Morgan. *Don't look,* she thought. *Please, don't look.*

At the end of the corridor, she slipped into the women's restroom and leaned against the door. Cold sweat pooled under her arms and beaded on her forehead. She swallowed the bitter taste coating her tongue and inhaled slowly through her nose.

"Jana?"

"I'm in the bathroom. I can change here. Morgan won't be hunting for a scruffy kid in a baseball hat."

"Good. Can you duck out the back?"

"Yes. The service stairs are close." She slammed into a stall and hung her pack and white coat on the hook. She could hear Nate's harsh breathing. He must be scared, too.

"I can't pick you up. They know my car, and they'll be watching."

"What about a bus?"

Nate made a noise, and she could almost see him shake his head. "Too risky."

"No, I'd be invisible. I could be at your house in half an hour."

"Makes sense, but your place is closer. Safer. They won't expect you to head there after the fire."

She wiggled out of her scrubs and grabbed the jeans and sweatshirt, but needed both hands free to dress. "I'll hide in the garage."

"Okay. I'll rent a car and meet you there. Keep your hair covered."

"Nate?"

"What?"

Glancing around the graffiti-scribbled gray stall, she chewed her lip. "Be safe."

"You too, gorgeous," he said softly. An engine turned over, and the connection broke.

Jana shivered. Alone. She squared her shoulders, but a near hysterical laugh escaped. "Get moving, Sutherland. Standing naked in a bathroom doesn't accomplish a damn thing."

After zipping the jeans, she pulled on Nate's sweatshirt and stuffed her scrubs and lab coat into the backpack. She let out a long sigh. How long before she practiced medicine again?

Facing the sink mirror, she tucked the last strands of hair under the cap.

The door creaked. Her belly jumped, but she froze.

Parvati Singh hurried in, brushing a strand of long, dark hair into her messy bun. "Jana? Is that you? Someone was asking for you."

Jana blinked and scratched her neck. "I don't have time to explain, but can you help me?"

"With what?" she asked, bracing her hands on her generous hips.

"Did you notice the really full-of-himself guy by station two? Tall and blond with a deep tan?"

"The one in the leather jacket? He's hard to miss. He's chatting up the head nurse."

Parvati's eyes narrowed with puzzlement and then suspicion. "But he's the one asking for you."

"Can you distract him for a minute? I wouldn't ask, but I really can't talk to him now."

One dark eyebrow rose.

Jana's cheeks flamed, and she rubbed her temples. "Please? Two minutes."

The woman studied her. "Are you in trouble?"

"Yes. He's...a stalker. He threatened me. Just catch his attention for a moment so I can get to the service stairs. Don't tell him you saw me."

"Youngsters." The woman shook her head, but started to open the door.

Jana put out her hand. "Parvati, he's dangerous."

After exactly one minute, Jana slouched out the door and down the corridor, carrying her flip-flops. Seventeen steps later, she swiped her badge across a scanner next to the door.

When the release clicked, she darted into the dingy beige stairwell. With her pulse echoing in her ears, she raced down the two flights of stairs toward the garage and receiving dock. Her bare feet made dull thuds on the cold metal.

Just before she reached the exit to the garage, a door to the stairwell opened, and a male voice growled, "Where's this go?"

All the hairs on her nape bristled.

"Th-the physician's garage," Parvati said in a shaky, but very loud tone. Damn. Morgan must have forced her to open the door.

Slap! Parvati shrieked.

Jana winced and crept forward. She kept moving, avoiding the garage entrance, and passed a janitorial closet.

Footsteps pounded on the stairs above her.

The noise echoed through her bones and turned her legs to jittery spandex.

An impulse to scream and cover her head and curl into the fetal position shook her to her toenails. Rounding a corner, she eased through the door to the receiving dock as quietly as she could.

Behind her, the door to the parking garage squeaked open.

She jumped down from the platform and scrambled along the side of a produce delivery van. Jana cowered by the wheel while she slipped back into her flip-flops. She heaved in one ragged breath, then another. Rotten vegetables, diesel fuel, and the smell of her own fear filled her nose.

A hefty man wearing brown coveralls and holding a clipboard came through the door from the kitchens and scowled. "Hey, kid! What the fuck you doing? Get away from my truck."

Jana took off toward the open warehouse doors. She emerged into the bright light and headed for the busy street.

A bus tagged with obscenities lumbered down the block behind her. She signaled the driver as he drove past and hustled along the sidewalk toward the stop. When the bus finally screeched to a halt, a cloud of black exhaust mushroomed from the tailpipe, and she inhaled a noxious lungful.

Coughing, she hurried up the steps, digging for quarters. Her hands trembled, but she clinked the coins into the fare box.

Maybe she'd lost Morgan. She glanced behind her, and a twinge of guilt jolted her stomach. He would have caught her in the garage for sure, except for Parvati's quick thinking. Hopefully Morgan hadn't hurt her friend.

Jana tugged down her cap and observed her surroundings carefully as the bus passed the entrance to the hospital. No gunmen in leather jackets. Morgan hadn't followed.

She started down the littered aisle. When the bus swung into the street, the movement hurled her against the shoulder of a middle-aged man sitting three rows back.

"Mine, mine." He stiff-armed her and shouted hysterically.

Her heart lurched. Above the rancid stink of body odor and urine, she smelled years of dirt and poverty and the bite of madness. "Sorry," she said, her voice pitched low. She brushed her damp hands on her jeans and grabbed a pole, breathing through her teeth.

"Mine," he shrilled again and half rose from his seat with his hands curled into claws. Under his puckered brows, his eyes showed white all around. The bench beside him was heaped with a coat, bedroll, and a mound of black plastic bags.

Fear crackled like electricity along her nerves, but she showed him her palms and backed away.

"Better sit over here, boy." The younger of two women on the left side motioned. "That's Sammy's place, ya know. His home." Gray hair slicked back from the woman's thin face and accentuated her sharp cheekbones and weathered complexion. Bright, mismatched earrings bobbed from her earlobes. She wore layers of clothes in faded tropical-fruit-salad colors and patterns.

"Thank you." Jana slumped into the seat in front of

them, rolling her eyes at Sammy. When she smiled, the woman returned a grin.

"I'm Grace, and this is my mom, Ruth. We like company. Don't we, Mom?"

The wizened woman next to Grace didn't reply, just stared out the cracked window with her thin shoulders hunched forward, and her hands rubbing her cheeks. Grace's smile dimmed for a moment.

"I'm...uh...Jay," Jana said.

"Nice to meet you, Jay. This is a birthday treat for my mother. I saved up. She used to ride this bus to work a long time ago." She took Ruth's hand gently in her own, but the woman continued to stare. "I hoped she would remember."

Jana swallowed to push down the lump in her throat. "You're a good daughter." She slid across the cracked seat to the window and let the breeze cool her flushed face. Secondhand clothes, no home, no job. She was on the run, using an alias. A fugitive.

Not much difference between her and Grace, except for her six-figure student loans and the murder rap hanging over her head. Jana hugged her backpack to her chest and grimaced. Mine.

The bus slowed at the next stop, and her belly churned. Keeping her head down, she watched through her lashes while more people boarded. No one she recognized.

Her chin slumped into her palm. Somehow, she had to clear her name. She was a surgeon, damn it, but no hospital would even consider her with charges pending. She folded her knees against her chest and huddled against the window.

Assuming she stayed out of jail.

And stayed alive.

Stop. She chafed her arms. Worrying only drilled holes in her stomach. Time to exercise her brain.

Okay. So what did she know about Morgan? He gave her the screaming willies.

Did he kill Mike? Nate said the creep had a flimsy alibi for the night Mike was murdered. A ticket stub? She snorted. Easy to sneak out of a movie theater.

She leaned her head against the cool glass and stared at the traffic. Nate was a master at sweet, sexy torture, but he'd also asked her some important questions she hadn't answered. What had she missed the night Mike died? Her insides cranked tighter.

Mike had believed he had both the right and the duty to run her life. When she'd stood up to him and his you-don't-need-more-school-to-marry-me attitude, he'd left her apartment furious. Did he already know where he was going, whom he was meeting? Nate thought so, but Mike had never mentioned anyone to her.

Rubbing her temples, she dragged her memories from hiding and pictured the last few minutes before he walked out of her life forever.

Mike, with his fists clenched and red slashes riding his cheekbones, had planted his feet and squared his shoulders. If anything, he'd looked taller than six-four in his dark blue uniform. He'd looked a little scary.

"Get out," she'd yelled.

"You got it, babe. You won't see me again."

She shut her eyes and focused on the details. Had he left anything behind when he grabbed his keys and slammed the door?

Adrenaline pumped into her bloodstream, and she bolted upright. His phone. The belt clip Mike always wore had been empty. She was positive. He must have left his cell in her apartment, because Nate said he'd never found it.

She nodded sharply, grinning. The phone she'd seen in the attic trunk last week must have been Mike's, not her old one. Was it still there? Or had the phone been charred to slag? She forced her hands to relax around the strap of her backpack and glanced outside. Only a few more miles to what was left of her house.

At the next stop, a pack of teenagers wearing green bandanas boarded. Their retro boom box blared violent rap.

From his locked cage, the bus driver yelled, "Turn down that crap."

The tallest kid had plugs in his earlobes the size of nickels, a green Mohawk, and a green flannel shirt unbuttoned at his tattooed throat. He flipped the driver off and upped the volume.

When the punk leered at her with his empty black eyes, prickles inched down her back. She dropped her gaze and slumped lower in her seat.

"Better get off, Jay," Grace muttered. "They're gang members. See the colors? They won't like you're on their bus."

Jana grabbed her pack. "Can I help you with your mother?"

Grace shook her head and drew her mother close. "They won't bother us. We're no threat."

With her chin tucked against her chest and her heart thumping madly, Jana slipped out the back door and jumped off the bus two stops early. She broke into a trot, but no one followed.

She rounded a corner and spotted her old hybrid

parked down the block from her house. One small piece of luck. The tow company had replaced all four tires and left her car behind a derelict SUV with battered bumpers and a crunched tailgate.

Crouching by the rear fender, she ran her fingers inside the wheel well. A surge of joy pulsed through her. She loosened the wing nut holding her spare keys and patted the old hybrid.

She started the car and approached her home through the back alley. After driving into the detached garage, she quickly closed the automatic door behind her and took her first full breath in hours.

She squared her shoulders, marched through the side door, and unlocked the backyard gate. Nausea rose in her throat, but she inhaled deeply and stared at the blown-out windows of her home. Get in and get out fast. Find that damn phone before Nate arrives. She ducked under the yellow crime scene tape and opened the rear door with her spare key.

The blood drained from her skull, and a wave of dizziness swept her. Water dripped from the scorched ceiling. Paint and vinyl flooring had blistered. Her kitchen cupboards hung empty, hacked to pieces by the firefighters. Cartons of food were heaped on the floor atop broken dishes.

She went around the corner and gagged. The living room was a wasteland, oozing the overpowering stench of melted carpet. Shafts of daylight peeked through the gutted cathedral ceiling. She balled her fists against her chest and blinked away tears.

Her books lay in a charred, soggy pile. Irreplaceable family pictures were burned, destroyed beyond recognition. Her medical diploma had been ripped down, and the glass shattered. She pulled it from the frame, smoothed the dirtied parchment, and tucked it into her backpack.

Electronics gone. Desktop smashed. But why destroy all her possessions? She clamped her jaw, refusing to allow her gorge to rise. Didn't matter, she had nothing left, at least down here.

She tested the blackened stairs. The first collapsed under her flip-flop, and splinters gouged her ankle. "Shit, that hurt." She stopped to pull out the fine pieces of wood.

The second step buckled, too, but she didn't put her full weight on it. She hugged the inside edge and clung to the handrail as she climbed instead.

The upstairs was singed and water-damaged, but not everything had been completely burned. Maybe she could rescue some clothes. She was sick of yanking up Lani's jeans.

Jana pushed through the door to her room and found chaos. Open-mouthed, she stared at the devastation. Everything had been torn and shredded from the closets and drawers. She picked up the remains of a lab coat and traced what was left of her embroidered nametag.

She searched for her jewelry box. Nothing. Tears stung the back of her throat, and a sour taste filled her mouth. Her grandmother's earrings were gone.

Who? Some crazy jerk had trashed her possessions and violated her home. Her life. She squeezed her eyes closed, refusing to cry.

Focus. Mike's phone.

Breathless, she ran to the hall and dashed up the stairs to the attic. She cried out and raced to her upended trunk. The contents had been scattered and trampled.

She pawed through the pile. Buried under her old green scarf, the old-fashioned phone had wedged behind a joist. A giddy burst of glee had her chuckling despite the surrounding disaster. She stuffed it in her backpack along with the pink and blue baby quilt Granny McAlpine had stitched for her.

Pine boughs scraped the siding, and the house creaked in the wind. The heebie-jeebies raced through her. She couldn't stand to stay inside one more minute.

She shouldered the pack. Careful not to be seen, she slipped out the way she'd entered and dashed across the yard past the bullet-pocked grapefruit tree.

After closing the side door, she inspected the garage, and her skin crawled with a sense of violation. She hadn't noticed it before, but that sadistic asshole had also searched out here.

Chapter Fifteen

January 10, 3:35 p.m.

Braced against the garage wall, Jana tied her shoelaces, straightened, and rotated her shoulders. Much better. Thank heaven she'd remembered the kickboxing gear stowed in her trunk.

She tucked away her skimpy black silk and lace bra, heaved the bag onto the front seat, and grinned. Fancy lingerie might make her feel sexy, but she'd rather wear a cotton sports bra and running shoes. Too bad she didn't have a pair of her own jeans instead of her kickboxing shorts.

She checked her watch and tapped the baseball cap on the roof of her car. Where was Nate? Her anxiety multiplied by the second, and she couldn't swallow the enormous lump in her throat. Had someone trapped him at the morgue?

She'd call, but checking in could be dangerous for him. Punching her hands into the sweatshirt pockets, she paced the narrow cement strip beside her car. What a freaking mess, forced to hide in her own garage behind the torched and trashed remains of her home. How had she blundered into this insane minefield? And how would she find a safe way out?

Tires crunched on the graveled alley. Her pulse bumped above a hundred again, and her breathing grew fast and shallow. Nate? Or had Joe Morgan recognized her and followed?

The engine stopped right outside her garage. Rising on tiptoe, she peered through a frosted glass window. A beige SUV with Nate behind the wheel. Thank God. She let out a shaky sigh and poked the automatic opener button.

As the garage door cranked up, he ducked underneath and grabbed her by the shoulders. "Are you okay?"

A giddy laugh bubbled from her lips. She hit the button again to close the door and wrapped her arms around his neck, kissing him hard. "I am now."

Holding her tight, he smoothed her cheek. "You scared the hell out of me."

"Sorry." The door slammed shut against the concrete floor. She buried her nose next to his chest, inhaling his clean, masculine scent. In his arms, she felt safe for the first time in hours.

She raised her face, smiling at him. "I don't think Joe Morgan ever actually saw me."

"Good. And the bus?"

"No problem," she lied. "But I went inside my house. They ransacked the place, but somehow they missed it."

"Missed what?"

"Mike's phone. I remembered he left his cell behind the night he died. I've had it all these years, but didn't know."

Nate's eyebrows hiked. "You missed a cell phone? How?"

"I don't think I ever saw it at the time. I was a mess after he died, and my roommate, Liv, helped me move.

She must have packed the thing."

He rubbed his forehead with both hands. "I searched everywhere for that damn phone."

"I didn't remember Mike's empty belt clip until today. I'd done my best to block out his last few hours until we talked this morning." A blush warmed her cheeks as she handed him the phone.

He gave her a quick kiss before turning the clunky black plastic device over in his hands. "Right brand. I wonder."

"Of course, the battery's dead, but we can probably find an old charger somewhere."

"Let me try something first." He slipped off the back cover and battery, then handed them to her. "Hold these for a sec."

"What are you doing?"

Nate wiggled a square white and silver chip loose. "This little beauty is a sim card. Should have all his contacts. I'll see if I can swap it into my phone."

Her pulse sang under her skin. "You're brilliant!"

Shooting her a quick grin, he dismantled his own cell and replaced the sim card with Mike's. Nate snapped his battery back in and activated the phone. He pushed a few buttons and whooped happily. "Too bad I can't get to his voicemails anymore."

"Why not?"

"Long gone. Back then they were stored on the provider's mainframe. But I can check his contact list."

She leaned against her car, watching him pace while he furiously pushed buttons.

Suddenly, he stopped and gave a long whistle. "Hot damn!"

She peered over his shoulder. "Tomasini? The

hospital trustee?"

"Yeah, the slimy son of a bitch. This is what we need. See? Mike noted the address." A huge smile lit Nate's face, and his eyes sparkled.

"I don't understand. Why did Mike have his address?"

"He didn't. The contact info lists the construction site, the spot Mike was murdered." Nate tapped the screen with a finger. "And here's the payphone number from the last call Mike received."

Her heart squeezed to the size of a walnut. "You're saying Morrie Tomasini killed Mike?"

"Not likely, but Tomasini did set him up for the ambush, and you can bet that weasel knows exactly who was behind the murder."

She covered her gaping mouth with one hand and let out a growl. "So to cover up his role, he hired someone to kill me?"

Nate grimaced and crossed his arms. "Tried to chase you away first. Fits with having your house torched."

She bounced her fists against her thighs. "But why? I don't understand. They ruined absolutely everything, my clothes, my diploma."

"He wants you gone from Sereno. No home. No possessions."

"No job." At Nate's sharp glance, she added, "I quit after Raines suspended me without pay. I wonder if Tomasini had a hand in his decision."

"Likely. It's all connected, and Captain Greene's in on the plot. He's pressured the arson investigators to call your house fire an accident."

"Bullshit. I heard the explosion, smelled the

gasoline…" Her mouth tightened, and she heaved a frustrated sigh. "They can do anything, get away with anything, can't they?"

"Afraid so."

"Then how can we nail these creeps?"

Nate waved the phone in the air. "We'll take this to the FBI. Mike's phone will touch off an avalanche and bury Tomasini along with Joe Morgan and half of Sereno PD."

A smile twitched her lips. "Do we need snow shovels to escape?"

Laughing, he lifted her and swung her around. "You did it, Jana. You blew open the case. We'll expose the whole filthy corrupt organization, uncover the mastermind, and put every one of the crooks away. Tomasini might have started out as a small player and worked hard to go legit, but we'll nail him for his role in Mike's murder." Kissing her hard, he set her down and laid both palms on her cheeks.

She gazed into his face, and her heart kicked into a gallop. His deep brown eyes held hers. Her knees shook, but she started grinning like an idiot. She tried, but she simply couldn't help herself.

"Jana," he started, and then cleared his throat. The tips of his ears reddened. "You might not be ready for this, but you know I care about you, right?"

Her forehead wrinkled, but she nodded.

He took her hand and kissed her palm. "When we get to Hawaii, I want to spend time together. Work on us."

Knocked breathless, she gasped and choked out a long exhale.

"I think I'm falling in love with you," he added in a

rush.

Finally, she managed to hitch in some air. "But, Nate…"

"I have an old plantation house on the Kona Coast. We can hang out there. They need surgeons on the islands. And cops."

Her heart did a series of cartwheels. When she opened her mouth to speak, no words came. With her, Nate didn't act like a stud-with-a-scorecard who was only out for a good time. He made love to her with care and awareness.

Her pulse roared in her ears. She was so in love with him; she yearned to believe he might mean more than he'd actually said. But she couldn't just leave her career behind in ruins and risk her heart for an extended boink-fest in Hawaii when he'd never even mentioned marriage. One day, he'd tire of her, and she'd have nothing but a broken heart.

She swallowed hard and looked into his tense, beloved face. Tears stung the corners of her eyes. She smiled and gently touched his lower lip. "This is crazy. Until last week, we hadn't seen each other for almost ten years."

He kissed her hard and grinned. "I know. I want you in my life for a long time. We'll have plenty of time to figure out the details once we clear up this cluster fuck."

****

Crazy? Maybe. But dear God, he loved her, and it actually felt good to talk about a future together. He was moving too fast, was a light year ahead of her, but he could give her time to catch up. He'd told her he loved her, and he hadn't been hit by lightning or a sudden earthquake or tsunami. He hadn't even dropped dead on the garage floor.

Jana looked like she still couldn't take everything in. Her head tilted to the side and shook gently. But she didn't mean no. Her smile was soft, and her mouth was parted slightly. Bright color burned on her cheeks.

He couldn't breathe. Every muscle tensed, and his stomach jittered. Her long, cool fingers framed his face gently, and her beautiful hazel gaze captured his.

"I do know how much I want to be with you," she whispered.

Joy burst through him. His body hummed with heady, swirling heat. He gave a hearty laugh and folded her into his arms.

Her heart thumped wildly against his chest. His gaze fastened on her lush, moist lips. Shock waves of arousal scalded him and spread like wildfire. He hardened between one hungry breath and the next.

Everything inside him shook with need, but he had to keep her safe. He smiled down at her. "Terrible timing. We'll celebrate soon, and I'll show you exactly how sexy you are in a baseball cap." He pulled on the bill.

Trembling, she stroked his cheeks and kissed him fast and hard. "We could try gymnastics in the back seat of my car."

"Later. Don't know when Morgan will discover your trail."

She closed her eyes, and her smile glittered, but she eased away from him and took a deep breath. "Okay. What's our next step?"

"We need more evidence for the FBI." He thought for a minute and let out an agonized groan. "Damn. I have to go back to the station, get the old billing printout. Then I can prove Mike's last incoming call was from this number." He dropped the sim card into his pocket and retrieved his own.

"But the FBI can commandeer all kinds of old documentation, including phone logs. Don't we have enough?"

"Can't take the risk. Don't know for sure how far back they can go, or how long it'd take. No, we need the insurance. Five minutes in records, and I can grab the hard copy. I could kick myself for never zapping a duplicate for my file."

"You shouldn't go anywhere near there," she said, her voice low and creepy.

A chill crawled up his neck. "The evidence against you wasn't at the morgue, but maybe I can find it at the station."

Jana frowned and wrapped her fingers around his arm. "I have a really bad feeling."

"No choice. Once Greene scores a murder warrant, the FBI will slap you in cuffs first and ask questions later. And you wouldn't be safe in jail. Not in Sereno. Probably not anywhere in California."

She squeezed her eyes shut and tucked her chin against her chest. "Damn it! I didn't do anything wrong."

He swallowed hard. "Doesn't matter. I'll go to the feds with the evidence once we hit the islands."

She looked at him, wide-eyed. "Do you ever feel like the whole universe is dumping on you?"

Nodding, he caressed her jawline with his thumb and kissed her softly. "Right now we have to leave for the station before someone finds us, or catches on and grabs those phone records."

"I can't go near the place, even in disguise."

Every instinct rebelled at the obvious solution. He didn't want her out of his sight, not ever again. "I'll drop you at the house first. You can get Bruner ready and grab my evidence stash."

"No. If you insist on going, we'll get away faster if I drive my car back to your place."

"Jana..."

Her chin did that stubborn thing again. "You'd have to backtrack to drop me."

She had him there. His mouth twisted with frustration, while his mind churned faster than a fleeing suspect on meth. He tucked the baseball cap back over her bright, silky hair. "Okay, but wear this. Park a block away and sneak in. Move fast. We'll drive to Reno, and buy tickets for Hawaii right before we walk on the plane."

She held his gaze for a second and grinned. "I could create a decoy and throw them off our trail. Make phony plane reservations, maybe L.A. to Mexico or South America. If they think we're driving to LAX, they'll blanket Interstate 5 and Highway 101, but they won't find us."

"Very sneaky, Dr. Sutherland."

Color flooded her cheeks.

"Give me those bags, and I'll dump them in my trunk so we're set to go."

"This was all I rescued."

"Never mind, I have money. Find the cache box hidden next to the fireplace."

He hiked the backpack and duffel onto his shoulder and wrapped his arms around her. "Kiss me again."

"Please stay safe," she murmured against his lips.

He kissed her slow and easy and glanced at the backseat with regret. "Now get moving and don't worry." He handed her in and forced himself to watch her car disappear.

Fastening his seatbelt, he gunned his engine and sped onto the street. His jaw clenched so hard his teeth ached. Why hadn't he twigged to Tomasini sooner? That creep had known something vital, but he'd played him for a fool after Mike died.

****

Ten years earlier.

With his partner dead and Jana a zombie, rage seized Nate, triggering an adrenaline surge that hadn't run dry. His jaw set, face contorted with anger, he rammed his fingers through his hair.

Why had Mike died? Who pulled the trigger? Nate slammed his fist against the Crown Vic's steering wheel and stared into the last dregs of a gray sunset. A bitter taste filled his mouth.

In his gut, he knew Joe Morgan had Mike's blood on his hands. The asshole's alibi was too flimsy, and he had an attitude. But where could he find evidence to break Morgan?

Nate sucked in a harsh breath. Think, Kapulani. Think.

Mike's snitch, Morrie Tomasini. The creep claimed Morgan and Wendell ran a drug ring. He claimed he'd had a pigeon's eye view from his convenience store across from the school. Claimed he'd just happened to see a deal going down.

Nate rubbed his palms over his eyes. Man, he wished he'd gone with Mike and met the sneaky bastard. No way to change the past, but he could track the snitch.

His lips twisted in a grim smile. Tomasini knew who was behind the murder, and he'd force him to squeal.

Nate shoved the beat-up sedan into gear and peeled out of the station parking lot. Two days since he'd slept, maybe more. His body and brain ached with exhaustion, but he scoured the town, checking one dive after another.

Finally, he tried the Last Chance. When he walked through the door, his stomach burned. He and Mike had downed plenty of beers at this bar with their buddies on the force. No cops here now. Tonight the place seemed unreal, like a hideous scene straight from a low budget sci-fi flick.

The overhead lights were low, and the place looked dull and dirty. Near the bar, neon beer signs flashed garish color over the room, throwing shapes and angles into sharp relief. There was nothing warm or welcoming.

Nate peered into the shadowed booths lining the walls. Faces looked warped, and the smell of stale beer, cheap perfume, and unwashed bodies fouled the air.

He checked the last booth—four guys around the right age and two matched Tomasini's description. They'd been drinking, probably all night. One character rambled on in a gravelly voice, his words slurring together.

Planting his feet wide, Nate crossed his arms. "Which one of you jokers is Tomasini?"

One man elbowed the guy next to him with a sharp, "Hey! Whatsa cop want with you, Morrie?"

Tomasini faced Nate and twitched his shoulders. "Who cares? I'm clean. Ain't done nothing." Eyes shuttered, the sleaze turned away.

Nate grabbed the snitch by the collar and hauled him off the bench. Tomasini's cronies focused on their drinks, avoiding even a glance in Nate's direction. Was one of them the brains behind Mike's murder? Tomasini knew something, and by God, he'd find out what.

Fueled by adrenaline, Nate had no trouble frog-marching the fat slob out the door. He let him drop on the wet pavement, whining and sucking air. "Mike Gordon's dead, and you know who killed him!"

"No!" Tomasini's eyes widened.

Nate smacked a fist against his hand, and fury radiated from him in waves. "Don't give me that shit. Morgan shot Mike, and we both know it. Spill it, scumbag!"

"All I know is Morgan sold drugs at the high school, he and that waste of air, Wendell. But they're pussies. No way they'd kill a cop."

Nate crowded closer. "Tell me."

"Come on, man. Don't hurt me no more. I was trying to help." Tomasini's head sank into his hands, body shaking with noisy, wheezing sobs.

Nate glared. Pitiful. He turned on his heel and stalked away. That loser would never have the brains or the balls to pull off a con or plan a murder.

****

"Damn Tomasini. The crook deserved an Oscar." Nate drove into the library lot and let the car idle while he eyed the police station across the street. MacLean slouched near the front entrance.

Goose bumps rose on his neck and marched down his back in parade formation. The setup didn't feel right. Nate sensed danger, and his cop radar niggled at the edge of his mind. He pulled on his earlobe. Should he turn the car around and race back to Jana? No, he had to try. Without hard evidence, the FBI would blow him off.

Turning off the engine, he slipped around the building and in through the secured back gate to the PD. The lot was mostly empty, just the captain's car and one cruiser. If his luck held, he'd slip in and out before anyone alerted Greene.

His breath rasped quick and jagged as he tiptoed down the deserted stairs. With another hasty glance around the empty corridor, he ducked inside the records office and locked the door behind him.

His heart raced, but a smile twitched across his face. He'd timed it right. The desk stood empty. Afternoon coffee break. Or Friday happy hour at the local bar, if his luck held.

He dodged around the counter and pounded the computer. Wendell, Douglas. Sweat dampened his collar while he waited for the computer to crank out the case number.

Nate pulled the file and leafed through the reports. Damn. No physical evidence in the file, but Nichols had been right. Hair and blood samples were out for DNA testing, and that sure looked like the coroner's signature.

Filled with disgust, Nate loosened his tie. Hair would be easy to plant, but blood? Couldn't get that from a cheek swab. A cold tendril of fear clutched at him. He remembered the big bandage on Jana's scalp after Wendell shot her.

How long before the test results came back? He scanned the paperwork and scowled. Today. He couldn't push a button and incinerate the DNA samples, but losing this report might slow the creeps down.

He had one more thing to steal before he left. He knew where to find the box from Mike's cold case. How many times had he visited that corner of the basement? He ducked around the shelving, pulled out the phone log, and stuffed it inside his jacket.

Footsteps clomped down the hall.

His pulse rate doubled. Nate bounded over the counter, grabbing the door just as the knob rattled.

"Hey, I was waiting for you," he said cheerfully and stepped aside to let the clerk waddle in, balancing three doughnuts and a frou-frou coffee. Good thing she couldn't hear his heart hammer against his ribs. "Where you been?"

She raised her eyebrows until they disappeared beneath her scraggly, straight black hair and looked pointedly at her stash. "What do you need, Sergeant?"

"File on a new case."

"Write down the details on a request slip, and I'll get to it." She glared at him over her half-glasses, and one corner of her lip twitched. "After I finish my break."

He checked his watch. "Uh, okay. Out of time, anyway. Captain's waiting. I'll come back later." With a quick salute, Nate rolled into the hall before she could grill him.

He couldn't leave without sanitizing his files, so he'd have to brave the bullpen. He took the stairs, three at a time, took a deep breath, and then strolled past dispatch. He turned the corner, and his stomach clenched.

"Kapulani. Front and center," Greene hollered across the noisy room.

Damn. No chance to get out clean. "Just a sec." Nate set his phone alarm for two minutes and sauntered into the office. Time for some theater.

He grinned at Greene and seized the chair in front of his desk, but it took full effort to meet the captain's gaze. Going for relaxed, he leaned back and crossed his arms to hide his hands. "I'm close on the Wendell murder case. About ready to nab my suspect."

"You found that red-headed bitch?"

Nate scowled and bit his lip. "Not yet. She went to ground after setting that fire." He shoved a hand into his hair to act more frustrated. "But I got a good snitch. Just waiting for him to call back." Easier to lie to this jerkwad than he expected.

"Then what the fuck are you doing here?"

Nate shrugged. "Been working all night. Came in for coffee and a cleanup." Tough to keep the smirk off his lips. The captain was rotten, but not stupid.

"Here's the warrant. Now get moving," Greene ordered with a smug sneer.

Nate's phone buzzed right on schedule, but he almost jumped out of his skin.

Raising one finger, he grunted, "Kapulani." His pulse pounded in his ears while he listened to the dial tone. "Yeah. Yeah, I got it. Oh, man. L.A.? Which flight?" He grabbed a message pad from the captain's desk and scribbled some numbers.

After closing the phone, he ripped off the top sheet of paper and waved it in Greene's face. "I got a lead.

I'll catch Sutherland at the airport before she splits."

"Need a SWAT team?"

He blew air through his lips. "Nah, be better if we kept this quiet, right?"

"Sure. You can handle one useless woman." The captain nodded sharply, but his eyes shifted over Nate's shoulder. Sucker was pretending to be satisfied, but that was another lie.

Nate ordered his body to remain at ease. No twitch, no blink. Hands still and away from his face.

Greene rose from his chair and closed the door to his office. "I've had my doubts about you, Kapulani, but now you seem to understand the reality."

"Uh...yes, sir. Got to go with the flow." He gave a sharp nod. "The reward's better, too."

When the captain pounded him on the shoulder, Nate clenched his jaw. He'd love to punch this lying son of a bitch in the gonads. Sure would feel good, but pounding the guy wouldn't get Jana to safety.

Greene sat on the edge of his desk and leaned forward. "Reward, huh? Tell you what. You haul in her skinny ass, and you'll get a fat reward."

Don't flinch. Just look him straight in the eye. He had to believe this act or Jana would die. Nate showed the guy some teeth and nodded. "That's my plan, sir."

Greene shook his hand. "Dismissed."

Resisting the urge to wipe off the slime, Nate grimaced as he hurried toward the bullpen. That'd keep the captain happy for an hour or two.

One last thing to do, delete all his personal info so it'd take longer to find them. Then he'd never have to return to this shithole.

The letter of resignation burned through his pocket.

Man, he'd love to stuff that paper down the asshole's gullet. As he crossed the room, he gave MacLean a thumbs-up and a buddy-buddy smile.

Chapter Sixteen

January 10, 4:35 p.m.

Driving an indirect route to Nate's, Jana checked her mirrors again for a tail and poked a lock of hair underneath her baseball cap with jittery fingers. Nobody obvious. No black pickups with silhouettes of naked women.

She searched her memory. Where had she first met Morrie Tomasini? She'd seen the creep somewhere, long before she started at Sereno General.

Last fall at the hospital benefit, she'd had a sense she knew the guy and had made a fool of herself, asking him if he'd ever been a cop. He hadn't replied right away, but had turned his flinty brown leer on her and hit on her like she was a fluff-headed call girl.

It had been a stupid question. Ten years ago, she'd known everyone on the force, because she'd finished her work-study internship at Sereno PD only a few months before Mike died.

Shoving the cap lower, she maneuvered through the midday traffic. No, the lecher had never carried a badge. But she'd met him somewhere before, and she had a hunch she'd been with Mike at the time.

She focused on people she and Mike had socialized with, ticking off their usual haunts. Not their Friday night cop rendezvous. Not a neighbor of Mike's. The university? No, Tomasini was older and didn't seem the type.

Jana mentally sorted through her dates with Mike during the few short months they were an item. Maybe the time he took her to dinner at the fancy Chinese restaurant.

Smiling, she sat up straighter. After a great meal, he'd ordered sake and stuffed a solitaire onto the end of her fortune cookie. She'd shut that evening out of her mind for years. Funny, but it didn't hurt to remember anymore.

When she'd returned to the table from the restroom, Mike had been talking to a man wearing Bermuda shorts and a garish shirt. A hefty, balding man. She remembered the shiny spot on the back of the big guy's head and his butt-white legs covered with thick, kinky black hair.

Mike had glanced over at her with a smile. While she waited a couple tables away, the two men finished talking. Mike called the guy Morrie as he turned to leave.

Shit. That guy was Tomasini.

He was older now, although slimmer and in much better shape. Somewhere along the line, he'd gotten a first-class hair transplant, but the jerk still had the same hard, brown eyes. A chill swept over her, raising goose bumps. If he'd lured Mike to his death, no wonder the guy had flipped out when she reappeared.

The light turned red, and she stopped. Shuddering, she put her hands over her face and rubbed the tightness from her forehead. At the benefit last fall, she'd talked to him about money. Donations for the hospital, of course. Her heart pumped faster. But in his mind, he probably thought…

The car behind her honked, and Jana squealed. The light had turned green. She sucked in a long, ragged breath, grabbed the wheel, and moved forward. Did he think she would demand blackmail? Damn. She'd said something about money the other day in Raines' office, too. And it wasn't as if she could waltz into his office and say she was sorry about the misunderstanding and had no intention of blackmailing him. My God, she'd blundered into a nest of scorpions.

Now that Tomasini had plenty of both power and money at risk, he would have investigated her and discovered her relationship with Mike. The man couldn't have helped seeing her as a potential threat to all he'd achieved, and she'd unwittingly confirmed his fears. He'd probably orchestrated her job loss and torched her home, determined to drive her away before she exposed his sordid past.

A cold weight twisted in the pit of her stomach and shuddered through her. Had the gunman shot at her to scare her away? Or to eliminate her permanently?

Didn't matter. Once she and Nate were safely were away from Sereno, they'd turn over the evidence they'd uncovered. Then the FBI would swoop in, interrogate Tomasini, and identify the mastermind behind Mike's death.

Jana parked around the corner from Nate's and locked her car with shaky hands. In the open, she was vulnerable. A sniper could hide anywhere. Cold sweat trickled down her back, and she glanced around the quiet streets.

On legs quivering like grape jelly, she hurried toward safety, passing a row of stumpy eighty-year-old bungalows with knee-high weeds and dead grass for lawns.

She rounded the corner, quickening her steps. Her gaze darted back and forth. A gunman would've taken a shot by now. Unless Joe Morgan was waiting inside Nate's house to ambush her.

She ducked behind some bushes across the street from his house and surveyed the area. If she ignored the trash in the street and the peeling paint, the neighborhood looked almost welcoming.

An express delivery truck roared past on the busy cross street with a squad car cruising close behind. Did they have a warrant out for her yet? She crouched lower, her stomach turning flips.

When the squad car continued on, she dug the house key from her pocket and bit her lip. The last hundred yards seemed like miles. Once she hit his front yard, she couldn't control the fear rising in her throat. She sprinted across the lawn, through the side gate, and dashed up the steps two at a time.

From inside, Bruner gave a sharp bark.

"Bru. It's me. Quiet." She rammed the key in the knob. Finally, she was safe with the door locked behind her.

She sank to the floor, and Bruner kissed her face, bowing like he wanted to play. When she hugged the big dog, her laughter had a hysterical edge.

"We're going on a trip, Bru, but it'll be okay." She ruffled his ears, and her pulse steadied. "It'll be okay."

Nate would turn over the evidence and clear her name. Mike's killer would suffer the justice he deserved. "Practicing medicine in Hawaii and spending time with Nate. What's not to like?" She winked at the dog.

When Nate trusted her to come here alone, he'd made her his partner. That was a huge step for him. "No time to daydream." She dashed into the living room and retrieved the metal box. At the bottom, she found a fat canvas bank bag, opened it, and gaped at the wad of money. Thousands. They wouldn't have to use plastic and risk being tracked.

A backpack with his workout gear hung on a hook in the den. Jana dumped the contents and crammed the papers and cash inside. Next, she pulled her credit card from her cell case, went on the Internet, and reserved two tickets from LAX to Rio on her phone. When she finished, she tucked her phone in her back pocket.

She headed for the enclosed back porch. Leash, food, a plastic bowl, and a water bottle. She stuck the supplies in the duffle.

Bruner bounded up with his favorite blue squeaky ball, his tail wagging. She had to smile. "Okay, boy, but only one. We're traveling light."

The big dog's ears perked up. He darted across the kitchen toward the garage and snuffled at the threshold.

The garage opened, and a car door slammed. Bruner's tail wagged faster. Must be Nate. She keyed in the alarm code. Grinning, she lifted the bag and moved toward the door. She was ready.

A gun blast echoed from the garage.

The dog let out an ear-shattering howl. He pawed the steel door and barked frantically, digging to get out.

Jana's heart faltered. Nate? Had he fired at someone?

She dragged Bruner away, terrified another bullet would tunnel through the metal and hit him.

But the dog yanked free and rammed against the door, barking ferociously.

Her insides twisted, and her breath came in shallow gulps. She had to reach Nate now. He could be hurt.

"Sit!" she hissed and lunged for his collar. She missed, but Bruner sank to his haunches for a split second. She grabbed the dog with one hand and wrenched the doorknob.

The garage door was open with Nate's rental car inside.

No noise.

No movement.

No one she could see or hear.

She crept onto the step. Where was Nate? She froze. Fear, sharp and bitter and corrosive, congealed in the pit of her stomach.

Nate sprawled face down on the concrete by the open car door.

She sprinted for him. Kneeling at his side, she checked the gunshot wound and shifted him onto his back.

Her lungs seized. Too much blood. She yanked off and folded her sweatshirt, applying pressure to the massive exit wound below his collarbone.

She searched for a pulse at his carotid. Faint, but there. She started to breathe again.

Bruner nudged at her elbow, whining.

"Down!" she commanded, and the dog sank, snuffling Nate's hair and quivering.

"Nate. Stay with me. I'm calling for help." Her voice wavered. One handed, she dialed 911, put the call on speaker and doubled the pressure.

The dispatcher answered, and Jana shouted,

"Officer down," adding the details. "Hurry."

She could keep him alive, damn it.

But his face was gray, and the blood continued to pump. The awful metallic smell choked her.

Oh, God. Even in a fully equipped ER, she'd have to fight hard to stop the bleeding. Here, he didn't have long.

He gave a low groan and opened his eyes. "Run, Jana," he gasped. "Get the bag and run."

She leaned closer to his face so he could hear her, see her. "Help's on the way," she choked out, blinking away her tears.

"Run," he said with more force and gripped her arm. Blood trickled from the corner of his mouth and over his cheek. He arched his back and wheezed in a gurgling breath.

"I love you, Nate. Don't you dare die."

His face contorted with agony, but he focused on her. "Love," he murmured.

Another spasm hit, and the light dimmed in his eyes.

She held on, but his breath whispered out.

His muscles went slack.

"No!" she wailed. The raw cry erupted from deep inside her. Pain and helpless anger rolled through her.

This couldn't be real, couldn't be happening. Half her soul had been blasted away, shredded into nothingness.

Nate was gone. She stared in horror at her bloody hands.

Bitter tears stung her throat. Dear God, why hadn't she died instead?

Gray numbness slipped over her. She swallowed

hard and placed a kiss on still lips to say goodbye.

She hated to leave him, but it didn't matter. He was beyond help, his great heart shattered by one of Tomasini's creeps.

Anger flared from the abyss within her. She'd make them pay.

She searched his pockets for Mike's sim card. Nothing. Where did he put the damn thing? Trembling, she struggled to hold her terror in check. What had Nate meant, get the bag? She shook her head, but couldn't clear the cold sludge swamping her mind. She stood. The room spun for a moment, and she grabbed the car door for balance.

The scene dropped into sharp focus. She stumbled backwards, staring. Nate's blood pooled under him, seeping across the garage floor. Bright red.

Chapter Seventeen

January 10, 5:25 p.m.

A gunshot echoed. Jana flinched and clamped her hands over her ears. Where? To the east, but close.

Bam! Bam! Bam! She jumped with each horrible report.

Glass shattered. Her car? Oh, God. The killer had to have found her car and knew she was here.

With his muzzle on his paws, Bruner crouched near Nate, shaking. The dog reared and his pitiful howl raised every tiny hair on her body. Jana grabbed his collar and hauled him inside the house.

They had to leave, had to get far away from Sereno fast.

How?

Panic dripped through her veins. She stood stock-still. Her car was probably history, and if they followed Nate here, they'd be watching for his rental.

She glanced down. The knees of Lani's jeans were soaked with blood. A hysterical laugh bubbled up from nowhere. Didn't matter what she wore, she wouldn't survive two minutes unless she got her skinny, freckled ass out of this house now.

She dug through the backpack for the leash and clipped it on Bruner. Hefting the bag full of hundreds, she moved a handful into her pocket before re-zipping the pack. She slapped the pack across her shoulders and tugged on the leash. "Let's go, Bru."

On her way out, she tied Nate's black down jacket around her waist and triggered the burglar alarm. Sereno PD might be full of crooked cops, but they'd react when they discovered one of their own murdered. If there were cops crawling all over the house, it might be tougher for the killer to take what he wanted.

She left the door ajar. Sixty seconds until the thing went off. Counting silently, she ran down the back porch steps, through the alley, and cut across the street, jogging in the opposite direction from where she'd parked. As she rounded the corner onto Lincoln, the first screech blared from the alarm, and a quick smile of bitter satisfaction touched her lips.

Patting Bruner's shoulder, she hurried to make the walk signal, thankful the baseball cap covered her red hair. "Just a kid and his dog, right Bru?"

Despite all the exercise, she shook from cold. Oppressive clouds hung over the city, obscuring the green hills. Might be snow on Mt. Hamilton by morning. After crossing the wide asphalt, she ducked behind a gas station and pulled Nate's jacket over her shirt.

She set off through the neighborhood. Weed-infested yards and foreclosed homes lined the street. Although she had the big dog trotting by her side, she still watched for squatters. She didn't need any witnesses.

The steady slap of her feet on the pavement masked the sirens at first. An ambulance and a pack of cruisers screamed closer, but stayed on the main road. Not a direct threat to her, yet. Not until they began searching for Nate's killer. Then she'd be swept up in the dragnet and arrested for Douggie Wendell's murder.

Murder.

Her throat knotted. The hideous sensation of holding Nate while he went limp in her arms flashed through her mind and overtook her consciousness. For an endless second, every horrible smell, sound, sight, and wrenching emotion was vivid and real again.

Nate's blood trickled through her fingers.

His gasp for breath echoed in her ears.

His fierce grip on her arm tightened and then went slack.

Jana faltered, caught her toe on a crack in the sidewalk, and fell. Rubbing her stinging palms, she clamped tight on the hysteria building inside.

Bruner nosed her cheek. Then he turned and strained against the leash. She had to wall off the memory and keep moving. Before she faced her grief, she had to reach someplace safe, someplace hidden.

Jana stood and set off at a run again. A single word resounded in her head with every step, so she chanted the cadence. "Dead. Dead. Dead."

Who could she turn to? Where could she go? Hawaii? Reno? The FBI? Every strategy she could imagine led to sure failure. All her options had vanished.

While she'd been in Sereno, her life had revolved around the hospital, but now she'd find no sanctuary there. She had no safe place to go and no proof of Tomasini's involvement. No leverage for the FBI to use if and when they questioned the guy. Her eyes burned but she shed no tears.

Brilliant! Dr. Jana Sutherland, board-certified

thoracic surgeon and fugitive with a murder warrant, chased by dirty cops and mystery killers. She had to go to ground for a few hours and rest, and find someone who could help her get out of town.

She and Bruner maintained the grueling pace, keeping to the shadows and away from the clogged commuter traffic. A cramp hitched in her side, and she slowed to a jog.

Bruner had started to pant. His long, pink tongue dangled out one side of his mouth. She was thirsty, so the dog must be parched.

Suddenly, Bruner tensed, and the hair on his back rose.

A small animal streaked across the road ahead and through a break in a chain link fence. A little red fox. Its coat glistened, almost sparkled, in the twilight.

The fence surrounded dry percolation ponds. Dark green algae scum stained the dirt and rocks. Tall weeds grew in clumps around volunteer saplings. She crinkled her nose at the smell, but it might provide a spot to hide while she and the dog had a drink. Could she take the time to rest? She had to. Something tugged at her, compelled her to follow the fox.

The instant she hesitated, Bruner dragged her through an opening in the cyclone fence, and they headed for the thickest cover. She pulled him behind a dense patch of reeds and eased the pack off her shoulders.

Groaning, she knelt and filled his bowl from a water bottle, but every muscle in her body protested. She took a sip of water and stretched her back.

What was a fox doing in this neighborhood? The animal had seemed very out of place. Eerie. Almost supernatural.

Her last encounter with Norah Redfox popped into her head, and Jana frowned. It seemed like half a lifetime since the bizarre woman had approached her at the fundraiser last night.

Her blood chilled as if made of frozen slush while Norah's parting words replayed in her mind. People you love will die. How had the woman known? Could her nonsense mask real psychic gifts?

She sneered. "Change the past? Get a redo? Bullshit."

But what if the impossible claims Norah made were true? What if she had saved those two boys after they'd drowned?

Jana plopped down in the dirt. What if she could see Nate again?

A wave of dizziness hit her, and her world tilted on its axis. She reeled and squeezed her eyes shut for a second, sucking in a lungful of chilly air.

Hope tickled at her heart, but she shook her head. No. She'd give her life to have Nate back, but bargaining with the universe never changed anything.

Dead was dead. Forever.

The best she could hope for from Norah was a place to hide and maybe help escaping Sereno. Jana pressed her lips together. The woman had mentioned her home in the Rose Garden District. An expressway and a major freeway interchange stood between her and that neighborhood. But the expressway wasn't far, and she could probably slip across before the manhunt started in earnest. She'd figure out the details once she had an address.

An engine rumbled on the street.

"Down," she commanded Bruner as she flattened. She peeked through the weeds, her nose buried in the sulfurous reek of rotting plants.

Her pulse kicked into triple digits. That damned black pickup cruised the street. As it passed under an amber streetlight, a chrome female silhouette flashed from the bumper.

The truck passed, but swung around and headed back toward them. Would she and the dog be invisible in the growing darkness? Trembling, Jana hugged Bruner tight until the rig vanished.

Finally, she mustered the courage to raise her head and look around. While she waited anxiously for the dog to finish his water, she dug out her cell phone and accessed her billing records. She memorized Norah's address before she turned the phone off.

Jana led Bruner back through the fence and along the residential streets. They jogged across a schoolyard, avoiding clumps of soccer players playing on a lit field.

Invisible.

Think invisible.

Pulse pounding, she climbed the ramp to the pedestrian bridge over the expressway and led Bruner along the raised cement path surrounded by a chain link cage.

A bitter January wind cut through her clothes, and she shivered. She tried to ignore the cars speeding on the highway below, but felt exposed, like she was center stage and naked under a spotlight.

An ambulance zoomed beneath her with a motorcycle cop escort, moving fast, but without lights or sirens. Nate? A great pain slashed through her heart. She blinked away the tears, gulped down a sob, and put one foot ahead of the other.

The overpass dumped them onto a side street at the edge of a rundown commercial area. She pounded along the cracked sidewalks. All the shops that weren't boarded up looked closed for the night.

The economic tailspin had hit hard. So had the booming crime rate. Heavy steel bars blocked the narrow entryways. Piles of rotting garbage flowed over the curb and onto the crumbling asphalt. No place she could duck inside and catch her breath. Even the derelict cars had no doors.

Keeping to the shadows, she loped past the single remaining streetlight. She shivered. The orange glow reflected from Bruner's eyes and gave him a vicious, feral look.

His ears alert, the dog trotted forward only a few inches from her side. Suddenly, his muscles tensed, and he planted his feet. An ominous, rumbling growl escaped his throat.

At the end of the block, a shiny black and white cruiser turned the corner. Searchlights swept the quiet street.

She only had a split second to decide before the light found them. The alley to her left. She tugged the leash, and Bruner surged past her down the stinking passageway and dragged her with him.

In the gloom, she hunted for a place to hide, flipping up the collar of Nate's jacket to shield her face.

Something black streaked across the path, and her stomach plunged. Her heart faltered, and then lurched back to life. She cursed silently at the mangy cat darting behind a putrid garbage can.

Bruner showed his teeth. Hissing, the nearly

skeletal cat bowed its back and howled. The sound bounced off the high brick walls.

Her pulse thudded in her ears. She hauled Bruner away from the animal and led him down the curving alley. She dodged the dim pool of light thrown by a bare yellow bulb that blazed above broken cement steps and a plywood-covered entry.

Shit. A dead end.

She jumped an oily puddle and ducked behind a Dumpster. Her quick, shallow breaths frosted in the cold air.

The cruiser slowed to a crawl at the mouth of the alley. Blue lights flashed and bounced off the buildings. A searchlight blazed, and she ducked to avoid the beam, cowering against the dog.

A car door slammed, and more adrenaline pumped into her system. Male voices. Had they seen her?

On her right, a metal security door hung crooked and broken. She took Bruner by the collar, moved closer, and squeezed through the opening. When she closed the bars behind her, they gave a horrific creak.

"Heard something," one cop shouted.

She shoved at the deadbolt, but it refused to move, rusted in place.

Footsteps splashed through water.

She ducked into a dark room thick with the smell of rotting cardboard, old beer, and rats.

Prickles marched over her skin. Watery moonlight filtered in through a broken skylight, and thick cobwebs trailed only a few inches above her head.

Outside, metal clanged and echoed like someone had kicked a garbage can. She pulled Bruner into the far corner and flattened behind a rough wooden table.

He strained against her, but she held his muzzle and whispered, "Quiet."

The bars covering the doorway screeched open. A beam of bright light flashed, searching the room.

She flinched and curled tighter. The beam bounced off the tabletop and legs, casting eerie shadows on the wall behind her. Her heart slammed against her ribs so hard she couldn't believe the cop would miss the racket. She held her breath until her lungs burned.

"Nothing," the cop yelled to his partner.

Shoe leather scraped outside the door. "Then move out. Captain sent out an APB. Another sighting reported across eight-eighty."

The light flicked around the room again. "Fucking cop killer."

"We'll find the bitch, and I can guarantee she won't survive the night."

A metallic bitterness lurched into her throat. They thought she'd murdered Nate. She swallowed hard to keep from being sick and clung to the quivering dog. She felt like someone had reached inside her belly, taken hold of her guts, and twisted.

A siren flared.

She buried her nose in Bruner's short, warm fur until the noise disappeared. Then she drew a full breath, but gagged on the reek.

She took a sip of water to rinse her mouth. Could she stay here? She straightened and glanced around the room. Something squeaked, and rustles filled the corners of the room.

No. She had to keep running. Norah Redfox was her only hope. Nate's only hope.

Jana put out her hand and felt her way along the

damp, moldy wall. She had to find another way out.

****

Midnight

Shivering with exhaustion, Jana huddled in the crotch of a cement maze. She rubbed her gritty, swollen eyes. Her body ached, and her stomach was chewing on itself.

Behind a stunted, spindly oleander bush, she curled closer to Bruner. Cars and trucks rumbled along the freeway overhead, and cloverleaf ramps veered in all directions. The air stank with exhaust fumes.

Tucked underneath and in a corner, they were protected from the winter drizzle, but an entrance lane merged into the sixty-five mile per hour chaos twenty feet below. She stretched Nate's jacket to shield the dog from the biting wind.

The whoop-whoop of a helicopter approached and hovered, loud despite the roar of cars. Bright searchlights flashed across the gravel and weeds below. A painful ache gripped her chest, and she clung to Bruner.

They were hunting her.

She squeezed deeper into the crevice. "They can't see us, Bru." But could the infrared sensors register body heat through concrete?

The helicopter swooped lower, blades churning the gravel. She choked back a terrified sob and buried her face against Bruner's warm neck. She had to find shelter before they caught her.

Finally, the chopper moved west, tracking the underpass boundaries.

She shifted Bruner off her lap, straightened, and slowly led him to the shadows that edged the entrance ramp. Huffing out a breath, she wrapped her arms around her chest and jiggled to keep warm while she watched for a long, dark space between headlights on the rain-slickened pavement. Cold sweat dampened her already frigid hands.

"Go!" she ordered, and they darted across the asphalt into the knee-high plants on the other side. As they barged through, the ivy leaves around them shuddered with the sounds of small animals scurrying away.

Ice shot up her spine. She pictured rats with fangs dripping with disease and grimaced. But she clenched her jaw and struggled ahead on numb feet. "Come on, Bru, run."

Bruner dragged her up the far slope, and they emerged at street level. She kept her head low, crouching while she scanned the area.

Tenements lined the litter-strewn road, with graffiti scrawled on the walls of burned-out shops. A herd of prostitutes wearing tight, garish clothes strutted on the sidewalk. A ragged couple huddled in a doorway and shushed their small child.

Fifty feet away, a hooker bent toward a luxury sedan, bargaining with a john. Their eyes wide, two pre-teen boys hovered in the alley closest to her and exchanged something on the sly. She pinched her lips together, and her stomach flipped. Had to be a drug deal.

Sereno's nasty but vibrant underbelly, and no cops in sight.

She had to keep moving. Her heart beat a tattoo as she lurched over the slippery verge. Feeling exposed, she urged Bruner along the road and down another embankment toward the river's edge. She wove between two cottonwoods toward the sound of flowing water and heard a frog croak.

"Good boy." She patted his head and stopped to rest, bending over with her hands braced against her knees.

"Hey!" a gruff voice shouted. A hand shot through the darkness, caught her arm, and jerked her backwards. Bruner's leash slipped from her grasp.

Booze soaked breath and stale body odor made her stomach lurched.

The tall, skinny Asian man, his thinning hair pulled back into a tail, wore filthy jeans and layers of tattered plaid shirts. He snatched off her baseball cap and leered at her through bloodshot eyes. "Look what we have here, Ray. We got us a girl!"

Bruner whipped around and bared his teeth.

Twisting hard, she planted a roundhouse kick against the bum's temple. She wrenched her arm free as he staggered backwards and sagged to the ground.

A second pair of strong hands grabbed the bag across her shoulders and yanked. Pain screamed through her arm sockets. She struggled, but the guy behind her shifted and wrapped an arm around her waist. He reeked of cigarette smoke.

Bruner growled deep in his throat and stalked closer.

"Let me go!" she shouted and elbowed the man in the gut. He grunted, but tightened his hold, so she stamped on his foot and dropped to her knees.

Snarling, the dog leaped.

The bum fell backward, screamed, and threw his hands over his face as Bruner attacked.

She swung around, her heart slamming against her ribcage. Her roundhouse had connected. Bum number one was out cold. She gave a quick nod of triumph and retrieved her muddy cap with trembling hands.

Jana whistled for Bruner and shouted, "Drop it!" The dog raised his head and pranced to her side. She could swear he was grinning.

She moved near enough to check the cowering man, but stayed out of reach. He had bloodied arms, but he'd live.

She picked up the leash and forced her feet to move. When her shoulders took the weight of the pack, pain stabbed through her joints. She sucked in a harsh breath, but adjusted the pack and trudged forward through mud and underbrush.

Brambles grabbed her face and clothes, but drawn by a vague glow in the distance, she slogged on. Campfires? But how could she trust anyone?

A couple hundred yards along the riverbank, the adrenaline fizzled from her system. Shakes overtook her, and emptiness and despair overwhelmed her.

She collapsed to the ground and moaned, "Nate." Curled into the fetal position, she wept. Great sobs wracked her body.

Bruner straddled her protectively. After a few minutes, he nosed her chin. Whining, he licked her face until she put her arms around his neck.

"Lady?"

Jana reared back and scrambled to her feet.

A hollow-eyed teenage girl wrapped in an old coat several sizes too big emerged from the brush.

Bruner sniffed the newcomer, but didn't growl. His stumpy tail twitched.

She sobbed in a halting breath and wiped her eyes. "My mom made soup. Wanna sit by our fire?"

Restraining a hysterical laugh, Jana shook her head and brushed off the leaves with one hand. But she kept a firm grip on Bruner's collar. "I have to find a way across the freeway."

"I'll show you the maze." The girl winked. "Anybody who knocked that creepazoid, Ray, on his ass is my friend."

Chapter Eighteen

January 11, 4:20 a.m.

Jana glanced over her shoulder expecting to see a big black truck bearing down upon her or a cruiser full of homicidal cops.

Bruner leaned against her, whining. With hands clumsy from the cold, she pounded on the carved wooden door for a third time. Finally, a light came on in the front of the white stucco bungalow. Her legs buckled, and she leaned against a pillar to stay upright.

A shadow crossed the sidelight, and the locks quickly released. "Dr. Sutherland. I've been so worried. I'm glad you came to me." Norah drew her inside and led her to the living room.

"I had no one else," Jana mumbled.

"Sit, please." The woman raised a hand. "No, don't worry about the couch. I'll bring you some towels."

Dropping her heavy pack on the floor, Jana obeyed, and Bruner crowded next to her. She smoothed her hands over his wet fur. He shivered as hard as she did, but sank on his haunches, resting heavily against her legs. "It's okay, boy. We're safe."

Norah returned with an armload of blankets and towels, but frowned and said, "Hot shower first. I'll take care of your dog."

Jana's throat was too tight to speak, so she nodded.

She shook so badly she let Norah herd her into the bathroom and undress her. Modesty didn't matter. Nothing mattered.

The steamy water stung her icy skin. Her fingers and toes burned as they defrosted. Hot tears flowed while she stood under the jets, but her body stopped quaking eventually. She felt drained, hollow, and battered.

The door squeaked. Jana poked her head out through the shower curtain and asked Norah, "Is Bruner okay?"

"I dried him and gave him food and water. He's in front of the fire on an old blanket, but he won't settle. I think he's waiting for you."

"Th-Thanks."

"These pants are probably too short for you, but they should do for now." Norah set a pile of clean clothes on the counter and slipped out.

Wearing the worn gray sweats and wool socks, Jana went into the living room.

Norah handed her a mug of hot chocolate, and Jana sat by the river rock fireplace on the sofa. She took a few sips. Her eyelids felt weighted down, and her shoulders ached.

Bruner limped over and settled his head on her thigh. Tight against her legs, he relaxed into sleep almost instantly and started snoring.

She set her cocoa on the rectangular glass coffee table, which sat atop a huge, hand-woven wool rug. The angular design, in blues, cream, and black, had the aura of age.

Norah studied her for a minute. Her full lips tightened into a thin line. "I know some of what happened yesterday. The other policeman died, didn't he?"

A painful sob clogged Jana's throat, and she nodded. Her heart felt so heavy, she didn't know if she could move. But if she let the pain overwhelm and paralyze her, there would never be hope for Nate. She blinked back scalding tears. "What must I do?"

Norah raised her chin. "You must go back tonight, before dawn breaks, and correct the distortion."

Gooseflesh prickled Jana's back and shoulders. She shuddered and rubbed her forehead with both hands. She had to be crazy to consider this nonsense seriously. Jana shook her head. "Why the urgency?"

"My spirit guide says the window for change has almost disappeared." Norah picked at a tweed sofa cushion with her fingernail. "But I know you don't trust my gift."

"I have no other choice." Jana folded her knees against her chest and wrapped her arms around them. Bruner raised his head, nudging her hand, and she patted him. "I'm prime suspect in the murder of Douggie Wendell, the guy who shot you."

"Ridiculous," Norah huffed. "Framed?"

"By crooked cops. They want me dead. They k-killed Nate."

"Did they also murder Mike Gordon?"

Jana swiped her cheeks with her palms. "I don't know. Nate said Morrie Tomasini set Mike up for the ambush."

"Did Nate know why you're in danger?"

"Tomasini thinks I plan to blackmail him. Nate and I found proof he was involved, but I don't know where Nate left the evidence."

"It won't matter."

"But I'm afraid you'll get caught up in this mess. The police could find me, or a hit man could come." Jana rose to her knees, more panicked than before.

"We'll finish our task before they can find you."

Her stomach shifted, and suddenly, the world she thought she knew seemed upside down and inside out. When she stared into Norah's calm dark eyes, her heart rate slowed a fraction. Maybe the woman's claims were real. "I don't…I need to understand. You claimed you fixed something yourself and saved your brother. Exactly what happened?"

Norah settled against the pillows. "The summer I turned ten, my big brother Aaron took us swimming near the waterfall. When my cousin Sammy panicked and went under, Aaron jumped in to save him, but they both drowned." She grimaced. "I remember the funeral. I felt itchy and squirmed on the pew. Although I couldn't put it into words, I sensed something was wrong. Everyone around me appeared out of focus, distorted."

Jana shifted on the cushions and rolled her shoulders. "Creepy."

"I didn't understand what was happening to me. I ran away on the walk to the graveyard. A little fox ran past me and disappeared into the bushes, so I followed."

Jana drew a sharp breath. "A fox? Following a fox saved us from Tomasini's assassin on the way here. I saw it run past and knew I had to hide."

"Ah! I thought my spirit guide had been active tonight. He manifests as a fox, sometimes sparkling with light. He can be very forceful."

"Yes, I felt compelled. While we were hiding, I remembered what you'd said and decided to come here."

"Good. So you understand why I followed the fox years ago." Norah nodded sharply. "I stopped running and sat on the riverbank, splashing the cool water on my face. Beside me, I found a medicine bundle tied together with a leather thong. Suddenly, I knew I had work to do and chanted like my Grandfather had taught me. As soon as I started, peace welled up from deep inside, and I heard my cousins playing and splashing exactly like before. When I turned around, Aaron was sitting on the old blue and white blanket."

Jana gasped and covered her mouth. "How did you know it wasn't a dream?"

"Everything was completely real and physical." She shrugged. "My mouth fell open, but I couldn't speak. Then Sammy yelled, and Aaron stood up. I knew what would happen next unless I could stop him, so I grabbed my brother's arm and hung on with all my might. He couldn't shake me off and dragged me with him into the shallow water."

"What happened to your cousin?"

"Sammy drifted with the current and caught a branch. He pulled himself out, but Aaron was furious. He didn't speak to me for hours."

"And you remember the way the events happened before?" Jana steepled her shaky fingers together while her mind raced. "What an incredible story. Did you ever tell your brother?"

Norah studied her hands. Her face was smooth and glowing in the firelight. "He wouldn't believe me. He never spent any time with my Lakota grandfather, never explored his spirit journey."

Norah's story seemed like a fairytale on steroids, but her body language radiated truth. "I'm ready for my redo."

"For a skeptic, you've come a long way."

"As a child, I spent summers with my Granny McAlpine. She had a gift for healing, and I was fascinated, yet repelled by her psychic…whatever."

"Her power?"

"I'll try to think of it that way." Jana swallowed hard.

"Good. But before we start, why don't you come into the kitchen with me? I'll fix some breakfast. We need to eat."

She left Bruner sleeping by the fire and followed Norah, pausing in the doorway.

Norah pointed a remote at the small television tucked in a bookshelf between cookbooks and shiny black clay pots. "I'll turn on the news."

Jana frowned at the wild-eyed reporter mouthing silent words. The local news anchor's blond hair was plastered to his forehead, and rain dripped from the edge of his umbrella. A swarm of police officers, including a canine unit, set up a perimeter in the background. She leaned closer and turned up the volume.

Nate's smiling picture flashed in one corner of the screen above a video of a blanket-covered stretcher. Her solar plexus cramped like she'd been sucker punched.

"Sereno Police Department released the name of their prime suspect in the murder of Detective Sergeant Nate Kapulani. The authorities suspect a lover's quarrel gone very wrong. A second warrant is also outstanding for this woman in the death of Douglas Wendell."

She stared at her ID picture from Sereno General, and the blood drained from her face. "Dear God. Captain Greene must be behind everything."

"The dogs tracking Dr. Jana Sutherland lost her trail near the 280 interchange. The storm has hindered their search effort. If you see the suspect, do not try to apprehend her. She may be armed and dangerous. The murder weapon, already implicated in several other murders, has not been recovered."

Captain Greene's taut, red face filled the screen, and nausea rose in her throat. He leveled his cold gaze at the camera. "Sutherland left a bloody handprint on the victim's car. Sereno PD will track this murderer and lock her away."

"Murderer? Me?"

"Finally, she is traveling with a vicious dog who savaged two homeless men in an unprovoked attack. I've given orders to shoot the animal on sight. The woman is—"

Norah clicked off the TV. "That sweet old dog was only protecting you." She set two plates of breakfast on the round oak table.

The smell of bacon made Jana's stomach reel. "I can't."

"You want to save Nate?" One hand on her hip, Norah pointed at the food.

Jana picked up her fork and shoveled in pale yellow scrambled eggs. They tasted like cardboard, but she managed a few bites. "How many people have you sent back?"

Norah raised her head and closed her eyes. "You'll

be the fourteenth. It's certainly not an everyday experience. I work, go to court, coach my niece's soccer team."

"You're a lawyer."

"You did research?"

Heat tinged Jana's cheeks. "Nate did, after you were shot."

"Good. Then you know who I am. A children's advocate isn't too scary." Norah flipped her dark hair over one shoulder and smiled softly. "I'm Lakota on my father's side. My grandfather's power passed to me, just like your grandmother's healing gift is part of you."

"I don't know about that."

Norah raised her hands, palms up. "Her power is part of the reason you're such a good doctor."

Jana stood and peered out the window. The storm had intensified. Wind howled around the house, and rain splattered against the glass. A flash of lightning lit the sky and outlined a huge eucalyptus tree. The white trunk glowed. Thunder rumbled across the city. A strong, ragged shiver ran up her spine. "I'm terrified."

Norah finished clearing the table. "Let's go sit by the fire."

Jana followed the woman through the open doorway. "Why did Nate die?"

"All the evil that happened stemmed from Mike Gordon's death. When you prevent his murder, the distortion will be reversed." Moving closer to the crackling fire, Norah lit the choir of tall candles along the mantel. "Sit down. Relax."

Jana's stomach gave a quick lurch, and her brain screamed in disbelief, but she sank onto the floor and crossed her legs. Within seconds, Bruner pillowed his head on her lap and heaved a huge sigh.

Norah reached behind her neck and lifted a leather pouch hanging from a narrow thong. "I need something of yours to ground the ritual. Something natural is best."

Jana glanced down at her hands. "Even my clothes are borrowed."

"A hair will do."

Jana plucked a few and held them out silently.

Humming a chant, Norah tucked the strands into her beaded sac. She grabbed herbs from the potpourri and tossed them on the flames. "Sweetgrass and ritual tobacco."

Acrid smoke burned her throat and eyes. She shifted, and Bruner roused. She stroked his warm, satiny fur. The dog snuffled his contentment. Her shoulders relaxed, but the gymnastics in her belly didn't stop.

"Better. You'll be the person you were at that time."

"But how will I know what I should do?"

"You'll have strong intuition and feel driven, but probably won't understand why. You might experience déjà vu." Norah asked nonchalantly, "Where and when are we targeting?"

Jana blinked at the mind-boggling question and shrugged. "I can only imagine one choice. My apartment the last time I saw Mike."

With her brow drawn in a tight frown, Norah opened her mouth as if to speak, but closed it again. She cleared her throat and asked, "Are you positive? That doesn't feel right to me."

"If I can keep Mike with me all night, he'll be safe.

I'll do whatever it takes to save Nate."

"Then focus your thoughts on that goal." Norah sat beside the fireplace, facing her and tapped a slow cadence on the rustic drum she held between her knees.

Jana rolled her shoulders and concentrated. She drew a deliberate breath of the pungent air and exhaled.

Closing her deep brown eyes, Norah added texture to the rhythm. Her chant gradually grew louder. The sounds coalesced into strange syllables and formed words Jana didn't understand.

Candles flickered around the room. Norah cast a long shadow onto the wall behind her that waxed and waned with the flames from the hearth.

Jana closed her eyes and focused on the slow, steady beat of the drum. At first, she saw only dancing lights, but then a picture of her college apartment flitted through her memory. Mismatched furniture, gaudy curtains hemmed with a row of fuzzy, harvest gold fringe. A tiny Formica table was littered with the remains of dinner.

A blurry vision of a tall man stood in front of her. Mike.

Her heart beat faster. Her pulse echoed in her ears and drowned out the drum. Her skin prickled. Dizziness swamped her senses, and tingling disorientation engulfed her, like she'd plunged into a dream.

Mike looked furious. His face was flushed, and his jaw tight. He raked one hand through his curly blond hair. Over the scents of melted cheese and jalapenos, she smelled his aftershave and the subtle tang of his anger.

The walls solidified, and the stuffy heat of that warm September night closed in around her. She curled her toes into the old shag carpeting.

The back of her throat burned with hot spices.

"Get out, and don't come back," her voice shouted. Her mouth shaped the words. They rasped across her tongue and seared her lips, but why did she sound so outraged? Her hands were clenched together, her heart raced, and her face burned. She closed her eyes for an instant and gave her head a quick shake.

Mike planted his feet and squared his shoulders. His fists clenched at his sides. Red slashes rode his cheekbones, and sparks flashed from his stormy blue eyes. If anything, he looked taller than six-four in his dark uniform..

She took a step back and dropped her gaze. The phone case on his belt was empty.

"Fine," he barked. "You won't see me again."

All the air was suddenly sucked from her lungs. Ghostly whispers blew across her neck, raising all the hair on her nape. Her mouth went as dry as the Mojave Desert.

A compulsion gripped her, tensed every muscle in her body. She couldn't let him leave.

"No, Mike. Don't go." She lunged for his arm. Her fingers grabbed the starched cotton of his uniform. She felt his body heat, and he flexed his arm muscles beneath his sleeve.

Suddenly, her hand was empty, and her heart convulsed. Sightless and deafened, she plummeted into a smothering void.

She tried to cry out, but pain seared through her, scraped every nerve ending raw, and twisted the marrow of her bones.

Her body thudded onto the ground, stunning her.

She lay still and gulped in deep breaths until the world stopped spinning. Slowly, the pain receded.

Bruner slept pressed against her thigh. Sitting up, she rubbed her eyes and took a minute to study Norah's living room. The fire blazed, and the candles flickered. She smelled wax, wood smoke, and sharp herbs. The hands on the clock had not moved.

But Norah's face had gone pale and gray.

Chapter Nineteen

January 11, 6:20 a.m.

Jana held her hand over Norah's thready pulse. The rhythm faltered. The woman's heart was failing. Time to start cardiac massage and call for help, but that would mean unavoidable exposure.

No choice. She couldn't let Norah die.

Jana stretched her patient out on the wool rug.

Suddenly, Norah gasped and convulsed. Her hands clutched at her chest, and her face twisted with pain. Color rushed through her skin. The woman moaned and curled into a ball.

"Norah? Norah, can you hear me?" Jana reached for a pulse and heaved a sigh. Her heartbeat was stronger and steady now, but far too fast.

"Hurts. Water?" Norah croaked.

Grabbing a comforter, Jana covered her and tucked a throw pillow beneath the woman's head. "I'll bring you some. Just rest."

She rushed into the kitchen and filled a glass. The cops were scouring the city for her and Bruner. How long before they stumbled across her trail?

She'd stabilize Norah and call the EMTs on her way out. She could borrow the woman's car and sneak back into Nate's garage for the sim card. Before he died, he'd told her to get the bag and run. He must have

213

put Mike's phone in with her kickboxing gear. She shook her head slowly. That's the bag Nate had meant for her to get, not the money bag.

But what if the police had already destroyed the evidence? If she could find the proof, would the FBI listen, or throw her straight in jail? She let out another long sigh. Maybe she could still drive to Reno and fly to Nate's parents for help. But why would they help a fugitive who was wanted for the murder of their son?

What about her folks? Would her dad forgive her and help? Didn't matter. She couldn't risk her parents' safety. She returned to the living room and knelt beside Norah to help her drink.

After the first sip, the woman grabbed Jana's wrist and struggled to sit up. "Bring me the drum. We must try again now," she said in a raspy, harsh voice.

Jana removed her fingers from Norah's pulse and put on her best you're-gonna-be-fine smile. "You need to be in bed."

Grimacing, the healer leaned back against the couch. Her face was gray, but her eyes and jaw held determination. "After we've finished."

Jana shook her head and propped a pillow behind her patient's head. "You're too weak."

"I made a big mistake the first time we tried."

"Maybe, but the police will be here soon. I should leave now, borrow your car, and run. You can tell them I stole it," Jana said in a calm, reality-sucks tone.

"Once more. If the ritual doesn't work, I'll give you my car and my blessing." Norah grabbed her hand with surprising strength. "If you don't go back now, you'll lose your only chance."

"I refuse to risk your life."

"The cops will find you soon anyway, and they'll kill us both."

Jana's blood chilled. The cold weight in the pit of her stomach burned like dry ice. "But..."

"Go back now or this reality will be inescapable. The dead will remain dead. You're almost out of time. You must correct the distortion and stop the murder while you still can or your cop will die. Forever."

Lightning struck directly overhead. Thunder shook the house, and Jana's hair crackled with static electricity. A fresh onslaught of rain hammered on the tile roof. Goose bumps crawled over her arms. "The ritual didn't work before."

Norah lifted her leather pouch. "It did work. I know it. I felt you go back, but you chose the wrong time."

"I saw Mike, heard him, touched him. I tried my hardest, but something wrenched me away."

"My spirit guide stopped the ritual, otherwise we both would have died because of my mistake." Norah's mouth drew in a tight line. "I didn't send you back far enough. Think. What event set you on this path?"

Jana raised her palms and gave a frustrated shrug. "I don't know. It could be anything."

"When did you meet Mike?"

Could she risk an answer? Norah wouldn't relent until they talked this through. Jana scrutinized her patient and checked her pulse. The woman's color had returned. Her eyes were clear, and her vital signs had stabilized. "I worked with Mike the semester before I graduated, and I had a crush on him for months."

"When did you begin dating?"

Thunder rolled again, but further away this time.

Exhausted, Jana stretched out her neck and rubbed her temples. "Two days before I finished my internship, he finally noticed me. He kissed me that evening."

"That morning is our target."

The gyrations in Jana's stomach eased. Her heart stumbled, but a deep sense of certainty poured through her. "That feels right. I didn't love Mike. I belong with Nate. I love him."

Norah flashed a wide smile and threw another handful of herbs on the fire. "Give me my drum."

Chapter Twenty

Part 2: Sereno, California

March 28, twelve years earlier, 6:30 a.m.
"Jana?"

She squeezed her eyes tighter, sighed, and stretched toward the sexy baritone voice.

A deep chuckle rumbled. "Hey, gorgeous. Bet you didn't get any sleep last night."

She sat up and focused on the man facing her. Strong features. An amazing grin. Dark hair waved onto his forehead, and his luscious, chocolate eyes were framed by crinkling laugh lines.

"Nate!" she yelled and launched over the seatback. "Oh, my God."

He laughed and took her by the shoulders. "Glad to see you, too."

Almost in tears, she touched his cheek, and stroked the hint of roughness on his square chin. Her thumb grazed his full lips.

He enveloped her hand in his warm grasp. His tanned skin was shades darker than her fingers, and his hand dwarfed hers. A warm rush of awareness formed inside her, and her blood pulsed faster in her veins.

With her hand still cradling his jaw, his intense gaze held hers as if he could see all her deepest secrets.

217

Everything inside her trembled, and fire burned up her neck and into her cheeks.

She jerked her hand away and scooted back against the seat of the well-worn sedan, staring at her running shoes and wishing she could vanish. Her heart pounded in her chest like she'd just done an hour of kickboxing. Kickboxing? Where'd that come from? She picked at a crack in the gray plastic upholstery and peeked up at him. "Sorry. I guess I must have been dreaming."

Nate flashed a wide smile, but there was something serious behind his expression. "I don't mind, but Mike will be back soon."

"Right, Mike." Tucking a loose strand of long hair behind her ears, she studied the streetscape. Still disoriented, she rotated her aching shoulders.

They were in the undercover sedan, parked in an industrial area of town. Low, flat-roofed buildings lined the narrow street. That's right—her first stakeout.

Kicking aside the empty coffee cups littering the floor, she slid toward the tinted window and stared out at the sunny spring morning. The velvet green of the eastern hills stood out against the clear, cloudless sky. "Who are we watching, again?"

"Joe Morgan. He owns the auto repair shop across the street."

She laid her arms on the seat back and rested her chin on her hands. "Is that Joe?" She pointed at a skinny guy wearing coveralls and leaning on a broom.

"No. That's the janitor, Douggie Wendell."

Wendell? She recognized the name, but from where? An image of his face shattered by a gunshot wound popped into her mind, and she shivered.

An engine revved, and a car raced along the street.

With a flash of tomato red and fuzzy dice, a late fifties Chevy convertible squealed into the driveway and stopped.

Nate let out a long, appreciative whistle. "Nice ride."

A thirtyish man with surfer blonde hair hopped out of the car. Pressed khakis, blue polo, orangey tan.

"That's Morgan." Nate waved a paper in her direction, with a picture of a much younger Joseph Robert Morgan in mug shot profile. "He's stayed out of trouble the past few years."

Outside the shop, the two men greeted each other, and the janitor followed Joe into the shop. "Are those the suspects?"

"Yeah. That'll teach Mike. He missed the grand entrance."

The front passenger door opened, and a man catapulted into the sedan.

Jana squeaked and jumped back.

"Watch the coffee, Gordon," Nate grouched.

"Relax." Mike grinned and passed out the cups. "Did you see Joe?"

Jana wrapped her hands around the hot mocha Mike handed her and sniffed the tantalizing fragrance.

"Yeah. Came roaring in, but didn't have anything on him."

"No suspicious bundles?"

"No, damn it. We've been waiting here for three hours, and that's all we got."

"Tomasini said they'd transport the drugs today." Mike popped the lid off his paper cup, blew on the coffee, and slurped.

"Right. How many hours have we sat here the past

two weeks? Nothing but coffee stains to show for the time."

"Patience, partner."

Jana's gaze ping-ponged between the two cops, and she scrunched her eyes shut, but couldn't clear the gritty, out-of-focus sensation. Listening to the byplay in stunned silence, she felt confused and off balance.

"Don't forget, today we have muffins to go with our coffee, thanks to our favorite little intern." Mike turned and focused his baby blues on her, grinning.

Her stomach jolted. "It's good to see you, Mike."

"Yeah, now that it's light outside." He gave her a slow once-over, and his eyebrows arched. "Nice outfit."

Heat blazed on her cheeks again. She'd dressed for Mike this morning, but now his scrutiny made her a little queasy. She glanced down at her forest green sweater and tight jeans. Frowning, she tugged at the hem, but couldn't cover her bellybutton ring.

When she spotted Nate's grimace in the rearview mirror, she shot him a rueful smile.

His lips quirked back at her, and he elbowed Mike. "How much longer are we going to sit on our butts?"

Mike shrugged. "Guess Tomasini had the timing wrong. Nothing will happen this late," he said through a mouth full of muffin.

"Some snitch you got, partner."

"Look, the high school's soaked with drugs, been getting worse all year. Somebody's supplying and somebody's dealing. Tomasini fingered this dude. You got anything better, tell me now."

"But Tomasini's involved," Jana blurted. Chilled, she frowned harder. That idea had popped out of nowhere.

"What?" Mike's eyes narrowed, and he studied her face silently.

Nate snickered.

Rubbing her aching temples, she stared at the floor again, but felt driven to add, "We've got to interrogate Tomasini. Find out what he knows."

Mike let out a long raspberry.

Determined, she sat forward, setting her mocha into the cup holder. Suddenly, the answer seemed so logical to her. "Look, Tomasini must have tipped them off. He's behind the drug dealing."

"What if he's using those guys as decoys? That'd be a real kick in the ass." Nate gave a halfhearted chuckle and sank his forehead onto one fist. "We're sitting here watching the auto show while he's doing business elsewhere?"

Jana griped the seatback. "That's it! What if he's misleading you on purpose to sidetrack your investigation?"

Nate nodded, no longer laughing. "She has a point, Gordon."

"Joe what's his name could be in on the plot, too. Where'd he find the money for his car?" She indicated the Chevy parked in the driveway.

"And that's a damn nice shop." Nate thumbed over his shoulder.

Unable to stop herself, she curled her hands into fists. "How well do you know your snitch? Trust him? We should focus the investigation on Tomasini."

"We?" Mike's eyebrows raised, and his mouth pinched into a straight line. "Look, we let you ride along to see what detectives do in the field. Doesn't mean a lowly intern gets to run the operation."

She sniffed. No matter how crazy her suspicions might sound, she knew she was right.

"Back off, partner. She's trying to help. Besides, she has an interesting theory. What do you actually know about your snitch?"

Mike scowled. "I ran a sheet on him. He's clean."

An unnatural certainty goaded her on. She didn't know why, but she simply could not let the subject drop. "My internship isn't over yet. I don't mind doing a little digging."

"Dig all you want, babe." Mike snorted and bounced back against the seat.

Her pulse shot up, and her jaw tightened. "My name is Jana. I hate being called babe."

"Sorry, Ms. Sutherland," Mike said, his voice thick with sarcasm. "Get this heap on the road, Kapulani."

Hunched in the corner, Jana stewed. She'd stayed awake late baking pumpkin muffins because Mike had said he liked them. Now she didn't want anything to do with the big jerk. She flashed him a dirty look behind his back, insulted. He'd treat her like some babe with her brains on her chest.

Mike didn't say a word to her all the way back to the station. It didn't take a genius to realize he was pissed, too. Good.

Nate parked the sedan in the department garage. When he killed the engine, she hopped out, relieved to escape.

"Gordon, we promised Jana a ride home. Want me to drop her off?" Nate asked, and she looked up at him gratefully.

Mike continued toward the entrance. "Whatever."

Nate smiled at her and clicked the locks on his

SUV. "Ready?" He handed her into the front seat and jogged around to the driver's side.

As soon as he slid in, she felt an overwhelming sense of safety. Her forehead wrinkled. Safe? Why? From what?

"Thought your idea had merit, Jana."

"You did?"

"Sure. Mike trusts this snitch, but he's given us a couple bum tips. Worth checking."

"I wouldn't mind doing some research this afternoon, if you think I can help. I don't have any plans."

"County records might have something, or maybe the library downtown."

"I could check Tomasini's background on the web, too, review his holdings, even search the FBI databases."

"Pretty serious about this?" He glanced her way, but returned his focus to the busy road.

"I want to do something. A six-month internship and all I've done is type boring reports into the computer, answer phones, and make coffee." She flipped her hand in disgust. "The work study grant kept my dad happy, but jeez."

Nate chuckled. "You want in on the action."

"Now you're laughing at me, too."

"Never. I like your dedication." He gave her a wicked glance, and her breath snagged.

The clatter of a cafeteria echoed around her. Nate bent toward her with a wicked gleam in his dark eyes and kissed her gently on the cheek. She tasted chocolate.

"Jana?"

"Huh? Sorry. I guess I was daydreaming again. I need more sleep tonight." She touched her cheek and felt warmth from his lips, as if the fantasy kiss had been real. Her body tingled, and she swallowed hard.

Nate parked in front of her apartment building. "This your place?"

"Yes." Jana grabbed the door handle and scrambled out of the car. Nate was faster and helped her onto the sidewalk, holding her hand for a half second too long.

Her gaze swept over his broad shoulders and back to his smiling face. She ached to brush the wavy lock off his forehead. She stared at his killer grin and swayed closer, but the surprise on his face made her cheeks flame. Dropping her gaze, she cleared her throat. "Well, thanks for the ride. Do you want the rest of these muffins?"

"You bet." Nate took the plastic bag. "When are you going to the library?"

"After lunch. I probably need to check county records first, before they close."

He touched her hand and set her whole body tingling again. "Want to meet me after? Have coffee or a sandwich?"

Her heart pounded hard and fast. She stared at the sidewalk and tried to hide her jumbled feelings.

"I mean just to hear what you found out on the investigation."

She tilted her face and smiled at him. "Just work?"

"Of course. We can sit outside. My pup can chaperone."

"Bruner?"

Nate's brows arrowed, and he cocked his head.

"How did you know his name?"

"I don't know. You must have told me before."

He studied her and shrugged. "Meet you in front of the library. Six thirty?"

"See you then." When he drove off, she hurried up the stairs two at a time and walked into the apartment.

Her roommate, Liv let the harvest-gold, fringed curtain drop, and stepped away from the window. "Who's the hunk?"

"He's Nate. Mike's partner." Jana hung her purse on a chair and grabbed a string cheese from the refrigerator.

"Yummy shoulders."

"Cute butt, too."

"Love how he moves, kind of like a panther." Liv turned from the front window and flopped on the couch. Petite and curvy with long dark hair, she dressed in vibrant colors. Today's choice was a deep amethyst. "But I thought you had the hots for Mike."

Jana wrinkled her nose and kicked off her shoes. She curled her toes into the seen-better-days avocado-green shag carpet. "Thought I did too, but not anymore. He acted like a jerk today. I'm meeting Nate later."

"Woo-hoo! Fast work. Where's your latest guy taking you?"

"Coffee and sandwiches after I finish at the library. But it's work, not a date." Jana tried for nonchalant, but a wide smile sneaked out. "He even encouraged me to investigate on my own."

"Are you sure you want to get involved with any cop, even if he is a hunk? I didn't want to say anything before this, but you've complained all along about how pushy those two guys are."

Jana frowned at the floor. Liv was right. It wasn't fair to encourage Nate when he was so much like her father. Best to ignore the crazy hormones. She gave her friend a swift kiss on the cheek. "You have a good point. Right now, I need to change."

She closed the door to her bedroom and gaped at her reflection in the full-length mirror. Moving closer, she studied her face. Odd. No different than a few hours ago. She shook her head. Maybe it was the light, but her skin seemed brighter, smoother, with a light tan and more freckles than she remembered.

She loosened the clasp holding her hair, and a coppery waterfall trailed down her back in rippling waves almost to her waist. The weight seemed heavy against her neck. She combed her fingers through the length and shivered. What would it feel like shorter?

Turning sideways, she glanced at her body in the mirror and traced the indent of her waist to the silvery bar crossing her belly button. She grinned. Her dad had gone ape-shit when she came home with a navel ring.

She peeled off her sweater and tossed it on the bed. Above her low-rise jeans, her tummy was tight and concave between her jutting hipbones. Even without a bra, her small breasts were high and somehow firmer than she expected.

She chose a pale green, scooped neck tee over a sports bra. The days were growing warmer, but she grabbed a light jacket for the evening.

Liv was right. She had more important goals and too much sense to get involved with Nate. Even though he did have yummy shoulders, and his melted chocolate eyes made her breath catch and her body hum.

Nate's dark eyes were very close. When his thumb

trailed down her cheek, she couldn't breathe. He tipped
her chin and kissed her. The blood sang in her veins.

Jana blinked and sucked in air. Her pulse raced,
and her body throbbed. She'd flirted with Mike for the
past few months, hoping to catch his attention. Why
had she worked so hard when she really wanted Nate?
She shuddered and made a face.

Whatever. Sex was nothing but pheromones
anyway. She'd finish her internship on Friday. Until
then, she could keep her attraction to Nate under control
and remember today was about work, not a date.

Jana shook out the kinks in her hands. Her next
step was to find the information she needed to prove her
point. Then they'd listen to her and investigate Morrie
Tomasini.

****

9:15 a.m.

Nate dumped his jacket on the chair and eyed his
partner across their crowded office. Jammed under the
window, their two scarred, oak desks faced each other.
Jana's small computer table was tucked in the corner
beside a file cabinet.

With an apple stuck in his mouth, Mike flipped
through a stack of pink message slips. He ripped the
fruit out and chewed. "Did you get rid of Little Miss
Detective?"

"Yeah, I dropped Jana at home." Nate held up a
clear plastic bag. "No thanks to you. She gave me the
rest of the muffins."

Mike's eyes lit, and he crooked a finger. "Hand
'em over, my friend. I need food. I'm meeting Tomasini
in—shit, I'm gonna be late." He made a grab for the
muffins.

Nate yanked the bag out of reach. "Hold on a minute. We can eat them on the way."

"We?"

"I want to meet this snitch, harass him about wasting our time again."

"No way. That'll piss him off."

"He'll get over it, unless he has something to hide."

"Don't tell me you believe the garbage Jana spouted?"

Nate's ears started to heat. "She's smart, and she had a point. But I have another reason for going."

"Wait." Mike punched his shoulder. "I smell a rat."

Nate scowled at his partner and hiked one eyebrow. "You mean rat fink? We're talking about your snitch again?"

"Why this sudden interest in Tomasini? Bet it's really Jana's hot sweater and sexy jeans."

"Yeah, she looked good this morning. You were wiping up drool, too."

"The girl is so damn hot, she makes my hands itch." Mike rubbed them together, leering. "But she'll be fair game tomorrow, and I'm going after her."

Something dark and primitive exploded inside Nate, pumped adrenaline into his system and tightened his fists. No way. He wanted to hogtie the son of a bitch and lock him in a holding cell. But he resisted the urge and tossed his partner a muffin.

"Thanks. Don't know what got into her. Damn it, she's not a cop. She should stick to her filing."

"My opinion? She's right about one thing. Unless we know what your favorite snitch is after, we don't know how far to trust his info."

"Come on. He wants a kickback, but he's clean."

"Maybe, but my gut tells me I should meet the charmer. You shouldn't have all the fun."

****

10:20 a.m.

Nate backed the Ford across the empty gravel lot and set the brake. He glanced around the quiet Japanese garden. "Why here and not at his convenience store?"

"Tomasini's cautious, afraid he'll kick off a gang war between the drug dealers and find his fat carcass in the middle of a shoot-out."

Nate shrugged and locked the car door. He pointed to the right toward the pagoda shaped tearoom. "Better check for eavesdroppers."

"I'll take a quick swing by the meditation gardens."

Nate nosed around the periphery. He moved silently along the thick bamboo hedge, past the massive wooden gates.

Deserted.

Dusting off his hands, he hiked across the arched moon bridge spanning the koi pond and up the wooded hillside.

Mike was talking to a beefy, stoop-shouldered guy in a loud, rumpled shirt and Bermuda shorts. His curly dark hair was thin on top, and sweat glistened on his face.

"Yo, Tomasini," Nate called. "Got a bone to pick."

Mike introduced them, adding, "Kapulani's pissed."

"We camped outside the joker's garage again and got nothing, thanks to your 'tip.'" Nate shot a narrow-eyed scowl at the snitch. "You're jerking us around."

Tomasini wiped his forehead with a handkerchief. "Relax, and I'll tell you what I overheard."

Mike leaned casually against a tall redwood and crossed his arms. "Whatcha got for us today?"

The snitch puffed out his chest, but his beer gut still hung over his belt. "Damn drug dealers. I hate when they hang around schools, but I know who's behind the ring."

"Yeah? I've heard that routine before."

"You're going at this all wrong, partner," Nate growled and elbowed past Mike, closing on the snitch. "Look closer at your source."

Tomasini's eyes shifted furtively. "I told ya, it's that stupid creep, Wendell, working outta Morgan's Garage."

"Wendell? The janitor?" Mike snorted.

Nate frowned. "No way the skinny freak runs a drug ring."

"Wendell's smart enough to see you two cops staking out Morgan's garage in your old Crown Vic again and change his plans, ain't he?" A sharp, calculating expression flashed across the snitch's face.

The gleam in his flinty brown eyes set off Nate's bullshit detector. "Is that what happened? Why didn't you give us a heads-up?"

"Only just heard. Don't know who tipped him off, but that's only partly why I'm here. You still interested in the rest?" The snitch poked some gravel with his shoe.

"Yeah, sure. What else you know?" Mike asked.

"At my store, I heard these kids talking about a drug deal that's going down Friday."

"Give me a break! You heard that while selling candy bars? You're lying, you weasel." Nate grabbed Tomasini's by the shirt and hauled him up onto his toes.

A chill prickled the back of Nate's neck. Why did he feel like he'd done this before? Mike raised a hand. "Back off, partner! We need details."

"Fine," Nate grumbled. He released the guy and flexed his hands. Time to hit the gym and work off some steam.

"Exactly what did you hear, Tomasini?"

A sleazy grin pasted on his face, the guy rubbed two fingers together.

"This tip works out, you'll get plenty," Mike added.

Tomasini shrugged. Then he turned and said over his shoulder, "Three thirty on Friday. The gas station near the school." He lumbered down the hill.

Nate scowled and heaved a handful of gravel into the bushes. Jana's intuition was on track. Tomasini was involved. He knew more than what he was feeding Mike. The weasel made his skin crawl.

Chapter Twenty-One

March 28, 6:30 p.m.

The library guard flipped through Jana's thick stack of printouts and handed them back to her.

She stuffed the papers into her empty backpack with a grin. That should squelch the strange inner voice needling her to hurry. She pushed past the exit turnstile and out the massive glass doors, blinking at the glare from the setting sun.

Nate rose from a bench, grinning at her. "Hey, Jana, come meet Bruner."

A brown boxer puppy with a black-rimmed white star on his forehead and white socks wiggled beside Nate. The dog yipped and tugged on his leash, straining toward her.

"Cute puppy!" She knelt to let him sniff her hand. Barking happily, he squirmed into her arms and showered her face with sloppy kisses. She giggled and rose, cuddling the puppy, but dodged his wet, pink tongue. "He's wonderful. How old?"

"Four months." Nate's puzzled grin widened, and the laugh lines around his eyes crinkled. He ran one hand through his hair. "Bruner's going absolutely nuts over you. Never seen him do that with someone new before."

She nuzzled the dog's soft velvet ears and gently

wiggled his jowls. "I think I'm in love."

"Tell you what, I'll share Bruner, but I'm ready for that sandwich. Why don't we let him walk off some energy? It's only a couple blocks."

She set the squirming puppy on his feet and stood, but Bruner crowded against her shins and gazed up at her, whining softly.

Crouching, she met the pup's black eyes and couldn't look away. Goose bumps shivered over her body, and fierce déjà vu assaulted her.

She knew this dog, and somehow, he was vital to her survival.

She tamped down the crazy notion and took a deep breath before turning to Nate with a smile.

"All set?" At her nod, he helped her stand.

For an instant, one strong hand rested at the back of her waist. Warmth seeped through her thin knit top. She glanced at him through her lashes, aware of his size and strength.

She smelled grapefruit. Nate's lips and tongue brushed hers. His big, strong hands cupped her bottom and drew her tight. Shuddering, she arched against him, making a hungry noise.

Jana snapped back to her senses. Dizzy and a little queasy, she blinked. Wearing her pajamas while Nate kissed her? Where were these weird fantasies coming from? They seemed so real.

Had an alien taken over her brain, or was she delusional like Granny McAlpine? Where was her self-control? Nate might have an adorable pup, but he was her boss, and they were working tonight.

Bruner galloped ahead, tugging at the leash. His outsized paws scrambled on the concrete like a cartoon character trying to get traction.

With a rumbling chuckle, Nate called, "Heel." The dog fell back and trotted at his side. "We already started obedience training. Two classes every week. He's a handful."

Something inside compelled her to leap to the dog's defense. "He's doing great for a puppy."

"Working on it."

A wad of paper skittered across the sidewalk in front of her. She tensed and bent to pick it up, suddenly flashing on a blighted urban neighborhood covered in trash and graffiti.

Druggies.

Pimps.

Hookers.

Shops boarded up or burned out, with homeless families sleeping in the doorways.

With her heart leaping in her chest, she scanned the area for threats. The last streaks of sunset faded from the horizon. An amber streetlight sputtered on and cast flickering shadows across the pavement.

The area around the university might be showing some age, but danger in Sereno? What an imagination. Next, she'd be wearing six layers of rags and feeding feral cats.

"What did you find today?" Nate asked. "Any dirt on Tomasini?"

His question refocused her thoughts. "Not dirt, exactly. I spent so much time at county records I barely got started at the library. He owns property all over the valley. A couple businesses, commercial buildings, his big place in Sereno, plus a cabin on twenty acres in the mountains."

"Guess he must rake in the bucks. Don't know how. Thought Mike said Tomasini managed a convenience store."

"He owns that store and three others."

"Huh." Nate frowned.

At the cross street, he punched the walk signal. Bruner sat politely, but wiggled in place, his tongue lolling, until Nate said, "Forward."

"I checked the property records on Joe Morgan's garage. It's not actually his. It's owned by Atlantic Partners, a brokerage Tomasini controls."

"Weird. Morgan's dad used to own the place. Wonder what happened?"

Lights blazed at the rustic sandwich shop down the road. But where was everyone? The usual crowd was missing tonight, only a few other students.

Nate guided her to one of the wooden tables scattered along a concrete path. The purple flowering plum trees looked inky beneath their clusters of small pink flowers. Clumped below the trees, daffodils glowed in the low spotlights.

"Haven't had one of their meatball specials in months." He pulled two bills out of his wallet. "Okay if I snag this table and wait here with Bruner?"

When their fingers met, awareness sizzled through her, and a gasp escaped from her throat. Her gaze locked with his, but her vision blurred.

Nate yanked off his white dress shirt and tossed it on her bedside chair. Well-defined muscles rippled across his naked back and shoulders. When he turned, she snaked her arms around his neck and tasted the warm tanned skin covering his collarbone.

Jana stumbled. Heat flooded her face, but she

managed to take the money without dropping it. Nate in her bedroom? Why was she having these crazy visions? How could she stop them before he noticed and had her committed?

He frowned at her and brushed her cheek with his knuckle. "You okay?"

"I'm fine," she said, moistening her mouth with her tongue.

His gaze fixed on her lips, and he inched closer. His eyes shifted and captured hers. Heat slumbered in those sexy, deep brown eyes.

She drew in a breath. He smelled good, like a mix of soap and something woodsy with a citrus tang. Warm, liquid need coiled low in her belly, and she leaned closer. But he stopped and dropped his hand to his side, grinning.

Her face flamed again, and she looked down. She still clutched the wrinkled bills in one tight fist, but her body throbbed, like they'd kissed for hours. "I-I'll go get the food," she blurted and hurried inside.

****

7:25 p.m.

Nate couldn't take his gaze off Jana. She sat beside him on the bench, bent forward and nuzzling Bruner. He wanted to kiss the freckles dusting the soft skin of her cheeks and nose. Her plush, sensual mouth would feel so damn good under his.

Her low-slung jeans were tight, shaping her slim hips and thighs. A thin band of pale skin showed below her sweater in back. She had gentle curves in all the right places, tiny waist and high, small breasts, just big enough to fill his palms. Or his mouth. But not tonight. Not while she still worked for him.

He flexed his fingers, and the wrapper from his sandwich crinkled. He dropped the paper and licked off the last dribble of tomato sauce. "Great meatballs, but I could use a bath." He swiped his hands with a soggy napkin.

Jana grinned wickedly. "Maybe I should let you hold your puppy for a few minutes. He'd clean you off."

"No, thanks, I'm golden." He tossed the tattered paper in the trash and rubbed his hands on his jeans.

She turned back to the dog. "You're such a little sweetheart," she said in a high-pitched, baby voice.

A cold spot formed deep in his guts. "For you," Nate said, but kept his tone light. Pitiful, Kapulani. Jealous of a freaking dog? So what if Jana and Bruner had a weird mind-meld going?

He'd envied Mike when she batted her lashes and flirted with him, and he was damn happy about whatever change came over her this morning. No question she'd started to respond to him instead, and if they weren't out in public...

Change the subject, idiot. "Uh...what will you do after graduation?"

Her face almost glowed. "Med school. My third acceptance came yesterday, the one I hoped for. All I have to do is send in my deposit."

His heart stumbled. Spicy meatballs knocked around in his stomach. "Where?"

"I want to go to Georgetown. Super program and far away."

Hell. He frowned. She'd be on the other side of the country. "Far away from what?"

She glanced up at him, her head tilted to the side.

"My father."

"He can't be that bad."

She shrugged and tucked her long, coppery hair behind her ears. "Not at all. He's a wonderful man, but I need my own space. My folks are helicopter parents."

He must have looked confused, because she laughed a little and added, "They're constantly hovering, especially the Colonel."

The spotlight above the sandwich shop door blinked out. Another followed, and Nate checked the area. "Closing time. You ready?"

She straightened. "Oh, I hadn't realized it was so late."

Nate untied the leash and held out a hand to help her rise. "Kinda quiet tonight."

"Midterms, but it's creepy with no one else on the streets."

He held her fingers a little too long while keeping tension on Bruner's leash. The dog trotted along obediently. "We're safe. Not like Sereno's crime central."

She shot him a sideways glance, but matched his stride.

The feel of her pale, slender hand in his, the texture of her delicate, cool skin had made him crave his hands all over her body. Blood pulsed thick and heavy in his groin. He wanted to claim her, wanted her taste in his mouth, wanted her long legs wrapped around his waist.

Get a grip, Kapulani. His brain was barreling down a super highway at a hundred miles an hour with his dick calling all the shots. But Jana was barely twenty-one, and he had to wait until she left the department. Even then, he'd have to take it slow.

His hands slid under her waistband and over the tight, supple curve of her ass. Angling his mouth over hers, he pulled her tight against his throbbing cock and hot pleasure wrenched a gasp from his throat.

Nate jerked, dislodging the vivid image, but his grip on Bruner's leash must have relaxed. The dog darted in front of him, aiming straight for Jana. He sidestepped, but didn't trip.

"Careful," she said with a light squeeze on his hand.

"Heel!" He tugged the dog into place. "My fault. Need to alpha walk the little turkey."

"Can I take him? Bet I can keep him under control." She took the leash and set off with the dog between them.

"Thanks." Flexing his now-empty hand, Nate glared at the prancing pup. He angled his body away from her, subtly readjusting his jeans.

X-rated fantasies? What the hell had happened to his control a minute ago? But he'd felt her smooth, warm skin and smelled the grass crushed beneath his shoes. Grapefruit? Why the hell did he smell grapefruit? He scratched his chin and shoved his hands in his pockets.

Near the intersection on the wide street to his left, a motor revved. He frowned at the souped-up white truck with darkened windows idling in the lane next to the curb. The driver gunned the engine.

Jockeying? Taunting the low rider next to him into a street race?

He reached around Jana to press the walk button. Time to beef up patrol and crack down on cruisers again. He'd say something to the lieutenant. Capturing her hand, he pressed a light kiss to her knuckles.

A faint blush tinged her cheekbones. She glanced ahead and stepped off the curb. "Light's green."

An electric tingle chilled the back of his neck.

Tires squealed.

The smell of burned rubber and brake linings stung his sinuses.

Adrenaline flooded his bloodstream. His pulse spiked, and he glanced sideways.

The truck roared off the line with its wheels cranked to the right. The rig fishtailed and skidded around the corner, angled toward them.

Toward Jana.

He pulled her back from the curb and jerked the leash.

Airborne, Bruner yelped.

Nate threw himself to the ground and rolled, dragging Jana and the dog out of the truck's trajectory.

One wheel bumped onto the concrete and caught the sidewalk edge, but missed them by a hand span.

A fender scraped the light post. Metal screeched against metal. Sparks flew.

The truck thumped back onto the asphalt and roared away without stopping.

"Asshole driver." His heart thundered like cannon fire, and cold sweat trickled down the center of his back. He stood and helped Jana up, taking back the leash. "You okay?"

She dusted off her jeans and cuddled the whimpering dog. "Just banged my knee."

"That idiot ought to be locked up and have his license yanked."

Moving closer, she leaned her face against his

chest. "Thank you. I didn't see him coming."

"Did you get a look at the clown?" He tucked her head under his chin and buried his nose in her hair, drawing a deep, shuddering breath of strawberry shampoo.

She gazed up at him, her eyes enormous in her pale face, and shook her head. "No, the cab was too dark."

"Me neither. And the taillights were out. Couldn't see his plates. Probably some drunk who started partying early." He stroked her long hair and let the adrenaline buzz flush out of his bloodstream. Threading his hand through the silky strands, he framed her face.

Her gaze locked on his, and her lips curved in a smile.

He backed her against the lamppost, covering her mouth with his.

Her arms shifted to his shoulders, and she sighed and pressed closer. Her mouth parted.

Fierce need clutched at him. He took her mouth, not waiting to coax her with gentle kisses.

She must have felt the same madness, because she didn't resist, but softened.

With one hand bracing her head, he explored the moist sides of her mouth and tongue. A hush fell over the night. He nipped her bottom lip and swiped the spot with his tongue.

She moaned and snuggled against him, her breasts tight against his chest.

Like a powerful drug, the taste of her fired his senses, sent blood roaring to his groin. The feel of her slim body pressed against his made him want to pleasure her until she was mindless, but he couldn't let her feel what she did to him yet. Too soon. He nuzzled her ear and tongued the sleek curve of her neck.

A horn honked behind them, and a teenager whistled out the window of a passing car. "Get a room!"

With a groan, Nate jerked back and rested his forehead against hers. He wanted to drag her to his cave now, tonight, and not come out. She might only have a few months before she left for school, but that'd be long enough.

He took a step away. Right now, he had to protect her and had to follow the rules at the same time. He smiled down into her beautiful face. "Come on, we need to return you to your car. I'll follow you home to make sure you're safe." He kissed her nose and led her across the street with his palm behind her waist. "In the morning, you can deliver the stuff you found at the library and wave Sereno PD goodbye."

Frowning, she shifted away from his hand, and her stubborn chin tensed. "I need to finish the investigation."

He shook his head. "Absolutely not. Too dangerous."

One auburn eyebrow quirked. "But I can help you figure out…" She stared at him in silence.

He managed not to growl no, but the idiot in the truck had reminded him her safety came first. "You're brilliant, Jana. You showed us a fresh angle. We'll bust that drug ring, no problem."

Chapter Twenty-Two

March 29, 9:05 a.m.

What was it about telling people stuff they didn't want to hear? Nate grimaced. Leaning back in his creaky walnut desk chair, he met his partner's glare. "I don't give a shit if you like what I said. You can't trust the guy."

Mike's jawbones jutted stubbornly, his nostrils flared. "Tomasini's a proven informant."

"Yeah, when he's ratting out the competition moving onto his turf."

Mike wadded a piece of paper and dunked it into the trash. "What about that string of burglaries?"

"East San Jose gang expanding their territory."

"The bank heist?"

"A dude from Oakland." Nate slurped his cold coffee and ran a hand through his hair. "Come on, Gordon. Think! We need a break on this case, and your snitch has given us squat."

"Time to prod Joe Morgan and see which way he jumps?"

"Long past time. But I say we investigate Tomasini first." Nate picked up a pencil and rolled it back and forth across his desk. "Last night at dinner, Jana showed me a list of his properties. The weasel must own ten million in Silicon Valley real estate. Hard to imagine he's strictly legit."

Mike paused, his eyes narrowed. "Hold on. You took Jana out to dinner?"

Cursing his big mouth, Nate avoided his partner's sharp stare and rapped the pencil against the desk. "I bought her a sandwich. She spent the afternoon working on our case."

"I'd call that a date, Kapulani." Mike stuck his nose in Nate's face. "I saw her first."

"No fucking way. Back off," Nate snarled. "You dropped her like a live grenade after the stakeout."

"Bullshit." Mike slammed both his hands on the desk and stood glaring at him. "You know I did it to teach her a lesson."

"Look, I agree she's hot, but she's smart. She's special, not another one of your party girls to play with and drop."

One glance at Mike's sly expression, and his gut plummeted. This conversation had gotten way out of hand, but he had to protect Jana from Mike.

A chilling sensation crept up Nate's spine. No, some other danger stalked her. He stared at the ceiling, buffeted by that eerie feeling again. Why was he so afraid for her?

"You listening, Kapulani?"

Nate shook his head. "Yeah. What?"

"I said, if she's so smart, we should bring her along when we shake down Morgan."

"No way. I won't risk her."

Mike hooted.

"Jana's not a real cop. She's just an intern, damn it! Tomorrow's her last day. She shouldn't play an active role in our investigation."

Flashing a wicked grin and his middle finger, Mike tipped his head toward the door.

Nate turned in time to see a blaze of hazel eyes and copper hair. His heart dropped and tangled with his guts. She had heard every stupid word.

He launched to his feet and sprinted into the corridor, but she'd already rounded the corner and disappeared.

Shit. Now he'd done it. The pencil in his hands snapped in half.

****

8:45 p.m.

Thursday night and Nate's favorite hangout, the Last Chance, boasted a half decent band for a change. He took another sip of his beer.

Jana walked through the door into the neon lit haze. She'd worn her hair down, changed clothes into another one of those too-short sweaters above a too-low, too-tight skirt. Her high heels made her legs look miles long.

He swallowed hard and glanced away. He'd ground the peanut shells in his hands to dust.

With a dazzling smile, she edged toward the group and was greeted by loud cheers from the guys.

Nate stood and offered the empty chair next to his seat.

Her smile didn't reach her frosty hazel eyes. With a searing glance, she moved past him around the table. She squeezed in next to Mike, laid a slender hand on Mike's bicep, and turned on the charm.

Grinding his teeth, Nate slumped over his beer. Rerun time at the Last Chance. Same old scarred wooden tables and dinged up air hockey. Same old minuscule dance floor. Same old Mike, putting moves on the sexiest girl in the place.

Mike snaked his arm over the back of her chair, too damn close to her shoulders, and flashed his lounge-lizard-on-the-prowl look. He leaned closer and mumbled something while tracing a finger along her jaw.

Nate's hands tightened around his mug. His knuckles showed white.

Over Mike's shoulder, Jana met Nate's gaze with an arctic glare. She angled back toward Mike, and her smile transformed her face, made her eyes sparkle. One side of her wide neckline slipped, exposing part of her bare, silky shoulder. A growl rose in his throat, and he lifted his mug to drown it. Man, she tied his insides in knots.

He peered through his half empty glass at them, couldn't help himself.

Mike took her hand and led her to the dance floor.

Damn. A slow one.

Nate picked up his beer and moved to the long bar. He perched on a stool and tried not to stare at the only couple on the floor.

Pathetic. He wished he could look away.

Mike pulled her closer and whispered against her ear. She arched her neck back and laughed. Yeah, Mike was clever. Too damn clever. The big jerk would get his face punched if he didn't stop holding her like that.

Nate took a long draw of his beer. Jamming an elbow on the bar, he leaned his chin on his fist. Shit, if this was what she wanted, he'd smile like nothing bothered him and keep his big fat mouth shut.

Glaring, he straightened. Like hell. He drained the

glass and wiped the froth off his mouth with the back of his hand.

The bleached blonde diva hit a last long note, and Mike's fingers crept toward Jana's ass. He drew her closer, and when she tipped her chin up to say something, Mike angled his head. A growl rumbled in his throat. The son of a bitch was going to kiss her.

With his jaw clenched tight, Nate rose out of his seat, but she dodged the kiss, and Mike's mouth landed on her cheek.

She pressed her lips briefly into a tight smile, patted Mike on the arm, and moved away. Alone.

He shook his head with a laugh. Hot damn, she'd brushed Mike off like yesterday's sushi. Hell. Women never brushed him off.

Nate dropped his gaze, but didn't wipe the gloat off his face before she glanced his way. She flashed him another frigid look, then sauntered back to the table.

His heart jammed up against his tonsils. Nate sank onto his seat and rubbed a hand over his jaw. She wouldn't give him another chance this side of purgatory, unless he talked to her and made her understand.

Mike shouldered through the crowd toward Nate, waving two fingers at the barkeep. "Couple more beers over here." Mike straddled the barstool next to him, plunked down a twenty, and picked up his brew.

The foam on Nate's fresh beer spilled over the top of the glass. He glanced sideways at his partner and chanced it. "You and Jana going out later?"

Mike took a sip of his drink and leveled his gaze. "Funny thing. Couple weeks ago, I figured we'd hook up, maybe long-term. She'd sent all the right signals.

Even stole a quick kiss once in the break room. Super hot."

Staring hard at the head on his brew, Nate listened, but kept his trap closed and his fists wrapped around his mug.

Mike punched him on the shoulder. "This morning you hit it smack on target. She's smart. She's funny. And hot?" He let out a low whistle that set Nate's teeth on edge. "But since last week, I get zero response from her. When I tried to kiss her just now, it was like kissing my sister. Nada."

Nate took his first full breath in an hour and smiled. When he'd kissed Jana last night, man, talk about a hot response. In two minutes, he'd had her trembling, soft, and kissing him back.

His warm lips traced her collarbone and one hand covered her naked breast. The other held her wrists captive over her head while she moaned and arched against him.

Nate shook his head at the erotic vision and fidgeted on the stool. With no blood left in his brain, his khakis fit way too tight. He wiped a finger's width of frost off his mug. Damn straight. Jana was absolutely nothing like his sister.

Even if she was going to school on the East Coast, even if she had years of medical training ahead of her— hell, even if she was living on the moon—he wanted her. Needed her.

She was his.

Not Mike Gordon's.

His, and his alone.

****

8:59 p.m.

Forget cops. Jana glanced at the bar and shot another hostile stare at their broad backs. There they were, slurping beers and elbowing each other. Probably comparing notes on how she kissed. Damn it. She'd looked forward to this party all week, and now those two jerks had ruined her fun.

She flipped her hair over her shoulder and pulled out her compact. Glaring into the tiny mirror, she scrubbed Mike's kiss off her cheek with the back of her hand.

Gritting her teeth, she checked the time. Liv would be here to pick her up in a few minutes. Next week, they'd have a blast on spring break. Maybe they'd meet some hot guys from UC Santa Cruz. Much better than pining after a thickheaded Neanderthal masquerading as a cop.

Who needed Nate's hunky shoulders or melted chocolate eyes or dissolve-your-bones kisses? His condescending attitude made her temper sizzle. Too much like her dad, Colonel James T. Sutherland. She huffed. Men who demanded a brisk "Yes, sir!" made her sick.

Besides, where did he get off, saying she was "only" an intern, not a real cop? She'd found evidence the real cops missed. The snitch those two bumbling idiots trusted had to be involved in something crooked.

She drummed her fingers on the table. What else did she need to convince them Morrie Tomasini was involved? She'd almost gotten Nate to buy in, but maybe his agreement was an act, and all he wanted was sex. Sneaky bastard.

Her hand stilled. What if she searched the police databases? Maybe the FBI files? Probably no point since Mike had already run Tomasini's sheet. But how deep had Mike actually dug, given he wasn't suspicious?

Tomasini hadn't been in California long. She swallowed hard. She had a creepy feeling he had a record wherever he came from, if she could find it.

Nate's expression was grim, and his somber eyes flashed with anger. He held a cell phone in his clenched fist. "Tomasini set Mike up for the ambush, and you can bet that weasel knew exactly who pulled the trigger."

Jana gasped and straightened. All the tiny hairs on her body stood upright, roughening her skin with goose bumps. Murder? She held the edge of the table and breathed slowly until her pulse calmed. She didn't know where her intuition came from, but it almost seemed like someone was whispering clues inside her brain.

If these creepy visions kept grabbing her, she'd have to swallow her convictions and call Granny McAlpine for a protective charm. Jana chuckled. No, maybe she should try psych meds first.

But wherever her suspicion came from, she had to investigate. If Tomasini had manipulated Mike and Nate, they were in danger, and the most likely place to find proof was on the office computer.

One side of her mouth twitched. She'd show them. She'd sweet talk her way past security, sneak in, and find solid evidence. Then she'd leave everything on Nate's desk with a look-what-I-found note, and she'd never have to see his damn sexy grin again.

Jana snapped her compact shut and dropped it into her purse. Her fingers brushed a plastic wrapped package she'd bought this morning. She pulled the rawhide dog toy out and opened the package. Chewing her lip, she juggled the bone in her hand and grinned at the wicked thought. She shouldered her bag. Why not? He'd have to go home and change. Wouldn't be able to follow her. Besides, Nate deserved it.

Putting an extra wiggle in her walk, she watched him watch her cross the room. Watched him drool into his beer and shift on his seat.

She leaned on the bar and gave him a wide smile, batting her lashes for effect. "I bought Bruner a toy. Will you give this to him for me?"

He blinked at her and opened his mouth, but she didn't give him a chance to reply. She suspended the rawhide bone with two fingers and plunked it into his full beer.

Nate's drink splashed over the bar and onto his lap. He shouted and bailed off the stool, but not in time to stay dry.

She covered her mouth and flushed. She hadn't meant to douse him.

Mike hooted and fished out the toy. Holding it over his head, he shouted, "She gave the man a bone!"

Standing mute, Nate glared at her, his dripping hands suspended at his sides. His khakis were soaked from belt to knee, and his face had flushed maroon.

Her heart stumbled, but she gulped and stuck her chin in the air.

"Nice one, Sutherland," Mike cheered.

A sprinkle of catcalls and a round of applause filled the joint.

She met Nate's gaze and sashayed out.

****

10:10 p.m.

Nate slammed his front door and threw his keys on the entry table. He stomped down the hall to change his freaking khakis. His jaw was clenched so tight his teeth hurt.

Where did she get off, pulling a stunt like that in front of his buddies? He'd be taking crap for years. Mike hadn't been any help. The jackass hadn't backed off, but cackled like a lunatic, and kept prodding Nate to go after Jana and show her who was boss.

He shucked his pants and wadded his boxers into a cold, wet lump before heaving them through the bathroom door.

Bruner trotted after him and nudged the pants, snuffling in a pocket.

"Want that?" Nate slipped on a dry pair of boxers before he pulled the soggy chew toy out of his soggy khakis with two fingers. "Here. A present. Pretty sure Jana likes you better than me."

The dog gave a sharp bark, grabbed the bone, and trotted toward the living room. Nate buttoned his dry jeans and followed, but found Bruner sitting on his haunches and whining at the door. "You had your walk, pal."

He flopped on the couch and tried to sort through the mess his big mouth had landed him in. Jana was pissed. He blew out a long sigh. Royally pissed. She didn't seem to understand he wanted to keep her safe.

Leaning against the cushions, he kicked his feet up on the coffee table. He was freaking sick of bone jokes. Didn't help that anytime he was within three feet of Jana, he went half hard and aching.

The dog picked up his new toy. With his stubby tail quivering, he dropped it at Nate's feet. Nate hurled the bone toward the kitchen, but instead of chasing after the rawhide, Bru returned to pawing at the door.

Nate rubbed his tense chin. Eventually, she'd listen. "No point in calling her tonight. She'd just hang up." He should let her cool off, wait until tomorrow. She had one more day on the payroll. If she didn't show up at the station first thing, he'd find her and apologize.

Bruner continued to whine, but bounded over to him and nudged his leg before pacing the length of the couch.

"Sit, Bru."

The dog obeyed for a split second. Then, barking furiously, he dashed to the back door.

Nate checked the porch. Nothing.

"What's wrong, boy?" He frowned at Bruner and followed him.

When he opened the door to the garage, the dog charged down the steps and put his paws up on the SUV.

"No. We're not going to the dog park, buddy. It's late. Maybe tomorrow I'll take you with me to Jana's."

The dog let out a long howl.

Shaking his head slowly, Nate scratched the back of his neck. He couldn't believe it, but repeated her name anyway.

Bruner pranced around the car, barking his fool head off.

Chapter Twenty-Three

March 29, 11:50 p.m.

Jana darted past dispatch toward Nate and Mike's office. A twinge of guilt fired her pulse, but she squared her shoulders. She still worked here. Right? And she had forgotten her jacket. The fact she'd come in this late to do more than retrieve it wasn't anyone else's business.

She turned her key in the knob and ducked inside the darkened office, leaning her back against the door until her heart slowed and gave her space to breathe. Gradually, her eyes adjusted to the darkness.

If she found proof the creep, Tomasini, was up to no good, Nate would understand why she sneaked in here. He might even forgive her for the stunt she'd pulled tonight at the party.

Her pulse throbbed at her temples. The embarrassment she'd caused him nagged at her, made her stomach twist. Yeah, he'd sounded like a pompous ass this morning, but maybe she'd stomped off too fast, jumped to a conclusion instead of giving him a chance to explain. She stood still, as if anchored in place.

Who had said those words to her? It couldn't have been Nate. She ran her hands through her hair, tucking the heavy mass behind her ears.

Should she turn on the light? No. If she left the

room dark, the officers on swing shift would assume she'd found her coat and gone home.

She felt her way across the room, found Nate's desk, and slid into his chair. She poked the monitor button and wiggled the mouse. The screen glowed an eerie blue.

Good thing he never shut down his computer, since she didn't know his password. But where to start? She tied her pain-in-the-ass hair into a knot and scooted closer to the screen. As part of her job, she'd accessed the FBI databases before, so she had the system online in two minutes. "Tomasini, Morrie" produced next to nothing. She hissed out a long breath and squinted at the screen.

No arrests in California. A misdemeanor DUI conviction in Massachusetts during the early eighties. A sealed juvenile record, too. Probably what Mike had found. But now she had a birthdate and prints.

"Tomasini's dirty," she muttered. "Just have to peer under the right rock." She spotted an alias in the earliest record. "Tom Tomas. Worth a look."

She swallowed to dampen her dry throat and continued the hunt. Her foot tapped against the chair rung as she searched the fingerprint database.

The screen filled with a dozen arrest records. She let out a squeak and clamped a hand over her mouth. Another alias popped up. Then another. Felonies in New York and Florida. Most recently, conspiracy and racketeering in New Jersey.

The birthdate matched. The prints matched. She did a silent victory dance in her chair. "Maybe now those idiots will listen."

Should she print the records and leave them for

Nate? She scrolled down. There were pages and pages of reports. Someone might hear the printer, but she had to take that risk.

She checked the paper supply and tented her jacket around the machine to muffle the noise. With her fingers clicking on the keyboard, she routed one document after another into the print queue.

Heavy, purposeful footsteps echoed out in the hall. Someone was coming this way.

For a second, she stopped breathing. "Almost there. Hurry," she whispered. With shaky fingers, she pressed print on the last rap sheet.

Keys clattered against the doorknob.

Her skin went cold and clammy, and her knees weakened.

"See you later, Flynn," Nate called, and a second male voice responded.

Her heart thudded against her ribs. Just as the laser printer spit out the last page, she flicked off the monitor and eased behind the coatrack. Lousy hiding place. The door shielded her, but if he did more than glance around the room, he'd spot her in a second. Squeezing her eyes shut, she stood still and prayed he was in too much of a hurry to check out the office.

Nate flipped on the light. With her face concealed by the folds of his raincoat, she couldn't see him, but his footsteps crossed the room.

"Come out, Jana."

Damn. Busted. Fixing her gaze on her feet, she stepped from behind the coatrack.

He waited in silence.

Blushing, she peeked at him and shrugged. Best to say nothing. He'd see through her lies, anyway.

Arms crossed, stance wide, he filled half the room. His square jaw tensed, but he remained mute.

Her face grew hotter, and she toed the floor. "How did you know I was here?"

"Your perfume."

She nodded and clasped her hands behind her back.

"And Liv told me where you were headed."

Jana's lips tightened. "The rat." She glanced at the door, but dismissed the possibility of escape.

With a loud click, he locked the door, and then took two giant steps toward her.

She swallowed with difficulty. The amused smile on his face made her jaw drop. "You're not angry?"

"No. I guess I deserved your surprise at the bar. Maybe what I said this morning was stupid, but you didn't give me time to explain." He reached for her and drew a finger down her cheek.

Her eyes met his, and she couldn't drag them away. "What you said hurt my feelings, but I overreacted. Well, just a little."

"Just a little," he repeated.

Her pulse reeled at the humor in his smile.

Taking her hands in his, he held them lightly and drew small circles on the backs with his thumbs.

She closed her eyes, absorbing the sizzling warmth of his touch that radiated through her body.

He dropped one hand and tilted her chin.

She peered at him through her lashes and was snared by his intense gaze.

"Did you find what you came for?" His deep voice sent more waves of heat along her spine.

With a quick nod, she answered his smile. "Did you?"

He cocked his head and searched her face. "Think so."

His lips brushed hers, and her eyelids fluttered closed again. The kiss sparked deeper sensations, muted her resistance. She shivered. Shaking off her growing lust, she arched back and said, "I found…"

"Shh." He touched a fingertip on her lips and drew her to him. "Later," he murmured against her mouth.

She stretched to return his kiss, nipping his bottom lip with her teeth. His taste washed through her. Heavy. Dark. Passionate. She knew the familiar taste and feel of him. Everything inside her trembled, and the heat low in her belly liquefied.

Tangling his fingers in her hair, he deepened the kiss and backed her against the desk. His tongue danced with hers. He molded his mouth to her lips, filling her.

Need stirred, fierce and hungry, and gathered strength. She snuggled closer, relishing the sinewy hardness of his arms and shoulders.

Didn't matter they were in his office, she loosened a shirt button and slid her palm across his taut belly, caressing his warm skin.

He explored her sides and waist. With each touch, tingles sparked along her nerves. He lifted her onto the edge of the desk, slipped a hand under the hem of her sweater, and traced her navel ring. "So sexy."

Her breath caught in a rush.

His hand moved to the underside of her breast. "Bare skin? Oh, Jana." Impatiently, he lifted her sweater. "If I'd known you weren't wearing a bra, I'd have thrown you over my shoulder and kidnapped you from that damn bar."

The image flashed into her mind and tightened the

raw need clawing at her. She moaned his name, a low, ragged noise humming from her throat.

He found a tight nipple with his thumb. When he stroked it, she pressed her breast harder against his fingertips.

Pleasure burst through her, exquisite torture heated her center. Warm, wet, and needy.

His mouth savored her nipples until they were hard and aching for more.

Her head swam, and her fingers dug into his back. She bit her lip, but couldn't restrain a cry.

Lifting her short skirt, his hands roamed over her thighs. He found her core through her damp, satiny panties and silenced her with long kisses while he built the need within her.

One broad finger slipped under the elastic and inside.

Sweet spasms pulsed through her, and she gasped.

He broke the kiss and smiled down at her. His dark eyes, black with passion, stared at her with an intensity that made her pulse leap faster.

Gathering her courage, Jana drew a hand along his fly and traced his erection, rewarded by his shudder. She stroked him through the rough denim and watched his eyes glaze.

"I want more," he rumbled, his breath coming in harsh gulps.

The ache magnified and doubled. She couldn't find the words, but she wanted all of him.

She sprawled on his naked chest, her head cradled on his warm, broad shoulder. "I want more, Nate. Make love to me again," she whispered against his neck and tongued the skin above his pulsing vein.

A brisk knock on the door jolted her back to reality. Her heart tumbled, and Nate swore under his breath.

Pulse pounding, she leaped off the desk and straightened her sweater and skirt, rolling her eyes at the ceiling. Another few seconds and they'd have been making love in the freaking police station. Had those crazy visions turned her brain to oatmeal?

He grabbed two jackets, tossed one to her, and draped the other over his arm.

"Sergeant?" the male voice demanded.

"Yeah, just a sec." With a guilty grin, Nate headed for the door.

She stuffed the printouts into her backpack.

"Hey, Lieutenant Greene." Nate turned to her and cleared his throat loudly. "Thanks, Ms. Sutherland, for remembering to log off your computer. Good security."

Her cheeks burned. "Uh, sure. Evening, Lieutenant," she said and dodged around the Watch Commander. With a super human effort, she strolled slowly down the hall instead of sprinting away.

"Idiot," she groaned and slapped her forehead. She'd acted like a sex-crazed tramp with her boss. And in his office? On his desk?

She shuddered. Thank God she was almost done working here. How would she ever face Nate again? Maybe she'd call in sick tomorrow.

Chapter Twenty-Four

March 30, 12:35 a.m.

Nate paused in his office doorway and shoved a hand in his pocket, watching Greene disappear toward dispatch. Why did he let Jana leave? He needed the info she'd found.

"Yeah, right." Nate heaved a sigh. She had him so turned on he'd hardly heard a word the lieutenant said. He shook his head, blind and deaf above the roar of his aroused body. Nope, he could tell himself he only wanted to see the evidence on Tomasini, only wanted to talk to her, but that was a crock.

He pivoted and stalked to Mike's desk. Rummaging around in the center drawer, he found a small purple box of condoms. He tossed it in the air and weighed the possibilities.

Three should be enough, and he'd replace the box before Mike missed them. Seemed kind of arrogant anyway. Unlikely they'd need protection at all tonight, the way she lit out of here. He dropped the box in his pocket anyway, locked the office door, and hustled toward his car.

He rubbed a hand over his jaw. The heat rose on his face, but a smile formed on his lips. Three more minutes alone with her and she'd have been naked and flat on her back. He squeezed his eyes shut and sucked in a guilty breath. Never mind that they were in his office. In police headquarters. And she still worked for him.

Right now he could barely walk for the aching, pulsing parts south of his belt. His body begged him to catch her and make love to her until neither of them could move.

When he clicked open the car door and slid behind the wheel, Bruner yipped and wiggled across the seat to greet him. The dog nosed Nate's hand and sniffed hard. "You were right, boy. We'll go after her. Now sit."

Gunning the engine, Nate squealed onto the main drag, but resisted flipping on the lights and siren, even though it felt like an emergency to him.

Seven and a half minutes later, he drove up behind her car just as she started toward the steps to her squat, stucco apartment building. He stomped on the emergency brake and bounded across the grass after her. "Jana, wait."

She glanced over her shoulder at him but flounced up the stairs with a toss of her hair.

He took three quick steps and hurdled the railing. Grabbing her wrist, he drew her toward him.

"Turn loose."

"Not yet." His heart thundered, but he refused to let her lock him out tonight. He cupped her neck, and his focus narrowed to her mouth.

She opened her lips as if to protest, but he angled his mouth and covered hers.

Her backpack thudded onto the cement porch. Her hands balled against his shoulders in brief protest, but he tightened his arms and molded her closer. She quivered and softened. Her fingers splayed out, and she traced his collar.

With a shudder, he smoothed his hands down her back.

He might have started the kiss rough, but once he'd claimed her, he took it slow and easy. He had all the time in the world. With each lick of his tongue and nip of his teeth, he wanted her more.

Her hands crept around his neck, and she flattened against him. His hard cock nestled against her belly. Pleasure spiked through him. She hadn't zipped her jacket, so he could feel the hard points of her bare nipples through their clothes.

He rubbed against her, and she gave a hungry, greedy cry. The delicate scent of her arousal wafted up and tore a groan from his throat.

The porch light flicked on.

When he broke the kiss, she arched her neck and met his gaze. Protective, possessive warmth surged in his veins. Her eyes were wide and glassy, her pupils dilated. Her full lips were swollen, slick, and parted. He kissed her quick and hard.

"Jana, that you?" The door opened, and a pretty, dark haired woman peered out. "Oh, I see Nate found you."

"Hey, Liv. Thanks again." He grinned.

Blushing furiously, Jana glanced over her shoulder at her roommate. "Yeah, we were just talking…"

Liv snickered. "Right. Why don't you come in and get comfortable while you 'talk'? I'm headed to my room to watch a video." She turned, but left the door gaping open behind her. "I'll crank up the sound so you can talk all you want."

Jana squeezed her eyes shut and hid her face

against his chest. "Want to come in?" she asked, her voice muffled.

From inside the SUV, Bruner let loose a pitiful howl and jumped against the window.

"Shit. He'll wake the neighborhood." Nate released her and cursed under his breath. Next time, he'd crate the damn dog and leave him home, no matter how hard the little turkey begged.

****

1:05 a.m.

Avoiding Nate's gaze, Jana stroked the puppy curled on a quilt in front of her brown plaid sofa. With her hands twisted together, she rose to her knees and groped for words. Why had she invited Nate inside? He was still her boss. Bad enough she'd acted like a wanton in the office. One little kiss outside, and she'd crawled all over him. What must he think? She forced herself to meet his eyes. "I can't believe Bruner just flopped down and went to sleep."

"Guess he wore himself out tonight." Standing close behind her, Nate laid a hand under her elbow and helped her up. His solid body radiated warmth, and her breath quickened.

She turned into his arms and leaned back to see his expression. His gaze swept her, triggering a tidal wave of heat that rushed up her neck to her face. She shifted away. "I printed a bunch of arrest records. Let me go get them."

"We can check the evidence tomorrow. Maybe next week," he said, his voice deeper than normal. With his hands on her waist, he drew her flush against him. "Right now, all I can think about is how much I want you."

Suddenly shy, she blinked, open mouthed. "Nate…"

"I know you might not be ready yet, but I have to be honest. I want to make love with you, Jana. Now. Tonight."

Her cheeks burned like they were flashing neon. She gulped and stared at her feet. She'd be honest, too. "I don't have much experience," she blurted. "Nate, I like kissing you, I even liked your hands on me, but I've only had sex a few times, and I'm not very good."

His eyebrows rose, and he chuckled. "In the office, it took only the barest touch and you came for me. Relax. Trust me."

"Relax? Tough for me to do when you're moving at warp speed."

He tucked her head against his chest and smoothed her hair. His breath warm against her scalp, he repeated, "Trust me. We won't do anything you don't want to do."

She shuddered and licked her lips, watching his gaze fasten on her mouth. The blatant need on his face bolstered her confidence, made her feel almost powerful. She could let herself be vulnerable with him.

Drawing a deep breath, she took his hand and grinned. "My bedroom? Liv already got an eyeful."

Laughing, Nate scooped her off her feet. "Wouldn't want to interrupt her movie."

She curled her arms over his shoulders and around his neck, feeling his muscles bunch. She snuggled against him and sneaked the tip of her tongue around his ear.

He jerked. His hand squeezed her bottom as she sucked the lobe into her mouth.

"Here?" he asked. At her nod, he backed through the bedroom door, kicked it shut, and laid her on the bed.

Flicking on the light, he took off his shoes and joined her. Liv was right. He moved with the grace and focus of a predator intent on the hunt. His eyes were dark and lidded with desire, his lips moist and firm.

With his body tense and steely, he kissed her again. His languid mouth worshiped hers with deep, unhurried caresses. He suckled her lower lip, and heat arrowed to the heavy ache between her legs.

She squirmed and reached for the hem of her sweater.

"We have all night. Let me touch you," he murmured against her chin. He shifted her hands above her head and held them there for a moment while he kissed her again. Rising on an elbow, he drew his palm over her sweater and skimmed each breast before concentrating on her nipples. He slowly moved the soft, textured fabric back and forth over the tips.

She trembled.

He toyed with the hard peaks through the knit. She sucked in a breath.

He shaped her breasts with his fingers, one after the other until the sweater clung to each one. He met her eyes. One finger trailed around a nipple where it poked upward, blatantly hard and aching for his touch. "Your breasts are beautiful."

"But don't you want to touch my skin?" she whimpered.

"Warp speed?" he teased with a smile and drew off the garment. He brushed her bare breasts with a feather light caress that left her skin tingling. He cupped one breast while he kissed his way down her neck and over her collarbone, then ducked to tweak her navel ring and tongued the soft flesh.

Moving with glorious patience, he kissed the pale mounds of her breasts, licked every inch before he finally settled and suckled a nipple deep.

The pull shot straight to her center, and she moaned his name. Straining toward him, she tangled her hands in his hair and writhed, rubbing her thighs together.

Teeth and tongue tugging gently, he bunched her skirt around her waist. He slipped a hand underneath her panties and grazed her swollen nub.

Unexpected tension tightened her nerves, and she spread her legs wider for him, trying to draw him closer.

His mouth shifted to the other breast, pulling in that tight peak.

Exquisite torture.

He parted her damp folds and slipped a finger inside.

She couldn't keep still under his hands. He spread her slick moisture, circling her nub with his thumb. He added a finger, stretching her, and pressed. The sensations spiraled.

"Nate!" Pleasure rose and crested in a deluge of throbbing waves as she pulsed around his fingers.

With a knowing smile, he shrugged out of his own shirt and pants. He was gorgeous, with smooth, tanned skin over well-defined muscles. A line of dark hair arrowed below his navel and nestled at the base of his huge, powerful erection.

Heat sparked in her loins and cascaded through her

body. Her hand stretched toward him on its own, but she hesitated and pulled back.

He lay next to her on his side and waited while she drew closer in her own time.

Licking her lips, she reached out and touched him. When her fingers slid around him and tightened, he closed his eyes, and a hum rumbled from his lips.

She stroked, awestruck at the feel of warm skin sliding over steel.

A moment later, Nate hissed and shifted her hand away. Kissing her hard, he eased off her skirt and panties. Then he sat back. His hot gaze swept her face, her breasts, her belly, and the triangle of hair between her legs.

She blushed again, fighting the urge to cover herself.

"Your skin's so soft and beautiful. Your freckles look like gold dust…" His breath hitched, and he shook his head. "I feel like I've said that before."

"Maybe in my dreams?" She framed his face with her hands. The evening stubble on his jaw rasped her fingertips. "But I think I'll die if you don't love me soon."

Grinning, he opened a foil packet and rolled the thin latex over himself. Then he settled onto the bed and spread her legs with his. Wiry hair rubbed against her thighs, and shivers cascaded through her.

He kissed her, and the heavy, pulsing part of him nudged against her. But he balanced most of his weight on his forearm and kept toying with her sensitive flesh when she needed him inside.

Her hands curled into fists against his shoulders. She loosened them and drew her nails over his back until her fingers dug into his buttocks and forced him closer.

He groaned and thrust.

Arching, she wrapped her ankles around his waist and drew him in.

He slowly worked his way deeper.

Stretched her.

Filled her.

But she needed him to move.

He touched her again, and she melted around his hardness.

Chapter Twenty-Five

March 31, 8:55 a.m.

Nate's whistle echoed through the department hall. The dispatch operator tossed him a quick salute. The phones were quiet, and the operators were talking and sipping their coffee. Not much going on this morning.

He turned toward his office with a smile on his face. No, a satisfied grin. He hadn't felt like this since...

Tilting his head, he paused in the doorway for an instant before entering the office. No, he'd never felt like this before.

Mike glanced up from a report and hiked one eyebrow. "Morning, partner. You're late."

"Been downstairs. Checked the evidence room." Nate stared hard at the inbox sitting cockeyed in the middle of his desk, where Jana's backside had shoved it last night. Straightening the box, he fought the heat that crept up his collar.

Mike dug a pen out of his center drawer, and Nate grimaced. If Mike missed his stash of condoms and made the connection, he'd never stop the razzing. Then he'd start on Jana. Nate shuddered. He'd rather be coated with chocolate syrup and staked over a hill of fire ants.

Better buy another box at lunch. He restrained a chuckle. Maybe a case. It had taken all his ingenuity to make those three condoms last until he left her place very early this morning.

"I asked what you were looking for," Mike shouted.

"Huh? Oh, yeah." Nate finally sat, wishing his ears would cool off. "Checked on the evidence from the drug bust last month. Prosecutor poked me the other day."

Mike nodded, clicking his pen a few times. "Anything reappear?"

"Nah. Don't know who screwed up, but that case is dead."

"Sucks. Ton of footwork down the drain." Mike kicked back from the desk and stretched his legs. "Been thinking about the current investigation. What about setting up a sting?"

"Flush the perps into the open? Makes sense."

"Morrie said the drug buy would be today."

"Yeah, like I trust your snitch."

"Got anything better?"

"Doesn't matter. Can't assume his info's solid."

"Maybe we should sneak someone in to nose around."

Frowning, Nate rubbed at the sudden itch on the back of his neck. "Where? Not Tomasini's store."

"The high school." Mike rapped the computer table where Jana usually sat. A grin spread slowly over his face. "She looks the part."

Nate sat ramrod straight and crossed his arms over his chest. "Undercover without training?"

"She'll be fine. The high school's low risk. It's the perfect setup."

The triumphant tone of his voice sent those fire

ants creeping through Nate's gut. "No way."

"Then we're back to Tomasini's tip."

Jana marched into the office, her high heels tapping a staccato beat, and her walk loose-limbed and confident. Her hips swayed. Her ponytail brushed tight slacks and showed off her tiny waist and curvy ass.

Nate concentrated on keeping his tongue from dangling out the corner of his mouth like Bruner's.

"I found it." Her hazel eyes gleamed. Mike glanced from one to the other, and his grin widened. "I'll bite, Ms. Sutherland. What did you find?"

"Proof that Morrie Tomasini, also known as Tom Tomas, is a crook." She fanned several dozen papers from her backpack on Mike's desk.

"Where'd you get these?" he asked, flipping through the printouts.

"The FBI database."

Nate cleared his throat. "We worked late last night." The morning light on her skin made those little freckles across her nose and cheeks stand out. He covered a smile with his hand. He couldn't wait until he could wake up next to her and kiss each one in the light of dawn.

Mike rubbed a knuckle against his chin. "So he's got a crooked past. There's nothing in the last few years. Nothing we can arrest him for. And no proof Tomasini's involved in the drug ring."

"How'd he buy all the property he owns? And what about his dummy corporation, Atlantic Partners?" She bumped the inbox aside and scooted onto the edge of his desk, right about where she'd been last night.

A blush highlighting her cheekbones, she turned sideways to meet his gaze and crossed her legs.

Those slacks did nice things for her ass. If he stretched, he could wrap his hands around her waist and scoot her backwards onto his lap.

"Nate. Would you pay attention?" Eyes sparkling, she chuckled.

He tore his gaze away from her sweet backside and focused on her face.

"Tomasini has a long list of felony convictions on the East Coast. Drug sales, extortion, racketeering," she pointed out.

"But nothing in California," Mike said.

"I haven't had time to track every connection or alias, but remember, I located arrest records for serious felonies. I want you to take him seriously. I want..." She lowered her lashes. "I wanted to keep you both safe."

"Have to admit she uncovered evidence we missed." Nate winked at her. His imagination had her under him and naked again. Maybe bent over the edge of the desk with those slacks around her ankles. He shifted in his seat, but couldn't get comfortable. Thank God today was her last day.

Mike pointed at the rap sheets on his desk. "Yep, but nothing we can show a judge. Maybe Tomasini is a lying sack of shit, but we can't justify a search warrant with these."

"No, but she exposed your crooked snitch."

"Exposed the danger," she interrupted, her eyes flickering wide.

His instincts twanged. "My gut says we need to move on this now. Drag the snitch in and question him. See what his story is. Maybe shove Joe Morgan in the next cell and apply pressure."

"No leverage. We need something on them first." Mike stared at the rap sheets. "No evidence, no leverage, no warrant."

Nate rose and paced the room, while Jana watched in silence, her gaze tracking his path.

Mike straightened. "Morrie said the drug deal would go down at the gas station this afternoon."

"Today?" Hands clenched on her thighs, she swallowed quickly.

"Yeah, but I don't trust him," Nate insisted.

"So we set a trap."

Furrowing his brow, Nate shot his partner a shut-your-mouth glare and swung back into his seat. "Don't even think it."

Mike stood facing Jana, his thumbs hooked in his belt. "You still work here. Want to help one more time?"

Nate smashed a fist on the desk. "No, she can't."

She startled and turned to him. "Can't what?"

"Go undercover." Mike's gaze swept from ponytail to high heels.

Nate locked his jaw. He wanted to shove her behind him and rip his partner's throat out.

But her face creased with an excited smile, and she leaned forward. "Cool. What do I do?"

"Simple." Mike picked up a pen and clicked it. "Dress like a student, maybe one of the slackers, and hang out at the high school. Find out where the drug sale's really happening."

Nate slammed both palms on his desk and shoved. His chair rocketed across the room and crashed into the filing cabinet. "No fucking way, Gordon."

"Relax, partner. We can score a warrant, no

problem. What could happen?" Mike flipped his pen in the air and caught it. "We'll wire her. She won't go anywhere near the actual buy. We can keep her safe."

Nate's gut twisted in a figure eight, and he threw his hands in the air. "You can't guarantee that. It's too dangerous. Scamming felons? Absolutely not."

That earned him a baleful glare as she hopped off the desk. "I'll volunteer."

Nate's shoulders sagged. "You're killing me, Jana."

Mike crowed and gave her a noisy kiss on the cheek. "That's my girl. Now, go get yourself dolled up and be back here at one. The grungier the better. I'll start the warrant." He headed out the door.

Smiling, she turned to Nate and laid a hand on his chest. "It'll be fine. I want to help, and the high school's not dangerous."

****

11:55 a.m.

A tall, purple-haired teenager dressed in black slouched against the office doorframe. How the hell did that kid get past security?

Nate frowned at her. His gaze traveled slowly up long, shapely legs in thick-soled, lace up boots over ripped, safety-pinned tights. He ogled the leather skirt barely covering her crotch. His gaze bounced to her face, and his mouth fell open. "Jana?"

Waving her arms in the air, she pirouetted. "What do you think?"

He rose and approached her slowly, taking in the skimpy black leather vest under an unbuttoned black shirt. The shirttails hung longer than her skirt in back, almost to her knees.

But the damn vee at the vest's hem played peek-a-boo with her bellybutton ring. She wore some kind of push-up bra, because the pale skin of her breasts mounded above the leather. Shit. His fingers twitched, and his cock pulsed. In that blatantly bad-girl-oozing-sex outfit, she was the most compelling disaster he'd ever seen.

Her hazel eyes twinkled through tons of black eye goo, and her silky red hair was gone. She looked like a porcupine with stiff, purple spikes he'd never want to touch, much less tunnel his fingers through. "Please tell me you're wearing a wig."

"Liv helped me cut it, but the color's sprayed in. It'll wash out." She ruffled the jagged hair on her nape and giggled. "The length's been bugging me all week. All that hair felt so heavy on my neck."

She whirled around again, modeling the Goth outfit. The black cross on her beaded necklace swung between her breasts, and chunky, wooden earrings dangled from her lobes. "It took half an hour to hook all these safety pins on, and Liv sacrificed a brand new pair of tights. Do you like my new piercing?"

"Uh..." A shiny chrome button above one nostril marred her face. He curled his lip. "Why?"

She laid her black-nailed hand on his arm and squeezed playfully. "Relax, it's fake."

Relief flooded through him and weakened his knees.

"I wish I had a camera so you could see your expression." Her laughter was clear and genuine.

He joined in. "Looks too damn real."

"It's magnetic. Liv had the nose ring left from Halloween. The dog collar, too. Bruner would look so tough wearing this. Grrr." She crinkled her nose and showed him her white teeth as she ran a nail along the wide, chrome-studded leather.

He studied her anything-for-a-lark expression for a long moment and then glanced overhead while he gripped his fraying patience. Did she think this was fun and games, a Halloween prank? How could he convince her to forget the whole scheme, strip off the costume and shower away those purple spikes?

Arms braced against the tile, he stared at the mangled bar of soap in his hand while hot water beat on his chest. Her pebbled nipples pressed against his back, and her wet, slick fingers circled his hard cock and stroked.

Lust spiked through him, made him stagger. He sucked in a breath and damped down the ache. Think about calculus. Think about income taxes. Think about anything but locking the door and taking her on his desk, hard and fast.

She glanced toward the hall. Closing the distance between them, she rested her hands on his shoulders and smiled.

Frowning, he shifted her to arm's length. God, she was so young. So innocent. "This isn't some dress-up party, Jana. And believe me, these creeps aren't playing Trick-or-Treat. You could be in danger. Last week, there was a stabbing at Sereno High."

Her expression grew serious; her face paled under the heavy makeup. She closed her eyes for a moment and leaned into him.

Sweeping her close, he held her steady. In the circle of his arms, she still felt and smelled like his Jana. "Are you okay?"

She rubbed her forehead. "I think so, but I've been having the weirdest déjà vu the past few days. I'm terrified for you."

An icy chill touched the back of his neck. "Creepy. You felt them, too? Then you should understand why I'm scared." He tipped her chin and studied her eyes. Normal, reactive pupils. Her color returned. "This sting's too risky. You don't have the undercover training to handle problems if anything goes wrong. You can't do this."

She blinked at him, moving out of his reach. "I can't explain why, but I know I have to."

"When you said déjà vu, what did you mean?"

One hand rubbed her jawline, and the faintest blush rose on her cheekbones. "I'm freaked out. At first, I had these flashes. About you and us. But now it feels almost like someone's talking in my brain. When people hear voices, they get locked up."

"You're not crazy, Jana. I..."

Mike sauntered into the office and released a long wolf whistle.

Nate glared at him.

"Hey, hot stuff. Love the clunky boots." Mike dumped a couple bags on his desk and held up a paper. "Spent all morning convincing Judge Pascal to hand over a warrant. You ready?"

Much as Nate wanted to, he couldn't stop her. "You can still back out."

She glanced at him, bit her lip, and nodded at Mike.

"Brought the wire. I can help you put it on in a minute." Mike flexed his fingers.

Nate snatched the electronics out of Mike's hand.

"I'll do it."

"Suit yourself." Pulling a banana out of one bag, Mike perched on the edge of his desk. He started to peel, looking eager for the show.

"Get out," Nate snarled.

Laughing hard enough to bust a gut, Mike hopped off and bowed. "Oh, and partner? Replace the condoms." He closed the door behind him, but his gleeful howls rang from the hall.

Nate gritted his teeth. "Mike enjoys giving me crap." For a nickel, he'd pound the guy into next week.

She turned to him. Bright pink color had flooded her cheeks. "He knows, doesn't he? About last night."

"Figured it out. Guess I'm kind of obvious." Nate watched her expression closely. In a department this size, rumors would spread fast, but he didn't care if the world knew. Would she?

"Good." A slow, disarming smile moved across her face, and she shrugged. "No secrets that way."

The cold spot in his gut melted away, and he released his breath.

She gave him a quick kiss, and then blotted the dark purple lipstick from his mouth with a finger.

Hunger roared through his system. He concentrated on not grasping her wrist and drawing her finger into his mouth. He'd left her bed only a few hours earlier, but she smelled so good up close. He ached to make love to her again.

Forcing himself to back away and work on untangling the wires, he hefted the receiver. "Take off your shirt and unbutton the vest."

"Mmm, Nate." She eyed him through half-closed lids as she shed the layers.

Her pale midriff and arms were bare above the low-slung skirt, and her fragile, black lace bra did incredible things for her breasts. His throat tightened. "Your skin is beautiful."

"You're giving me chills. After work, do you want to go home and play bust the bad girl?"

A warm claw of need grabbed him and shook him hard. He drew closer until he whispered against her nape, his breath stirring the fine hairs, "I want to reach inside that bra, pop your nipples out, and suck them."

She shivered and turned to meet his gaze, her pupils huge and dark, and her lips parted.

He glanced at the closed door and tugged his tie loose. The office had a lock, but how long would Mike be gone? "How about I throw you back on the desk again? Get you as hot as you're making me?"

Eyes glazed, she made a hungry noise.

Footsteps thumped in the hall, and he blew out a disgusted breath. Don't be an idiot. He kissed her hard. "Later. We'll have all the time in the world together."

Her brows rose, and her eyes rounded for a second. "I hope so," she said and brushed her hand across her cheek.

He concentrated on the pile of technology in front of him. When he passed her the tiny earpiece and tested the volume, his hands fumbled. But he clamped his jaw and kept from grabbing her.

She fluffed a strand of purple hair over the device. Invisible.

Lifting her arm, she allowed him to thread the wire down her neck and under her bra strap.

He glanced down her back, and his brows rose in unison. A tattoo snaked over the top of her ass, disappearing beneath her tight, low-slung skirt. "What's that?"

She peeked over her shoulder and smoothed a hand along the base of her spine. "A tramp stamp."

His jaw dropped.

Grinning, she added, "It's fake."

Chapter Twenty-Six

March 31, 3:15 p.m.

Nate slouched under the steering wheel of the old unmarked sedan. He'd backed the Ford into a library parking space. The view of the high school entrance was decent, but they were across the street and half a block away.

The two-story, Depression-era building, set behind a palm-studded lawn, looked solid and safe from afar, but Sereno PD fielded weapon calls a few times a month at the school, and you could get a buzz from the dope fumes just walking down the hallways.

They hadn't busted any kids for coke, meth, or worse yet, but he'd heard rumors. How far would drug-dealing scumbags go to make a buck? His jaw ached with tension. Any minute now, Jana would waltz right in, unarmed and half naked.

Mike leaned forward in the passenger seat and adjusted the surveillance monitor.

"Where are you?" Nate asked into the microphone.

Jana's car lock beeped in his ear, and he winced.

"Walking toward the front steps. Will you stop worrying? You're worse than my dad."

He kneaded the ridge between his brows and barked, "Damn it! I'm not your dad."

"Duh."

Nate cracked his knuckles for the third time. "Can't wait to meet him if he keeps you in line."

She snorted delicately. "Who says he does?"

Mike snickered and dug in the glove compartment. "We got any snacks? Didn't get much lunch."

"How can you eat?" Nate shifted uncomfortably. He rubbed the crick in his neck and itched to stretch his legs. No. He itched to chase after Jana and drag her back by her short, neon purple hair. Didn't matter if she hollered bloody murder, he'd have her smiling again after a couple hours in bed.

First, they had to finish this operation. He glared at his partner. Hands down, this sting was Mike's stupidest idea ever. The wire provided her some protection, but they were too far away if she got into real trouble.

Nate drummed on the dashboard while she climbed the imposing stone steps. She paused for a split second and glanced his way. Then the double doors closed behind her.

Goose bumps peppered his neck. He leaned his head against the window, watching the woman he loved take a huge risk with only the flimsiest safeguards.

He checked his mirror. His stomach twisted like someone had doubled him over with a right cross. Loved? He swallowed convulsively.

Hell. It didn't matter she was ten years younger than him. He was crazy about her.

He sank his chin onto his palm and scrubbed his hand over his mouth. What a blind, thickheaded, dim-witted, besotted fool. He'd fallen for a twenty-one-year-old college girl who looked like jailbait. Talk about thinking with your dick. He rotated his jaw to ease a cramp.

Talk about shitty timing, too. She'd head to medical school in September, and then what? At best, four years of jetlag and phone sex.

He closed his eyes. Jana was too young to imagine forever. Too many things she hadn't experienced yet. Her excitement over this assignment proved that. A sick feeling grabbed the pit of his stomach and spread to every cell of his body. Only a matter of time before she moved on and stuck him with a hollowed-out heart.

Ain't love grand?

A buzzer rang, and classes let out for the afternoon. Nate turned up the volume on the receiver and cleared the tightness in his throat. Teenaged voices echoed in the hallways and filtered through Jana's microphone.

Kids shouted.

Lockers banged.

"Nice rack," one jerk called in his new, crackly baritone.

Listening to her boots clunk along the hall, Nate's temper flared. Probably swinging her hips in that short, tight skirt and smiling at every pimple-faced punk she passed. Her footsteps stopped.

"Thanks," she purred. "Oh, I love your hot ear cuff."

Nate ground his teeth while she flirted, his hands clenching the wheel.

"Damn, she's got a hit. Zeroed right in." Mike laughed. "Too bad she doesn't want to be a cop. She's a natural."

Nate tugged at his earlobe and listened.

"I'm new." Her voice came through clearly. "And I sorta wanna, like, party tonight."

"Yeah?" answered the baritone.

"Wanna keep me company?" She drew out her vowels.

"Sure, babe."

She gave a little snort of disgust, and Nate choked back a laugh. She hated being called babe.

****

Jana batted her lashes at the tall, skinny slacker leaning against an open locker. The reek of marijuana nearly choked her, but she moved a half step closer and waggled a finger at him. "No, no, no. You gotta call me Jay-Jay."

His Adam's apple bobbed. He nodded, lank dark hair falling into his glazed-over, bloodshot black eyes. "Daren Chow."

"Hey, Daren. So, I wanna party, but I'm low on, uh, herbal refreshment. My friend, like, had to go outta town. Know anyone?"

His spine straightened, but he shoved his hands in the pockets of his jeans and shrugged. "I might."

Her pulse jumped like she'd hit a jackpot. "Can ya hook me up?"

The kid was silent for a minute, his gaze fastened on the cleavage popping above her vest. *Face is up here, you dork.* She gritted her teeth and shifted to give him a better view.

"Probably figuring he can score more than grass. Keep your distance," Nate's voice whispered over her earpiece, and she twitched.

She angled her head and ran a long, black fake nail up the line of the kid's buttons to his chin. "Daren?"

He jerked and met her gaze, a dull red blush lighting up his pimples. "I could buy ya some. Would ya like that?"

"Sick. I got money." She ruffled her hair with one hand, stretching to show off her navel ring. "Can I come along?"

He pinched his lips together and spoke in a nasal squeak. "Guy's kinda hinky. Only sells to certain people."

She pouted. "Whatever. I, like, get so horny when I'm high."

She heard Nate choke.

The kid's eyes popped, gaze traveling from boobs to belly to crotch and back again. He cleared his throat and nodded. "Yeah, I can help ya out. I'm meeting a friend by the oak. Come on."

"Gnarly," she cooed, her heart thumping double time.

"Don't be clever, Jana. Find out where the dealer's waiting and get out of there," Nate warned softly.

She followed the boy out the back door and grinned slyly. "I've been real lonely in Sereno. You know, I could, like, be real nice to someone who helps me hook up with the right kind of kids."

Daren stumbled, probably tripping on his hormones.

"Be careful." Jana hooked a hand through his skinny arm and squeezed the bicep. "Yum. I love muscles on a big, tall guy."

The giant oak behind the football field had probably been there a century before the school was built. She glanced at the new green leaves shading the meeting place. Two kids dressed in grunge band T-shirts under black leather jackets eyed her suspiciously.

"That's Ray," Daren nodded toward the taller of

the two, a lean-faced blond with tough, hardened eyes.

Ray broke away from the other kid and strode toward them. "Hey, man, no bitches. We gotta go."

Daren folded in on himself. His shoulders sagged, and his bravado evaporated.

Jana pressed against his side to bolster his confidence. She'd never get anywhere with Ray if Daren couldn't keep his shit together.

"This is Jay-Jay," he squeaked out. "She wants…"

Cold fury gripped the other boy's face, and her stomach dropped.

Baring his yellow teeth, Ray throttled Daren and shoved him backward. "I said no bitches. I need to make that meeting, and you know we can't take riders or our supplier will bolt."

Barely able to hear above the pounding of her heart, she showed Ray her palms. "No prob, man. I just wanna score."

Ray moved closer, spreading his legs and crossing his arms.

She retreated a step. "My connection back home is careful, too. But you can get a couple joints for me, right?" She gave him a crooked smile, shifting her hips. "Can ya get it soon? Me and Daren have plans."

Ray leered at her with puffy, pale blue eyes. When he rubbed his ear, his hand had a faint tremor that made her nervous. "What kinda plans?"

Feeling lightheaded, she shrugged and dropped her gaze. "Private plans." Ray had used something stronger than grass. She could handle Daren, but the creepy expression on Ray's face curdled her blood.

"Man, what happen to your chill, Ray?" Daren whined. "You're acting totally weird."

Ray pushed him again. His face beaded with sweat. "You drive, asshole. My old man grounded me and took my fucking keys. Haven't stolen 'em back yet." He pivoted and stomped toward the parking lot.

"Jana. We've been listening." Nate's firm, deep voice murmured through her earpiece, and she clung to his calming tone, willing her heart rate to slow. "That kid's hyped up. Probably on meth. You need to leave. Make any excuse. But leave. Now."

His command stiffened her spine. They had to catch Tomasini. No choice. "Not yet," she whispered and then hurried after the boys.

"Jana." Mike's voice sounded strangely rough. "Get the hell out of there. We'll find another way."

Ray took shotgun as Daren tossed her a wave and climbed into the driver's seat of a dented, but nearly new, Lexus. "Hang around, Jay-Jay. We'll be back soon."

"Cool, I'll be here." She shot him a stupid looking grin while she memorized the license plate number. "Are you sure I can't come with ya?"

"No!" Nate and Ray yelled, both loud enough to make her jump.

Daren ground the engine twice, but the starter didn't catch.

She leaned against her car door and bit her lip. Could she be so lucky?

The poor kid tried again, but the starter still didn't engage. The next time he cranked the engine, the grinding noise dwindled into clicks. Daren slapped a palm against the dash, and his head drooped to rest on the wheel.

Ray grabbed him by the shoulder and shook. "You

fucking, useless asshole. Did ya leave the fucking lights on again?"

An adrenaline spurt lit her system and launched her into action. This was her chance. She unlocked her own car and slid into the driver's side. After a quick turn of the key, the engine of her thirty-year-old Mustang purred to life.

She backed out of the space and stopped behind Daren's fancy, broken car. Grinning, she rolled down her window a crack. "Need a lift, guys?"

"Jana. Don't be an idiot," Nate barked. "You can't risk being alone with those meth heads."

She stared at her clunky boots. What choice did she have? "Sorry," she murmured.

"Come on, guys. Hop in." With a quick shrug, she closed her window.

"You better play this cool, bitch." Ray slammed the passenger door so hard the car shook and her ears popped with the pressure change.

She'd be in control while driving, right? What could happen?

The skin on her back goose bumped like a mob of insects was stinging its way up her spine. In the rearview mirror, her eyes looked huge and frightened, her skin ashen. She stretched her neck to start the blood flowing again and drew a deep breath. "Which way?"

"Damn it! You don't listen worth shit," Nate yelled.

"Head toward downtown." Ray buckled in. Then his shaky hands curled into fists.

Pulling out of the driveway into the late afternoon traffic, she glanced over her shoulder and caught sight of the department's gray sedan several cars back. Warm relief rushed over her, and she flexed her fingers and forced her grip on the wheel to loosen.

Nate's voice hissed in her earpiece. "Find out where and bail."

"Turn left here," Ray ordered.

"We're going to the park," Daren added.

"Shut your trap, Chow." Ray glowered, pounding a fist against his thigh.

Out of the corner of her eye, she saw Daren slink into a corner and sneer at Ray's back.

"Park? Not the gas station? So much for Tomasini's tip," Nate groused. "Okay, Jana. Get the details, and we'll take over."

Ray's gaze jerked sideways and started with the safety pin holding her ripped tights over bare legs and traveled up her body to fix on her chest. A hungry gleam burned in his eyes.

She wanted to squirm away from him, but she took a slow breath to calm her shakes and pulled out from the four-way stop. Shifting through the gears, she stayed under the twenty-five mile per hour speed limit. "Uh, which park? I'm, like, new around here. Remember?"

"That way at the next light. Couple miles." Ray pointed and sneaked his arm over the back of her seat.

A noxious cloud of body odor assaulted her nose. She choked, and her stomach went into contortions, while the jerk's fingers trailed toward her neck.

Shit. He'd find the wire.

Jana giggled and shoved his hand away. "Bad boy. Don't tickle me now. I gotta drive," she simpered. "Where's this park we're going to, anyway?"

Eyebrows raised, Ray angled in her direction and

asked, "So, where'd you live before Sereno?"

She glanced at him. *Could you answer my question, you freak?* But she disguised her irritation with a smile. "San Diego. So close to the border, scoring anything you want is no prob. And my folks kinda let me run loose."

"No kidding?" The kid ran a hand through his greasy hair and leaned closer, staring at her chest. "Run loose, huh? You're my kinda chick."

Every muscle in her body screamed with tension. She checked her mirrors again. Where was Nate? She'd lost them. Trying to keep her lips from tightening, she grinned wider and winked at the pig-in-human-skin stinking up her passenger seat. "No shit. I got them buffaloed."

"Yeah? Bet you'll be real grateful when I score you some good shit." Ray's clammy paw settled on her leg, and she wanted to backhand the bastard.

"We're a couple blocks behind. Got caught at a red light." Nate growled deep in his throat. "Find out where you're going."

Her stomach heaved, and her skin crawled. Her nose rebelled, but she had to do this. "I kinda forgot. Which way next?" she repeated, her expression innocent.

"Good. Stay in the car when you get to the location. Drop the punks off and split," Nate said.

Ray waggled his hand toward a wide driveway framed in oaks and eucalyptus and then readjusted his crotch. "Right over there. See the lot?"

"Sure." Cold sweat formed on her palms. She didn't know this part of town, and there wasn't a sign at the entrance. No way to tell Nate where she was. She searched for a landmark, something distinctive.

Her wheels bumped over the driveway curb. No matter what Nate said, she couldn't bear to be in the car with Ray for one more second. She scooted into the first space she found, grabbed her keys, and jumped out.

She made a show of fluffing her hair and straightened her shirt so the tails covered as much of her butt as possible. Glancing around, she squealed, "That's, like, so cute. Look, a fire truck. And, oh my God, an airplane." She headed for the playground.

****

Adrenaline jacked Nate's heart rate up another couple notches. "They're at the kiddy park." He dodged the local bus and ran a very yellow light.

"I'll call dispatch with the location," Mike said.

"Can you really, like, climb through the jet plane?" Jana trilled over the microphone.

"Sure thing." Ray's voice sounded too damn close for comfort. "Friend of mine loves to sneak in here at night and fuck his chick inside the thing. Says he loves the way her screams echo."

"Cool." Jana drew the word out and made it last two syllables.

Red mist blurred Nate's vision. His pulse throbbed in his ears. "What the hell are you doing?"

She blew out a noisy breath. "But I gotta get into the mood. You promised me some dope. Before I fuck anybody, I need to relax. Where's your contact?"

Nate skidded around a corner and punched the gas. He'd watched her for the past six months, and she'd never seemed reckless. But she'd changed, suddenly she seemed almost driven.

"This guy is kinda paranoid, ya know?" Ray's voice sounded jittery, wound tight. The kid had to be on meth and late for his next high. "Get in the car and wait until he leaves or you'll blow the buy."

"Chill out," Jana said in an exasperated tone.

"Come on, Jay-Jay. You want some good shit, don't you?" Ray pleaded.

"Pretend you don't know me. Your contact will never notice me here by the plane," she purred.

Nate wanted to punch somebody's lights out. Another red light. "Shit."

Mike sat up straight. "Hey, watch out for those women."

Nate pushed on the brakes while two little old ladies hobbled across the street in front of the sedan.

"A hot, juicy piece of ass like you? He's a coke head, always after a quick fuck." Ray's leer came through the speaker. "Hey, bet I can getcha a real deal on your weed. You ever fucked two guys at once?"

"She's going to get herself raped," Nate choked. He'd have to castrate the damned kids.

Her disgusted squeal morphed into a giggle. "I told you. Hands off until I can relax."

"Won't be able to drive this heap if you pound that steering wheel any harder," Mike said.

On the green, Nate tore through the last turn. He swung into the large lot, parked behind a grove of redwoods, and checked the area. Near the exit, Jana's car edged the curb.

"Hold on, partner." Mike grabbed his arm before he could bolt from the car. "I know you're spitting nails, but let the scenario play out. She'll be okay for a few minutes. We can protect her."

Nate glared at him, every muscle tight as steel cables. He sucked in a harsh breath and released it slowly. "You jackass. If you ever come up with a brainless scheme like this again, I'll—"

"Message received," Mike shot back. "Now, let's make the risk she's taking count and bust the perverts."

Nate managed a crisp nod, detached the receiver unit, and stuffed it into his shirt pocket.

"We'll need cover. Not much action this afternoon, only a few dog walkers."

"And the freaking slackers are huddled around Jana."

Mike strolled up to a middle-aged woman unloading a dozen dogs and struck up a conversation.

Trailing him, all Nate could manage was to nod and stick out a hand for the labs and spaniels to sniff.

He and Mike flanked the pack and moved within range of the playground.

One knee hiked over the other, Jana perched on the wing of the decommissioned WWII fighter. She kicked her clunky black boots in a seesaw rhythm, keeping the creeps away from her ass. Good thing. Two pimple-faced kids hovered, panting, just beyond her range.

Nate rolled his eyes. With that view, those creeps wouldn't notice a SWAT team in riot gear. He turned down the volume on her transmitter and adjusted his earpiece.

Mike followed him to a park bench thirty feet along the path and muttered, "Busy watching the show. They'll never make us."

Nate slouched on the bench, but his heart pumped so hard, he thought it would explode.

"Look, if you ain't gonna put out, I need some cash

now," the blond kid whined.

"Sure, Ray." Jana scooted backwards and pulled a wad of bills from her purse.

"Where'd she get that?" Nate demanded through clenched teeth.

Mike shrugged. "Didn't want her caught short if something like this happened."

"You got shit for brains, Gordon?" If his eyes could shoot daggers, his partner would be perforated. He grunted. "Time to move."

Mike raised a hand to shield his face and elbowed Nate. "Douggie Wendell just drove up." A dusty white delivery van crept through the lot and parked near the exit, but no one emerged.

"Stay here, Jay-Jay. Don't even watch," Ray ordered, but his voice squeaked. He cleared his throat. "Chow, move away from her and get your ass in gear if I signal."

Nate snagged an old newspaper off the bench and slumped behind it, concentrating on keeping his blood pressure from killing him.

With his hands held visible, Ray swaggered toward the car. He spoke through the half rolled down window to the man inside. After a long minute, he turned and motioned.

Daren hurried across the park toward the van.

Nate started to rise, but Mike put out an arm. "Wait."

"Now," Nate demanded.

"You'll blow this if you don't cool off. She's fine. Nobody's going to shoot at her."

Adrenaline flooded his brain.

He tasted dirt. Smelled fresh grapefruit. Saw it

splatter as he rolled Jana beneath him. Bullets whined past, dug up the lawn. Two more rounds smashed into a tree. Bark splintered.

A sudden spurt of panic brought him back to reality. Nate shook his head and inhaled deeply. Damn visions. Now he was a target.

"Bingo. He flashed the cash. The deal's going down." Mike stood.

Nate whacked the paper against his leg and followed. "You cover. I'll grab Wendell. He might be armed. Ready, Linden? Murphy?"

Over the radio, voices squawked, "Roger."

Mike held Nate back. "One…minute…more, partner."

"There. They've made the exchange." Drawing his weapon, Nate leaped forward.

Mike seized the kids as two cruisers skidded into place, blocking the entrance. Gun in hand, he ordered, "Drop and spread 'em." He ground his knee into one punk's back as he slapped on cuffs.

Adrenaline pumped through Nate's system, fired his muscles, and slowed time to a trickle. He stuck his service weapon against Wendell's temple and dragged him out of the car.

"You're under arrest. Assume the position." Felt damn good to bust the creep.

"I didn't do nothing," Wendell howled as Nate patted him down.

Nate pushed Wendell's chest flat on the trunk of the car and read him his rights. He cuffed him and confiscated a .45, and two dozen plastic baggies of drugs.

The creep's face turned a sour green. "I don't

wanna go back to jail. Please, man. I'll tell you whatever ya wanna know."

Mike patted down the last kid and stowed him in one squad car. He turned to Nate. "See what Wendell has to say, partner. I'll go bust their chick."

"Stick her in the sedan," Nate barked. He flipped Wendell and yanked him to his feet. "Who do you work for? D. A. might cut you a deal."

Wendell snuffled and spewed a string of curses. "Joe Morgan. He set me up. He's the guy ya want."

"Need more than that." Nate growled nose to nose, with his hands fisted in the creep's shirtfront. "Where's the supply? Who delivers?"

Wendell's thin shoulders shook. "Morgan arranges everything. I swear, I never seen nobody else."

Chapter Twenty-Seven

March 31, 6:50 p.m.

Cuffed in the backseat of the undercover sedan, Jana focused on her bootlaces. She glanced up, and her cheeks burned. With his mouth drooping, Daren stared out the window of the squad car like a kicked puppy.

Her new buddy was headed for jail, but if she hadn't given him a ride to the kiddy park, he would have missed the drug deal and might never have been arrested.

She pursed her lips and turned the other way. Bullshit. When she'd met him in the school corridor, he'd reeked of marijuana, and Ray had practically frothed at the mouth. They'd both have gotten caught. If not today, soon.

She felt chilled. The twilight had deepened, but that wasn't the only reason she was shivering. She'd come too damn close to being gang raped.

Drooling Daren wouldn't have started anything on his own, but Ray had crowded her, promising her drugs. He'd touched her legs and pawed her chest like she was fresh meat on a serving platter.

Nausea knotted her stomach at the memory of Ray's finger tracing the tops of her breasts. She closed her eyes and swallowed the rancid taste in her throat. She'd done her best to laugh it off, string him along, but she'd been shaken and was very aware of her vulnerability. She was relieved to see Nate and Mike arrive.

One hand braced on a squad car roof, Nate shoved Wendell in and, with a wide grin, slammed the door. After the last black-and-white left, she struggled out of the sedan. Wishing she could pull her shirt closed to cover herself, she cut across the playground sand toward the entrance.

Toward Nate.

She stopped in front of him and held out her wrists. "Please take them off."

Silently, he removed the handcuffs.

"How's it going?" she asked. He hadn't said a word to her yet. Shivers raced over her again, and she wrapped her arms around her waist.

With hard eyes, Nate inspected her from head to toe. "We'll talk later."

She dropped her gaze.

He turned his back and barked, "Mike, get on the horn with dispatch. Relay orders to search the auto shop and arrest Morgan."

She chewed her lower lip between her teeth. Yeah, he was pissed. Tough. She'd made the choice, taken the risk, and Nate Kapulani would just have to get over his anger. Or not. She tapped him on the shoulder.

He pivoted, his jaw rigid as obsidian, and silently eyed her again.

"Sorry to interrupt, but I'm cold. There's some yoga gear in my trunk. Okay if I change?"

"Keys?" he demanded, his palm outstretched.

She pinched her mouth closed and dropped them into his hand.

"Linden," he called.

A curvy blonde in a crisp Sereno PD uniform jogged up. "Yes, sir?"

"Escort Ms. Sutherland to the restroom so she can change. Her clothes are in the trunk of that old Mustang in a…" Nate frowned at her.

"Green nylon bag," Jana supplied.

Keys in hand, Kathy Linden hustled toward Jana's car and popped the trunk.

Nate glared at Jana and lowered his voice. "While you're changing, clean up. You have more crap on your face than a heavy metal band."

****

7:05 p.m.

Jana dried her face with the rough, brown paper towel and squinted at the pockmarked metal mirror. Pale skin, red-rimmed eyes. Her nose and chin felt raw, both from the cold and from scrubbing with the gritty hand soap. Add in neon freckles and "Violent Violet" hair clashing with her tomato-red yoga wrap, she looked like a fourteen-year-old who'd sneaked into her big sister's hair products.

"I think you've finally got it all off." Kathy grinned and nudged her with an elbow. "You know, you're a damn lucky girl. How long have you and the sergeant been an item?"

Heat rushed up Jana's neck and burned her cheeks. Her mouth moved, but nothing came out.

"Come on, you can tell me. Is he as hot between the sheets as he looks?"

"We haven't been together that long."

Kathy's eyebrows rose. "Give me a break. A stud like Nate? Mmm-mmm."

When Jana didn't respond, Kathy mumbled thoughtfully, "Man, he can stash his gun in my holster any time he wants."

Jana wanted to sink through a crack in the cement floor. Pretending she hadn't heard Kathy's last comment, she ducked her head and grabbed her yoga bag. "Sorry this took so long."

"No problem. Let's see what's happening outside."

Jana trailed Kathy past the swings and the decommissioned fire engine toward the parking lot. She drew a deep breath to loosen the fierce knots in her stomach. Where did Kathy get off, lusting after Nate? Damn it. Kathy didn't love him.

Heat flooded her face again, and her heart began to sprint. Love him? Crap. Jana slapped her forehead. She loved Nate. She'd fallen head over ass for a hunky cop almost ten years older than she was.

Shaking her head, she let out a long, forlorn sigh. He'd never take her seriously.

She'd broken all the rules last night and let Nate make love to her way too soon. Squeezing her hands into fists, she growled and kicked at the sand, sending a tall spray pinging onto the metal merry-go-round.

They'd only had one date. One measly take-out sandwich, and she'd given in. She'd invited him into her bed and given him a night of incredible, swinging-from-the-chandeliers sex.

He'd left her sated, almost boneless. Last night, she'd come more times than she could count. Today, each step still sent pleasurable pangs to her sensitive flesh. When she thought of him, raw desire clutched that hollow place low inside.

She ached for Nate, only Nate, but he could have

any woman he chose. Kathy wanted him, and she was beautiful, curvy, and way more experienced.

A grimace twisted her lips. She loved him, but maybe sex was all he'd ever wanted from her. After all, he'd shown up at her apartment with a pocket full of condoms, expecting to score.

****

Nate's heart clenched, and his body heated. Jana shuffled across the playground toward him with her eyes lowered as if she was deep in thought. Her face was finally clean again, but with that crazy purple hair sticking up, she looked even younger. Beautiful, but so young.

He traced the grooves framing his open mouth with his thumb and index finger. Hell. He hadn't meant to be so rough on her a minute ago, but she'd scared him shitless. As soon as he got off shift, he'd decide exactly what he'd say to her.

"What are you grinning about?" Mike sauntered over and punched Nate's shoulder.

"Nothing."

"Dispatch says they caught Morgan and found the dope hidden in a couple toolboxes in the storeroom. Several kilos, plus coke and crystal meth. Nice bust, partner."

"Here." Nate handed Mike an evidence pouch holding plastic snack bags crammed full of drugs. "Make sure it's locked tight. Don't want this case fucked up, too."

"Got it." Mike nodded.

Jana approached warily. She'd slipped into a cover up and wrapped it tight, but her anxious expression worried him. "Are we going after Tomasini now?"

"What?" Mike asked, a puzzled expression flashed on his face.

"You know he's behind this." Her stubborn chin jutted forward.

"Wendell rolled over on Morgan, just Morgan. Tomasini probably knew something, but there's no proof," Nate growled, exasperated. He'd planned to wrap up this bust and drag her home. Then he'd make it clear why she would never pull a stunt like this again.

"Morgan didn't implicate Tomasini, either," Mike said. "All Morgan admitted was that he arranges a delivery once a week."

"Those two will lawyer up, but that might work to our advantage, if Tomasini was involved." At her frown, Nate added, "A good defender will push them to spill what they know fast, figuring the D. A. might cut a deal."

"But we can't wait. Those creeps had a supplier, and someone's making meth. That means a lab." She poked a black fingernail at his chest. "Tomasini owns the perfect place, his cabin in the Santa Cruz Mountains. We should go check." She grabbed his wrist and met his gaze.

His heart jolted, but he shrugged. "Need a warrant."

"No. We can't afford to wait." Her cold hand trembled.

She looked so scared that he draped an arm over her shoulders, and she shivered under his touch. He softened his tone, "We'll keep an eye on Tomasini, put the pressure on, but that's all we can do today."

Eyes narrowed, Jana flashed him an are-you-shitting-me glare, shrugged off his arm, and stomped toward her car.

****

Idiot. He'd never listen. Jana shook the kinks from her arms and tried to clear her thoughts. The compulsion didn't make sense, but something continued to nag at her. A tingling numbness flowed through her body. Her brow furrowed. She knew with utter conviction they had to go after Tomasini tonight.

With her elbows braced on the roof of her car, she rested her chin in her hands. Maybe she could convince Nate she was right. Or maybe she just needed to trust him, let him do his job. Given enough time, those losers would squeal and put Tomasini behind bars.

She'd helped bust the drug dealers today, despite all Nate's protective worries. A tiny smile tugged at her lips. Maybe he cared a little, and everything would eventually work out. She should relax.

A hot, metallic smell seared her nostrils. Blood trickled from Nate's mouth. A spasm twisted his body, and the light in his eyes dimmed. He went slack in her arms. Bruner reared back and howled.

Jana's heart thundered against her breastbone. Raw panic clutched her throat and left her breathless. With her chest heaving, she bent forward and leaned against the car until her knees would hold her.

She looked at her hands, expecting to see his blood caked under her fingernails. Adrenaline fired her muscles, seared her cold cheeks.

Nate was a dead man, and Morrie Tomasini had ordered his murder.

Again.

But why was she so certain? She massaged her forehead.

Shivering, Jana huddled before the fireplace. Hunted. Paralyzed by grief. Behind her, a woman with long dark hair threw herbs on the fire and smoke curled into the room.

The woman stared straight at her. "You're almost out of time. Before dawn breaks, you must correct the distortion and stop Tomasini, or your cop will die. Forever." The woman's voice sent shivers through her.

Jana sobbed in a ragged breath and straightened. She wasn't done yet. More than anything, she wanted Nate to live, so she had to stop Tomasini. Tonight.

She blinked back scalding tears.

Think. Think. Think.

The only location Tomasini owned where he could get away with drug production was his cabin. She beeped open her door and double-checked her notes for the address.

When she glanced up, Nate was headed toward her car, stone-faced. One look at his expression told her he wouldn't listen. He'd stop her, and then he'd die.

Panic grabbed hold of her and fogged her brain. She slammed the door and shoved her key in the ignition. Before he could cross the parking lot, she started the car and peeled out onto the main drag.

Her phone buzzed a few seconds later. She flipped it to speaker and stuck it in the cup holder.

"What are you doing?" he bellowed.

Good, he was angry. He'd follow her.

He'd survive.

"We have to finish this tonight," she yelled, but kept her focus on the road ahead.

"God damn it! Didn't you already put yourself in enough danger today? The guy's a gangster."

Driven by a freakish sense of urgency, she ran a four-way stop and turned right. Horns blared, and brakes squealed, but she ignored them.

Nate roared her name. "Give us time to squeeze Morgan and Wendell. A little pressure and they'll cave. Listen!"

"No, you listen. You can't die. Not again."

"What the hell does that mean?"

"I can't explain now, there's no time. I have to stop Tomasini tonight."

Silence.

"Where?" he finally asked.

"His cabin. The one past Summit Road." She screeched onto the freeway and jammed the gas.

Chapter Twenty-Eight

March 31, 8:20 p.m.

Tendrils of fog wove between tall redwoods and crawled down the gully edging the treacherous mountain road. Jana swung around a hairpin turn, and her headlights picked out a rosebush gone wild. Thorny canes sprawled over the rough track and screeched against her car. The noise grated through her and ratcheted her already taut nerves even tighter.

Dodging a huge pothole, she passed a row of decrepit mailboxes. The road turned downhill, straightened, but narrowed where winter rains had washed out a chunk of asphalt, like a giant had taken a huge bite out of the hillside.

She hunched over the steering wheel and stared into the shadowed blackness beyond her high beams. With the cloudbanks hiding the moon, the night was dark up here away from the city lights.

Chills oozed along her spine.

She spotted a hand-painted road sign stuck on a huge evergreen. "Madrone Cutoff. Finally." She heaved a sigh and veered left. Her car rattled. The tires crunched on the graveled lane.

Along the rough, winding road, the cabins were sparse, mostly set back with no streetlights. Driving slowly, she followed the track and searched for address numbers.

After about a mile, she spotted a steep driveway leading to a split-level cabin fronted by tall trees. A dim glow showed from one of the upper rooms. Her headlights caught the reflective glimmer of the numbers on the mailbox.

She continued on and U-turned at the dead end. Driving back past the cabin, she squinted to double-check the address. "A match!" she crowed and stopped at the next wide spot in the road. From here she could watch the house behind her without being seen.

When she flicked off her lights, the beams disappeared under a blanket of inky darkness. She shivered and reached forward, but turning them back on would be foolish.

The night pressed in on her and squeezed the air from her lungs. She swallowed the prickly lump in her throat, trying not to think about the sheer cliff a few feet to her right where the roadway fell off into a canyon.

She shook her head to clear the mental fog. How did she get here? She searched her memory, but most of the trip was a blur.

Her stomach twisted into a tight, hard lump. She was by herself. Unarmed. Suddenly, her impulse to find Tomasini seemed foolhardy. She rubbed her temples, fighting waves of panic. What lunatic urge had driven her to confront an ex-con alone?

Jana wrapped her flimsy yoga cover up tighter to keep warm and dug her cell phone out of the cup holder. She turned the phone over in her hands.

Lights flashed on the road ahead. A painful ache gripped her chest.

The whoop-whoop of the helicopter neared.

Searchlights flashed across the gravel and weeds below, hunting for her. Eyes wide, she clung to Bruner.

Her heart raced, and she panted like someone had been chasing her. Bright headlights blazed through her windshield, snapped her from her terrifying vision, and pinned her against the seat.

She peeked over the steering wheel. Two car doors slammed, and a shriek caught in her throat.

Nate's broad-shouldered form was silhouetted in the glare. She exhaled a shaky breath and popped the locks. He'd followed.

Mike slipped into the backseat and flashed a lopsided smirk.

Nate took the passenger seat. With his eyes narrowed and his jaw rigid, he looked like he wanted to throttle her.

But the woman's voice in her mind insisted his life was at stake. Raising her chin, Jana met his angry stare. "Tomasini's place is up the steep driveway behind me. There's one light on inside."

"Could be for security," Mike offered, studying the area through her rear window. "No vehicle out front."

"But he might be inside." She laid a hand over Nate's, but gave Mike a quick glance, too. "Please. Can you at least take a look?"

Mike cleared his throat. "I'll report our position to dispatch. Be right back."

The door closed, and they were alone. Silence sat between them like an elephant in a tutu.

He rubbed his neck with one hand and met her gaze. "Go home. Now."

Her stomach dropped three stories at his grim expression, but that damn voice compelled her again.

"I'll bet Tomasini's car is around back."

Nate squeezed his eyes shut for a second.

She bristled and reached for the handle. "Fine. If you won't investigate, I will."

He grabbed her wrist and spoke through clenched teeth, "I ought to cuff you and haul you back to Sereno."

"You know I'm right." She yanked her hand from his grasp and glared into his furious dark eyes. "We have to do this tonight."

Nate threw himself against the seat, muttering about headstrong women. "If Mike and I check the place, will you forget this critical mission you've dreamed up?"

"Deal. But I'm coming with you." She stepped out of the car.

"No!" Nate slammed his door so hard the car rocked. He sprinted toward her, blocking her path, and captured her in his arms. "Stay inside."

The undercover sedan's headlights winked out, and darkness closed over them. Her heart jumped. She couldn't see his expression, but his grip relaxed. "I know you're mad. You're worried about me, and I understand why. The drug bust was really dangerous. But I'm freaked out. I keep having those weird premonitions I told you about. If we don't stop Tomasini tonight, I'll lose you forever."

Nate gathered her against his chest and cradled her head. His warm breath feathered through her hair. "We can check the cabin, but Tomasini's dangerous, Jana. I don't want you anywhere near him." His voice lowered. "Please."

She could make out Mike perched on the hood of

her car. "Nate's right. Stay put. Lock your doors. We'll be back in a few minutes," he said in a hushed tone.

She started to object, but then relented. Finally, she was alone in her head again. "Be careful," she warned and crawled into the car.

Guns held at ready, they disappeared into the night.

Goose bumps raced over her, and she chafed her upper arms. A lopsided moon emerged from behind dark clouds and outlined the tall trees. Shadows cast by the watery, gray light fell across the narrow road.

A trickle of dread played on her neck, pulling the tiny hairs erect. She clenched her fingers together to stop them from trembling.

She stared at the dashboard clock. The hands jerked as each second ticked past. She rubbed her palms against the Lycra covering her thighs.

Ten minutes, and they hadn't returned. She speared her hands into hair still stiff with purple hairspray and grimaced. Maybe she should call dispatch again. She bumped her head against the seatback.

No. If Mike had already requested back up, a distress call would get her in even more trouble with Nate. She really shouldn't worry. They were cops. They could handle this. She huffed out a quick breath and crossed her arms. Or maybe Nate was trying to teach her a lesson.

An eon, no, two more minutes crept past. She worried her cheek and tasted blood on her tongue.

A shaft of moonlight lit the road in front of her car. Something streaked over the cliff edge and across the asphalt. An animal? It stopped at the base of Tomasini's driveway and glowed. Almost sparkled.

"Move!" The command reverberated in her brain,

and she felt a dire urge to follow.

Jana clicked the locks and eased her door open. The hinges squeaked, and the overhead light flared. Wincing at the brightness, she flipped off the switch.

Dry leaves and gravel crunched under her thick-soled boots. The rutted road made it impossible to walk silently. Why hadn't she put sneakers in with her yoga gear?

Fifty feet from Tomasini's house, she crouched behind a Monterey pine. Deep in shadow and built of dark wood, the cabin was much larger than she'd first thought. The top level extended above the garage and up the hill, so the cabin looked more like a fortress than a home. But light glowed around the edges of a shuttered window beside what might be the main door.

She listened for movement.

Nothing. No voices.

The fog had thickened again, dimming the moonlight. "Nate?" she called quietly through the mist.

No answer.

Her pulse skittered. Sucking in a breath, she crept closer. Smoke swirled from the chimney, and the next gust of wind bore a caustic taint overlying a more familiar odor. Her eyes stung, and the uneven pounding of her heart raced even faster. She couldn't identify the chemical reek, but she recognized the smell of marijuana.

Cold sweat trickled down her back. With probable cause, Nate and Mike had gone inside.

Leaning against a redwood, Jana pulled out her phone and called 911, explaining the situation to dispatch in hushed tones. They had the location from Mike's call, but he hadn't requested back up, and response time would be at least fifteen minutes. She slammed her heel against the tree. Too long to wait.

Another blast of smoke assaulted her nostrils. Coughing, she grabbed the rough bark for support. Damn it! Unless she kept going, Nate would be dead forever. She straightened her shoulders and climbed the steep drive, moving from shadow to shadow.

The garage doors hung unevenly, and a side entrance stood ajar. She peered through the gap. Rows of shelves crowded with dark shapes choked the entire space. Slowly, she pushed the door open. A twig snapped under her heel, and she winced. She'd have to take off the damn boots.

With clumsy fingers, she untied the laces and stepped onto the cold cement in her stocking feet. An open trapdoor in the ceiling allowed a narrow beam of light to filter into the garage. The room reeked of old motor oil, dust, and mice, but she moved through the clutter without making a sound. She crossed the room to the metal ladder attached to the trap door in the ceiling and listened.

"Don't move. You hear me, cop?" a man shouted in the room above the garage, panic and anger roughening his voice.

"Drop the weapon," Nate ordered.

Icy tremors crawled over her skin. She grasped the ladder and eased up the rungs. With each step she took, the heat and moisture increased, like stepping into a sauna.

Holding her breath, she peeked through the opening into the room above. Jana blinked, squinting into the blinding glow of dozens of fluorescent light fixtures. Startled by the glare, she shaded her eyes with one hand. Shiny silver foil lined the ceiling and walls, intensifying the light.

Oversized pots crowded every corner. Row upon row of marijuana plants stretched toward the artificial sunlight, filling the room with green leaves and the pungent smell of skunk laced with mildew and garden chemicals. Off to the right, steam leaked through a sealed door, and the intense odor burned her throat and tripped her gag reflex.

Arms raised high, Nate and Mike stood between two rows of towering plants. With his back to her, a large man in a wife beater and baggy shorts held them at gunpoint. Tomasini? Her stomach tightened with dread.

The ex-con waved his weapon at the two cops, blocking their escape. "Stand still or I'll shoot. I know my rights. You entered without a warrant."

Mike's gun lay on the floor at his feet, and she'd never reach it. She squeezed her mouth closed and fought the urge to heave.

With shaky hands, she climbed back down the ladder and searched the shelves for a possible weapon. A length of galvanized pipe lay near her feet. Better than nothing. She closed a fist around the crude club and pulled in a steadying breath.

When she peered into the room again, Nate's eyes widened. He jerked a step away from Mike, brushing against a tall plant.

Tomasini's head swiveled toward Nate. "I told you, stand still or I'll shoot."

Jana eased onto the wooden floor. Her pulse thudded so fast and hard she was afraid Tomasini would hear. But he kept the gun aimed at Nate.

"Drop the weapon," Nate said. "You do a little gardening, even cook some meth. Big deal. But you're too smart to shoot a cop."

She took a quiet step, careful not to rustle the plants around her.

Mike paled. He'd spotted her, too.

Tomasini waved the gun. "You stupid fuckers. You'll never pin this on me."

Nate shrugged and spoke calmly, almost casually, "You got us there, but one way or another, we'll shut down your operation. You had a nice setup for a while." He slid another pace away, and the snitch's gun tracked him.

Jana's heart rammed into her throat, and she fought the red mist crowding her vision. Lungs screaming, she tightened her clammy fingers around the pipe and crept nearer. Close enough to see Tomasini's bald spot.

Nate stiffened.

"Damn it, cop. I swear. If you even twitch again, I'll kill you." Tomasini retreated a step.

She raised the pipe and slashed toward his head.

He must have seen the movement. His finger squeezed the trigger as he twisted.

Her ears rang. The round smashed into a planter and sent a swarm of leaf green confetti flying behind Nate.

She swung again.

The pipe struck Tomasini's knee. He cried out, but he kept hold of the gun and fired another round.

Nate gasped and fell, clutching his chest. Blood seeped between his fingers.

A glacial heaviness cascaded through her like a slow motion mudslide. She couldn't stop what was to come, and she couldn't bear to watch Nate die. Again. The pipe clanged to the floor.

Tomasini grabbed her. When he ground the gun against her temple, the hot barrel singed her skin. She smelled the man's fear, felt the sweat soaking through his clothes.

His left arm squeezed her throat, choking her. Spots blurred her vision, and the room darkened. Desperate for air, she clawed at his arm.

Tomasini flinched and loosened his grip on her throat, but ground the gun barrel tighter against her skin.

Mike had dropped and retrieved his weapon. He'd come up in a crouch, but stopped dead and stared at the gun pressed to her head.

"Drop it. Drop it right now, or she dies!" Tomasini yelled. Dragging her with him as a shield, he hobbled toward the trapdoor.

Mike laid his gun on the floor.

"Kick it away," Tomasini shouted, and the gun clattered across the floorboards.

Moaning, Nate struggled to raise his head.

Adrenaline surged through her veins. He was still alive. She had a chance.

Jana lifted a foot, twisted, and put her full weight against Tomasini's injured knee. Then she went limp and slipped through his grasp.

Tomasini howled, "Bitch!"

She grabbed the pipe and hurled it at him, but missed. He ducked through the trap door just as Mike fired.

Footsteps sounded across the garage floor, and the door downstairs slammed shut.

Too shaky to stand, Jana crawled to Nate. His eyes were closed, his face pale and flaccid.

Pressure.

Stop the bleeding.

Her heart raced so fast she thought it might shatter, but she put her palms flat on his chest and leaned into the wound.

Nate groaned, and his eyelids lifted briefly.

"Stay with me, Nate," she begged.

Mike moved to her side, holstering his weapon. "How is he?"

"Bad, but the bullet missed the aorta this time."

"This time?"

"Give me your shirt!"

He ripped it off, and the buttons scattered across the floor. He folded the shirt into a pad and held it next to her hands.

She lifted her hands enough to let Mike slip it underneath and put her weight on the makeshift bandage. "Hang on, Nate. Please. Don't die again," she choked out.

An engine started, and Mike cocked his head as the noise roared past the cabin and down the drive. "I need to go after Tomasini."

"No! Backup's coming." Frantic, she seized his arm, her hand sticky with Nate's blood. "You can't go now or you'll die, too," she shouted along with the voice in her head.

Mike froze, staring at her wide-eyed. Then he nodded as if he suddenly understood and kissed her cheek. "Take care of him while I call medevac."

Two loud explosions shook the frame of the house, and she shielded Nate with her body.

"Damn. Had to be the cars." Mike pulled his radio from his belt. "Tomasini made sure I couldn't follow. Let's get out of here. What if he rigged this place to blow?"

Chapter Twenty-Nine

April 1, 9:00 a.m.

Nate glared at the bank of monitors chirping incessantly, just loud enough to set his teeth on edge. Whenever the morphine haze wore thin, jagged slivers of pain stabbed through his battered body with each beep. He was sick of the damn noise, twenty-four seven. Sick of the stink, the puking, and the pain.

He jerked his head sideways, away from the racket, and fiery demons in spiked shoes tap-danced on his chest and shoulder. Nausea gripped his guts.

He drew slow, shallow breaths until the agony relented. Carefully, he opened his eyelids. Warm spring sunshine filtered through the blinds, but he was stuck inside, tied to the hard, narrow bed, watching a clock tick. At least the old codger in the other bed had left this morning. No more sitcom reruns blaring at top volume.

He shifted against his pillows and fiddled with the bed control, but couldn't get comfortable, not with so many freaking tubes dripping stuff in or draining stuff out. Not with his left arm and shoulder immobilized.

"Hey, partner." Mike bounded into the hospital room with an annoying grin on his face. "Arraignments went great. Ready to go back to work?"

Nate grunted. "Gimme a day or two."

"At least they wired you back together." Mike's grin widened, and he gestured at the ropes and pulleys. "Looks like the puppet master dumped you off for repairs."

"Whatever." Nate rolled his eyes, restraining a chuckle. "Didn't lose any moving parts."

"Got an update for you." Mike slouched into a low-backed chair and stretched out his legs. "The DEA squad figured out why Tomasini blew up the cars and not the house. He had a vanload of cash hidden in the pantry."

"Confiscated?" At Mike's satisfied nod, Nate said, "'Bout time we had good news. Any word on the weasel?"

"Vanished. Can't believe he got through the perimeter."

He shrugged and sent the jackhammers back to work on his shoulder. "Don't beat yourself up. There's nothing else you could have done after he destroyed the cars."

"Too bad the backup units didn't nab him." Mike scuffed a foot on the floor, with his mouth and eyes set in tight lines. "I should have stopped the creep."

"You made exactly the right choice," Jana said as she entered the room. "You called medevac and that saved Nate's life."

At the sound of her voice, Nate's lips curved into a smile. "Hey, Jana." The dark circles under her eyes had disappeared. Her skin was fresh and clear with a little trail of freckles on her cheekbones that he loved to kiss. But she still looked more like jailbait than an almost college grad headed off to med school.

The obnoxious purple was gone from her hair, but

she'd spiked it with loads of goop. Once he was out of this damn bed, he'd convince her to keep it soft and silky.

He flashed on washing her hair and then taking her in the shower, pictured being buried deep inside her with water streaming over her slick skin. The blood in his groin stirred sluggishly.

God, he needed her in his life. His lips thinned, and his fist tightened on the bed rail. Jana was so young, and her parents had always protected her, especially her dad. The Colonel would probably kill him if he knew what Nate wanted. What they'd already done…

She put down a DVD player, earphones, and a stack of disks before she sat in the chair next to his bed. "I figured you were going crazy in here, so I brought you the latest thriller on disk and some tunes."

"Thanks."

Surreptitiously, she checked his vitals on the monitors.

"I'm fine," he grouched.

She stretched over the rail, touched his cheek, and kissed him, careful not to jostle the bed.

Her warm lips tasted of honey. He wanted more, but when he strained toward her mouth, she dodged.

The damn demons polkaed across his chest again, and he sank back against the pillow with a groan.

Gently, she covered his free hand. "Feeling better, Detective?"

The warmth in her wide hazel eyes seeped through him, driving out some of the lingering pain. He gave her fingers a quick squeeze and met her gaze. "Yeah, I am now."

Mike cleared his throat. "Feds posted a warrant for

Tomasini. Besides the million plus in cash, they're impounding property all over the valley."

Nate nodded. "Good. With a price on his head and no resources, maybe his connections back east will eliminate the problem for us."

"Our snitch had his fingers in a lot of pies, but I doubt we'll hear from him again."

Sounded good, but didn't feel right, so Nate made a noncommittal grunt. "Never know. We destroyed his West Coast network and cost him a bundle. Tomasini might want payback."

"Not this week." Mike's mouth quirked. Hands planted on the armrests, he pushed off and rose from his chair. "Gotta go. Lieutenant Greene's got me buried in paperwork. Better get started." With a brief salute, he swaggered out the door.

Moving as few muscles as possible, Nate smiled at Jana. "Wouldn't mind getting shot again if I could skip the paperwork."

The sudden look of distress on her face had him backtracking. He groped for another subject. "What's that?"

She glanced at the manila envelope on her lap, crossed her legs, and angled her lower body toward the exit. She faced him, her expression serious. A tiny muscle beside her mouth twitched. "It's my enrollment forms and tuition deposit."

"Med school?"

Biting the inside of her cheek, she nodded, but seemed unable to meet his gaze.

His stomach twisted. He stared at the ceiling while the wall clock clunked through a never-ending minute.

He loved her more than life, but no matter how

much he wanted her, he couldn't keep her here. He couldn't hold her back, and it wouldn't be fair to tie her to him before she left. His eyes stung. Closing them, he rubbed his thumb along his index finger. "I'll miss you, but D. C. isn't too far."

Jana fiddled with the envelope on her lap, stood it on end, and then tapped it against a thigh. She leaned forward and grasped his hand. A fiery blush highlighted her cheekbones. "I'm going to say this, even if I sound foolish. At least I tried."

"Nope. Still my turn." He curled his fingers around hers. "I care about you. A lot. But you're young. You need a chance to finish school and decide what you really want."

She squared her shoulders and faced him. Her gold-flecked green eyes took on heat that stole his breath. "I love you, Nate."

His pulse kicked to double time. He swallowed the boulder in his throat and flashed her a tender smile. "You think you do right now, but we haven't known each other long. One date's not enough."

She shifted back and stared silently at the floor with her arms crossed around her stomach as she rocked in her seat.

He winked, forcing a smile. "Hey, we had some good times. No reason we can't keep in touch."

"If that's the way you feel." She stood and pivoted toward the door.

His heart thudded heavily in his chest. "Jana. Wait. Don't go yet." With a groan, he grabbed for her hand, but missed. Pain screamed through his shoulder and lit fire to his chest, but his heart ached even worse.

She stopped in the doorway and turned back

toward him.

"That for Georgetown?" he asked in a shaky voice.

Tendons stood out under the pale skin of her neck and hands, but she sneaked a glance at him through her lashes. "No. I was accepted by some other schools, too."

"Where?"

She met his gaze. "Stanford."

He cocked his head. "You'd stay around here? Live this close to your parents?"

"I don't care where I go to med school."

"You'll make a kickass doctor." His grin felt like it'd split his face. "Would your dad kill me if I dragged you to Vegas?"

Forehead scrunched in a frown, she shook her head slowly. Then she stepped closer, and her eyes sparkled.

He drew her hand to his lips. "I love you, Jana. Marry me. I don't care when or where. Next week isn't soon enough."

A broad smile lit her face.

"But if you want to go to Georgetown, I'll survive four years of jet lag and phone sex."

Epilogue

January 1, present day, 7:30 p.m.

Jana gazed through the sliding glass door at the crimson and indigo sunset. A leafless sycamore tree was silhouetted and warmed by the brilliant colors of the January sky.

Nate's laughter rang out from their son's bedroom, followed by a high-pitched childish giggle.

Grinning, she rested her head against the sofa cushions, closed her eyes, and let her body relax. She'd had a busy week, but maybe this would be a quiet weekend, even though she was on call.

She'd been so shocked when Norah Redfox appeared in the ER early New Year's Day, she'd babbled incoherently. But the emergency surgery on the woman's sister had gone seamlessly, and Jana expected a complete recovery.

"Come on, Tiger," Nate said from the hallway. "Give Mom a goodnight kiss."

Two-and-a-half-year-old Michael shuffled in, wearing blue footy pajamas and a wide smile. He clung to Nate's big hand and clutched his favorite stuffed fox to his chest.

Her heart ached with love for both of them.

Sprawled in front of the fireplace, Bruner raised his head and gave a long yawn, then scratched the old studded leather collar around his neck. He stretched out on the rug and drifted back to sleep.

Michael climbed onto her lap, and Jana nuzzled his dark wavy hair, inhaling the scents of baby shampoo. "While you were helping Michael with his pajamas, Norah Redfox called."

Nate's eyebrows lifted. He perched on the arm of the sofa. "Why'd she call here? Worried about her sister?"

She smiled up at him. His dark chocolate gaze snared hers, and her breath caught. Warmth and need ignited deep within her. "No, she wished me a happy anniversary."

"Anniversary?" The line between his brows furrowed. He cocked his head and tugged an earlobe.

"Don't worry, I'd almost forgotten the event myself. I'll explain later." She chuckled, smiling to herself. Exactly as Norah had predicted, when Jana worked hard to remember, she could still hold both versions of the past ten years in her consciousness. Tonight, the two timelines would finally knit together. She'd overwritten the evil thriving in Sereno after Mike's murder and eliminated the distortion.

"Darn. Thought we had an excuse to celebrate." He tipped her chin and kissed her softly, stroking the corner of her mouth with his thumb.

Blood pulsed under her skin, moving liquid heat to her core. "We always do."

Nate kissed her again, deeper, and then broke away. A wolfish grin lit his face. He stretched his arms toward their son. "Bedtime, kiddo."

But Michael faced her and laid a small hand on her cheek, his big brown eyes serious. "Mommy? Sing me chariot?"

"Again?" She sighed but started to hum the old spiritual Granny McAlpine had always sung to her. Michael settled back on her lap.

Nate sank beside her on the sofa and laid a strong hand on her shoulder.

Across the living room, a light bulb popped.

Dizziness flashed through her, leaving a giddy sense of wonder and déjà vu. When she'd envisioned this scene before, it had seemed impossible.

She covered Nate's fingers with hers. Would he believe her? "Let's sing together. After we put Michael to bed, I have a story I can finally tell you."

A word about the author...

Along with teaching, Joy began her writing career by publishing children's historical fiction. She later found writing romantic suspense fulfilled her need for travel and romance.

She lives with her husband and two dogs near Silicon Valley and the mythical town of Sereno.

http://www.ejbrighton.com